INTERCEPTED

INTERCEPTED

Alexa Martin

JOVE
NEW YORK

A JOVE BOOK
Published by Berkley
An imprint of Penguin Random House LLC
375 Hudson Street, New York, New York 10014

ISBN: 9780451491954

Library of Congress Cataloging-in-Publication Data

Names: Martin, Alexa.
Title: Intercepted / Alexa Martin.
Description: First edition. | New York : Jove Book, 2018.
Identifiers: LCCN 2017060279| ISBN 9780451491954 (pbk.) |
ISBN 9780451491961 (ebook)
Subjects: LCSH: Single women—fiction. | Football players—Fiction. |
Man-woman relationships—fiction. | GSAFD: Love stories
Classification: LCC PS3613.A77776 I58 2018 | DDC 813/.6—dc23
LC record available at https://lccn.loc.gov/2017060279

First Edition: September 2018

Printed in the United States of America
1 3 5 7 9 10 8 6 4 2

Cover design and illustration by Colleen Reinhart
Book design by Kelly Lipovich

To Derrick.

For everything.

ACKNOWLEDGMENTS

This book would not have happened without Kristine Swartz and the amazing team at Berkley. Thank you for turning my dream into a reality.

My rockstar agent, Jessica Watterson, you are everything dream agents are made of. Thank you for always having my back, listening to me ramble, and never judging my love of KA and jeggings.

Brenda Drake, thank you for creating Pitch Wars and presenting me with the opportunity of a lifetime. Kara Lee Miller and Meredith Ireland, thank you for choosing me. Thank you for believing in me more than I believed in myself and thank you for teaching me your ways. I am eternally grateful to you.

Nattie and Lin. Thank you for reading the hot messes I sent you over the years and thank you for never calling them hot messes. I hope every writer has friends like you in their corner.

My WAGS—Meghan, Kelsey, Emilia, Cicely, Tracy, Mia, Jill, Melissa, Lacey, Kirbie, Sarah, Christina, Jessica, Keisha, Caroline, and so many more. Thank you for taking me into your tribe when I was a nineteen-year-old girl and showing me the woman and friend I wanted to be. Of all the things being an NFL wife has brought me, you ladies are by far my most treasured.

The bra, you know who you are. Thank you for supporting me always.

All the kissing—you're the best writing tribe a girl could ever ask for.

Abby, thank you for being the best sixth-grade locker partner, freshman roommate, and friend I could ever ask for. Taylor, you are the strongest woman I know. Thank you for always being my voice of reason and of course, for experiencing the summer of '03 with me. Brittany, I've never come across someone as brave as you and I'm patiently waiting to see you conquer the world. You three are my ride-or-dies. None of this would have happened without your support and friendship. I love you all.

My grandma would have loved this and I have faith she's watching and smiling, knowing she sparked my love of reading. My grandpa would have pretended to not love this, but secretly he'd be thrilled. I miss you both more and more every day.

Rhonda, thank you for being the best mother-in-law a woman could ever ask for.

Mom, thank you for always believing in me.

DJ, Harlow, Dash, and Ellis, I love you to the moon and back. Thank you for being so patient with me throughout this process. Of all the things I am, being your mom is by far the best. Derrick, I still remember when you walked into that leadership class fifteen years ago. I hoped for one date. Who would've thought that all these years later, I'd be just as smitten as ever? Thank you for supporting me through this crazy ride. I am so in love with the amazing life we've created. Our love story will always be my favorite.

One

FOR THE FIRST THREE YEARS, IT'S FUN BEING A PRO FOOTBALL PLAYer's girlfriend.

"Marlee, let me see your hand! Did Chris propose yet?" Amber asks.

I'm in year ten.

"Still naked." I wiggle my fingers in front of her the same way I did last week and the week before that . . . and the week before that. #HeDidntPutARingOnIt

Sometimes, I like to hashtag my life. #CheaperThanTherapy

I sip my margarita. "When it happens, I promise to let you know." *Or, you know, keep asking every time you see me.*

"Marlee." Courtney sighs. She stands at the head of the table clutching a glitter-coated gavel. "We made exceptions for you to join the Lady Mustangs. Try to acknowledge that and save your little side conversation until we've finished."

"Sorry, Court." Every time I call her Court, she strains her Botoxed forehead and glares in my direction, so obviously, it's the only thing I call her. Well, sometimes I call her bitch, but she doesn't know about that.

"As I was saying, the annual Lady Mustangs Fashion Show is in three weeks. Everyone *must* attend the next meeting so we can discuss the outfits for you and your husbands."

I catch her eye again. She raises her chin, and her fat-injected lips form an actual smile.

"Oh, I'm sorry. In your case, Marlee, you and your *boyfriend*." See? What a bitch.

"Thanks for the clarification, Court, but I understood." My fingernails dig into my palm as I fight the urge to ask if one of her husband's girlfriends will be joining the festivities.

"I didn't want you to feel like you were being excluded."

Hmm . . . including me by pointing out my differences. Makes so much sense. I don't know if she's trying to convince herself, me, or the rest of the Mustang wives, but she isn't succeeding with anybody.

"You're so thoughtful," I return with an equal amount of authenticity.

Courtney is the president (how obnoxious) of the Lady Mustangs, the charitable organization consisting of the wives and girlfriend (singular) of the Denver Mustangs. We get together every Wednesday during the season to plan different events to benefit the community. There is an unspoken rule—each woman only gets one season to lead—but surprising nobody at all, Courtney didn't think the rules applied to her. This is her fourth year as president. Her husband, Kevin Matthews, is our quarterback, but her head is bigger than his. And that's saying a lot. There are football players and then there are quarterbacks—which are an entirely different breed. Courtney has also made it her mission during her reign of terror to put me in my place, a spot well below her. She doesn't seem to realize I'm fresh out of fucks to give.

"As I was saying, now that the season has arrived, everyone needs to be here every week. No excuses." She looks toward me again.

So I've missed some meetings, sue me. But, unlike Courtney, I have an actual job that includes more than lunching. We also live in the day and age of email, something that seems to evade her.

"Remember what we always say? We work hard to inspire our husbands' on-field success with our off-field dedication, support, and achievements."

Vomit.

Honestly, besides the constant pressure to prove I'll be the best football wife ever, the only reason I keep coming to these awful things is because it gives me an excuse to drink in the early afternoon. I focus on the Colorado sun shining down on our rooftop patio table as I sip my oversized margarita, listening to the music as it switches between seventies pop and nineties hip-hop—until Courtney's shrill voice pulls my attention back to her.

"Is there anything else that needs to be discussed today?" Courtney asks. After a quick glance around the table confirms there's nothing else to be said, the gavel slams into the table and glitter explodes off of it, covering the table, plates, and floor.

Fantastic.

Like the waitstaff needed more of a reason to hate us beyond the ten separate checks, no dressing/no flavor orders, and the three women who sent their meals back because they spotted a carb.

Whenever these meetings end, the switch flips from good deeds to gossip central.

"Can I have a chip?" Naomi says. "Salad is so stupid. Why don't you ever tell me not to order one?" She draws my attention away from the brewing gossip storm as she reaches to my plate without waiting for an answer. Not that she needs one, she does this every week. And every week she still orders a salad—like the calories don't count if I'm the one who orders them. #WhoNeeds-Science

"What if I was going to say no?"

"Were you?" She crunches into the chip in a manner so un-Lady-Mustang-like, I'm surprised Courtney doesn't slam down the gavel again to reprimand her.

"No, you can have the rest, I'm done. Playing nice while Power Trip Barbie threw her jabs stole my appetite."

I love Naomi. She has never questioned the authenticity of my relationship because of my lack of a gaudy diamond decorating my left hand. She's the first to call me to get together when the guys are out of town. She also doesn't partake in the hype some of the other women do when it comes to the faux fame of being an athlete's wife.

"Don't mind Courtney. She's just pissed they're bringing in another quarterback, and Kevin's reign as leader supreme is coming to an end . . . not surprising considering how he played during preseason." She doesn't even finish the sentence before she's grabbing the untouched taco still on my plate.

"Wait. What? When did that happen?" I ask.

"They announced it this morning. How do you not know these things? As a wide receiver, this affects Chris more than anyone else, except for Kevin." Her eyes never meet mine, and if I didn't know better, I would've thought she was whispering sweet nothings to a taco.

"The season started. Chris isn't around to tell me these things, and I don't have ESPN alerts sent to my phone like the rest of you freaks. Who'd they get?"

Instead of an answer, all I get is one flawless, manicured finger in my face while another points toward her mouth as she chews what was left of my lunch. Rolling my eyes to the heavens, I try to gather patience while she takes an eternity to swallow and chase it down with her watery Diet Coke.

"Gavin Pope—he was the Bears quarterback," she says with shrug.

She's all nonchalant while I, on the other hand, contemplate grabbing my chest and calling 911. My heart is racing so fast, I'm afraid I'm seconds away from keeling over. The sunshine now feels like a heat lamp, and my straightened hair against the back of my neck starts to curl.

"Holy shit. Are you okay? You just turned white."

"Actually, I'm feeling a little queasy. I think I drank my margarita too fast." I'm well accustomed to explaining away my distress around the wicked wives, and sitting by Naomi, hearing the one name I work overtime to avoid, is no different. "I think I'm going to head out, rest a little before Chris gets home."

"Good, go and feel better. Call me later if you need anything." Naomi's watchful gaze follows my shaky movements as I put enough money on the table to cover my bill and offer a small apology for the glitter they'll no doubt be cleaning for the next six months.

"I will, thank you." I give Naomi a hug, shout a quick goodbye to our table, and get the hell out of dodge.

The problem with a rooftop patio is there's no quick escape.

How is this my life? I know Lady Luck has never been too fond of me, but it's just cruel that out of all the quarterbacks and all the teams, Gavin Pope ends up on the Mustangs.

Halfway down the stairs, my knees are knocking so hard I have to stop and let the wall support me. My breathing won't slow, and I'm dizzy from all of the scenarios spinning in my head.

"Are you okay, ma'am?" an unexpected voice calls from behind me. I jump back and hit my head against the sports memorabilia–covered walls. One of the pictures crashes down, landing at my feet. I bend to pick it up and my shaking hands almost drop it twice before my nerves calm enough to look at it.

I forget where I am. Instead of a restaurant in a Denver suburb, I'm back in that Chicago high-rise. The guy I'd just had the hottest night of my life with—the one who told me he was an investment banker—has framed pictures of himself in his apartment. But instead of a suit, Gavin Pope wears a Bears hat with the NFL commissioner's arm draped over his shoulders.

"Ma'am?" The waiter's voice startles me back to the present.

I shake the memories of the Chicago police officers staring at my tight dress, smudged mascara, and just-been-fucked hair as I ran out of the high-rise and focus on the picture frame in my hands. It's not Gavin. Instead, it's my boyfriend, both feet in the air, football locked tight in his outstretched arms.

"I'm fine. Thank you." I hand him the frame, and then I'm running again. I don't stop until I'm sitting in my car. But once I'm inside my Prius, the news hits me all over again.

Gavin Pope.

Here.

Like a tsunami, each memory of that night hits me like another wave. His eyes as he watched me undress. *Crash*. My tongue dancing against his. *Crash*. The way he took me to the edge of euphoria over and over and over again. *Crash. Crash. Crash*. I'm drowning with the sinking realization that all of my hard work to bury every panty-dropping, toe-curling memory of that night was for nothing.

Not only did fate decide it'd be fun to remind me of him, it threw him right smack-dab in the center of my life. I mean, it's not like the quarterback holds the wide receivers' careers in their hands or anything. How could this possibly go wrong?

I guess it depends on whether Gavin Pope even remembers who I am.

Two

CHRIS AND I LIVE IN WHAT I FONDLY REFER TO AS THE SEVENTH circle of hell—oddly enough, that's located in Denver.

We are both native Denverites; we met in high school, and somehow, Chris lucked out by being drafted by the Mustangs and never being traded. In the NFL, getting to play at all is odds defying. And staying on the same team for more than five seasons is a damn miracle.

With Chris's awesome income, the money I get from my freelance design jobs, and no kids, we should be living the high life. Denver is the coolest city with the most eclectic, vibrant mix of people. But we don't live in an industrial condo downtown or a historical bungalow in Washington Park.

No, no, no. Chris and I—just the two of us—live in eight thousand square feet of obnoxious marble and crystal covered extravagance in the gated community of all gated communities with all the other Mustang starters in #TheLandWhereHighSchoolNeverEnds.

I grew up middle class. Chris grew up loaded. His dad is still the most sought after plastic surgeon in Colorado—a common topic between the other wives and I. And to this day, I still have no idea who the hell Chris is trying to impress. I guess showing your daddy you're a big boy includes ugly chandeliers and gold leafed wallpaper.

After hearing about Gavin's arrival, I knew Chris was going to be upset. And because I'm such a wonderful girlfriend, I made him my world famous red velvet cake to help ease the pain. I absolutely did not make it in an effort to eat my own feelings. And the extra bowl of cream cheese frosting hidden in the back of the fridge isn't for that either. Sweet decadent denial.

"Fuck Coach Jacobs!" Chris's entrances tend to have a flair for theatrics, but he has outdone himself this time. His deep voice echoes off the gallery art–lined walls. His heavy feet against the white marble causes them to rattle. But the crowning glory on this manly display of fury is the way he launches his workout bag across the kitchen the moment he sees me. Almost as if in slow motion, I watch his Nike bag soar over the island into my favorite teal cake stand holding my beautiful, iced to perfection, world famous red velvet cake. Both fall to the floor with a frosting-padded thud.

"What the hell, Chris?" I walk over and start picking out cream cheese–covered ceramic. I'm contemplating whether or not to still eat the parts of the cake that didn't directly touch the floor when Chris starts yelling again.

"Are you really more worried about a fucking cake than me right now?"

Well . . . yes.

"Of course not. It's just a mess, and I don't want either of us to cut our feet." Lies.

Bye, cake. I'll miss you.

I stand up to look at him and when I do, I realize leaving the cake for later is for the best. Chris's normally mocha complexion has a cherry hue to it, and his full lips are pulled into a thin, straight line. If I didn't know him better, I'd think he's about to cry. "Holy shit. Are you okay?"

"No, I'm not fucking okay! That piece of shit Jacobs brought in another quarterback. Fucking Gavin Pope. Even the guy's fuckin' name is pretentious." His eyes are focused on the coffered ceiling and his hands never stop roaming his not-quite-bald head.

In all my time knowing him, I've never seen him so worked up over football.

"Kevin and I were solid. I was his receiver. With him throwing me the ball, this was going to be my biggest contract year yet. And that rat, son of a bitch, knew it. He doesn't want to fuckin' pay me, and he thought bringing in some pretty boy was going to stop me. Fuck that. He's got another thing coming."

"I thought Pope was supposed to be good?" Not like I'd know, or that I've looked up his stats once a week, every week for the last four years or anything.

"It's not about him being fucking good, Marlee!" His attention snaps toward me. It seems he didn't appreciate that little tidbit. "Do you listen when I talk to you?"

"First of all, yes, I do listen. Second, check yourself. I get you're pissed and taking it out on Nike bags and innocent, baked-with-love cakes, but you will not take it out on me. I'm not Jacobs, I didn't make this trade. I want to help you, but not if you're acting like I'm the enemy here." #99ProblemsButChrisAintOne

"Fuck. I'm sorry," Chris says. He looks properly chastised, and resisting the urge to dust the dirt off my shoulder is almost too much for me to handle. "This was going to be our year, baby. I was going to be the number one receiver in the league; we were going to fly to Hawaii so I could play in the all-star game. I was going to get the franchise tag and the contract we've always dreamed of so we could start our family the right way—on top. Now Jacobs is putting it all at risk."

I hate the way the dormant butterflies always take flight the second Chris mentions starting a family. If he was waiting for money, he could have proposed six years ago. But instead, every year passed without an engagement and another item added to his pre-marriage bucket list. But at last, Chris is nearing the end of his list. Plus, a few weeks ago, one of my rings went missing, and when I asked him about it, he got all jittery and nervous. I've wanted to be Mrs. Chris Alexander since I was sixteen and now, nearly eleven years later, the time is almost here.

"What can I do? There has to be something we can do to keep you in your number one spot." Stepping over the long-forgotten mess on the floor, I make my way around the kitchen island (or, more accurately, the kitchen continent) to Chris and wrap my arms around him. I've always loved how when I hug him, my head rests right above his heart.

"There is something you could do. I invited the wide receivers over next Tuesday. It'd be great if you make dinner."

"Of course. Should I make Nonna's lasagna? Is TK coming? He loved it last time." Between the circles he's drawing on my back and the rhythmic thumping of his heart beneath my ear, I'm at a serious risk of falling asleep in this kitchen.

"Sure, but make double because I invited Kevin and Gavin too."

I pull back from Chris so quickly, you would've thought he told me Jeffery Dahmer was coming for dinner. Even though . . . Gavin has eaten me before.

Dammit.

Don't go there now, Marlee!

"Gavin? Why would you invite him? Weren't you just complaining because he's on the team?" I try to cover my reaction with confusion. The last thing I need is for Chris to catch a whiff of what Gavin's name does to me.

"I don't want him on the team, but he's here and the best thing I can do now is try to butter him up. Feed him some food, play some poker, try to bond with the guy. I need him to want to throw to me. So can you do it?"

I can't.

I cannot cook dinner for Gavin Pope in the home I share with Chris. Granted, my one night with him happened during the break Chris wanted . . . okay, he'd pretty much dumped me, but still. Aren't there rules about this kind of thing?

"I have a few projects, but their deadlines aren't for a couple of weeks. I'd love to do this for you. I gotta do my part to support Team Alexander."

"That's why I love you—you always put the team first." His lips crash into mine and when he pulls away, the anger he walked in with is nowhere to be found. Chris's smile is so bright, the contrast between his brown skin and freakishly white teeth nearly causes me to squint.

"You know me—they don't call me Marlee 'Team Player' Harper for no reason." And if they knew what Gavin and I did, they'd be calling me that for a whole lot of other reasons. "Speaking of, I gotta feed my man. Do you want me to make you a plate?"

"No thanks, babe. I'm gonna head back to the facility. I left early because I was pissed about Pope, but since you calmed me down, I'm gonna finish watching film. First regular season game's this weekend. I have to be ready now more than ever. You don't mind, do you?"

"Nope. Go do your superstar prep. I'll clean up here and knock out some work." I roll onto my tippy toes and kiss his chin at the same time my palm stings from slapping his ass.

"I'm not sure how long this will take, so don't wait up."

Fine with me. I have an entire Tupperware filled with cream cheese frosting, an unopened bottle of wine, and unwelcome feelings to avoid.

"Okay, but try not to burn yourself out too early in the week," I call to his back as he's walking out of the kitchen.

"Always looking out for me. Bye, babe!" I barely hear the words before the rattling of the art alerts me he's gone, and the only sounds left are the alarms bells in my head.

Holy shit.

I'm going to see Gavin Pope again.

Three

I MAY NOT FOLLOW FOOTBALL CLOSELY, BUT WHEN IT COMES TO going to a game, I can rival the most devout fan with my intensity.

What can I say? As soon as they scan my ticket and I step through the turnstile, I transform into an obnoxious, psychotic football soldier. Except instead of camouflage, my uniform consists of impractical heels, skinny jeans, and a football jersey that has been cut, sewed, glued, and covered in Swarovski crystals. But don't let the bling fool you—I know how to make the sun hit it at the right angle to temporarily blind the toughest of opponents.

"Marlee, I swear to god, if you cause a scene like the one you did in preseason, I'm *never* coming to a game with you again," Naomi says beside me.

I don't know what her problem is. Those tools in the seats near us spent the entire game either yelling that our players sucked or talking about how much better they had been back when they played. If you ask me—which, in my defense, I felt they did for saying it all within my earshot—if you're sitting in the stands instead of on the field, you have no right to say anything. It's not the players' fault your career peaked. And when you're old enough to be the rookie's dad, it's probably time to put your glory days to rest.

But Tool One and Tool Two weren't very receptive of my advice and caused a little bit of a scuffle. It's not like I would've let anything happen to Naomi. Not only have I taken boxing classes religiously for the last three years, my boy Lenny, the attendant for our section, loves it when I give him a little action.

"First of all, I did not start that."

"Marlee! You called them football rejects and told them the only thing they could do with a football was shove it up their—"

"Whoa, whoa, whoa! You know better than to repeat my war crimes outside of the battle." I stop walking with no warning and the guy behind me mutters a few curse words as he makes his way around us. "And do you not remember the shit he was saying about Dre? Your husband? Don't get me wrong, I'm glad you stay calm because one of us needs to, but you were happy when I said something. You can't take it back now."

"Maybe a little bit, but don't do it again. I can only imagine the joy Courtney would feel finding out you were starting fights at games."

"Courtney can borrow the reject brothers' football and shove it up her—"

"Marlee! Naomi! Don't you girls look the cutest? Just sparklin' with support." Dixie's southern twang rings out. She stands between us with her arms hooked through ours. "First game of the season. Can y'all believe it? How blessed are we? Our men out on the field, living their dreams. I'm praying god protects them all today."

I love Dixie. She's every southern stereotype rolled into one loud, giggly, gossipy, heavy-on-the-Jesus-and-the-hairspray, one-hundred-pound pixie. She's no Naomi—then again, nobody is—but she's high on my list of favorites.

Dixie always tries to convince me to join her Bible study and says things like "bless your heart" and "aren't you just precious" as if my life both amuses and frightens her. She's told us many times how she held her virtue tight until the day Tucker married her. When she asked how long I had lived with Chris and I told her, I swear she almost threw holy water on me. She has yet to save me, but she isn't tamping down her efforts.

"Aren't we all?" I might not be the biggest believer, but I know what comes after Dixie's "God-Fearin' Woman" act. I don't care who I'm with or where I am, when Gossip Dixie arrives, I settle in.

"We sure are. Speaking of all of us . . ." She tugs on both of our arms and pulls us in close, drawing the eyes of damn near everyone around us. The three of us look like a confused version of Charlie's Angels. "Did you hear Kevin isn't startin' this week? Poor Courtney's just tore up. When I walked into their box earlier, her eyes were swollen and bless her heart, whatever makeup she uses didn't even begin to touch the circles under them."

She's the original Gossip Girl.

"That's horrible, poor thing. She's such a delicate flower. I hope she'll be able to make our Wednesday meeting. What will we do if she cancels? Email? That'll *never* work."

Naomi's full-on glaring at me now. Dixie, on the other hand, looks like I told her the higher the hair does not actually make her closer to god.

"Oh my. I didn't even think of that! The fashion show is too close to chance it. And if any of those little girlfriends try to take the good outfits, there will be problems. I don't want to have to get ugly at a charity event." When she realizes what she said, she drops Naomi's arm and pulls me into a hug. She stands there with her arms wrapped around me for what feels like an eternity before she whispers in my ear, "Of course I didn't mean you. You're already a wife in all of our eyes, you just need to make it right with the lord."

"The game's almost starting." Naomi grabs my hand and pulls me free from Dixie's embrace. "The elevators to club level are getting really busy; you'll want to get on one before you miss kickoff."

"Thank you, I would've been pitchin' a fit if I missed it! Will I see y'all downstairs at halftime?" Dixie asks.

Downstairs is where family and friends can go and stock up on free food and drinks. So there's only one answer I can give. "Absolutely."

I don't know why Dixie goes because she shares a box with a few of the other offensive linemen's families, and they're stocked to the brim with treats and goodness. I suspect it's so she can gather information on the one-comma club members and bring it to her fellow two-comma members.

The one-comma club is the majority of the team, the poor schmoes who make under a million dollars per season. The two-comma club is for the demigods who make over a million. Get it? It's terrible.

"I'm obsessed with her," I tell Naomi, smiling at Dixie, who's waving like a fool, her teased, sky-high blonde hair bouncing along with her movements before the elevator doors slide shut.

"Me too. It's like listening to a charming alien when she talks." Naomi links her arm through mine. "But you need to be careful who you talk to about Courtney. I doubt Dixie would say anything, but any of those other worker bees would love running back to their queen with dirt on you."

"I'll tell Courtney it was you. It's not like it'd be the first time they got us confused." I laugh, but I'm not joking . . . and Naomi knows it.

"Don't you dare." She pulls her arm away from me and turns to me with wide eyes.

"But I like to be you. It makes me feel tall."

Poor Naomi. We're both biracial, but our caramel skin is

where the comparisons end. She's five foot eight inches, I'm five foot two inches. She has green eyes, mine are brown. She wears a size two, I wear . . . not a size two. We look nothing alike, and I can't tell if they really don't know or if it's another jab where they can only remember the married person's name.

"No. You can never be me at a game. All I'd need is to look online and see reports of me causing a scuffle in the stands."

Fair point.

"But you have to admit, 'Scuffle in the Stands' would be an outstanding headline," I say.

Naomi and Dre got married while they were still in college, so she never had to navigate the waters as a girlfriend. Which was good for her because—and god love her—the poor girl damn near breaks out in hives if she even thinks about getting involved in confrontation. Even so, she still stuck her neck out for me when it came to the Lady Mustangs. I'm one of the few live-in girlfriends on the team, and Chris wanted me to join, but it was met with pushback from the wicked wives.

Naomi never told me exactly what was said at the meetings leading up to me joining, but I know she left her comfort zone to have my back. Because after she went to the Mustang's General Manager and he extended me a formal apology and a personal invitation to the group, Naomi's seat in the hierarchy was long forgotten. Now she lays as low as possible when it comes to drama of any sort, and I make sure to be her voice every now and again.

We make our way to our section, navigating the already rowdy fans and avoiding spilling our Blue Moons. When we make it, Lenny is standing at the top, looking his typical grumpy self.

"Lenny! How's it going? Are you feeling a win today?" I ask. He doesn't crack a smile, but he can't fool me—I know he loves me.

"Eh. Who knows with these putzes they call players? One of them could've had their precious feelings hurt on the tweeter.

When I played, we played for glory, your fellas just play money."
Every week for every season Chris has played for the Mustangs,
Lenny has been guarding the seats to section 112. And every
game, he rants about the same thing. "There's no honor with you
kids. All you want is attention."

"I can always count on you to tell it how it is. Let's hope the
only players with hurt feelings are the Raiders." I pat him on the
shoulder.

"Yeah, yeah. Don't start any trouble today, my hip's been acting up. Wait a few more weeks so I can join in."

"Me? Start trouble? You know me better than that." My hand
goes to my chest, but he still doesn't crack a smile. He just looks
up and mutters something under his breath about frustrating girls
before scolding me for causing a traffic jam in his section.

After the dangerous trek down the cement steps, I catch up to
Naomi, who's in her seat taking selfies while switching from sunglasses to no sunglasses and back again.

"Lenny told me no fights, so you're safe . . . for today. Unless
you don't put the phone away, then I'll be fighting you." I look to
the field in time to see the captains from each team walk to cen-
terfield for the coin toss. "Come on, Nay, it's game time!"

I recognize number twenty-nine as Dre, Naomi's superfine,
chocolate drop, cornerback extraordinaire. He's standing next to
number eight, Brendon Davis, our kicker, who manages to send
my heart rate skyrocketing every time he goes to kick, and number twelve, who is new. All I know about number twelve is he's
the reason football pants were made.

"Your Denver Mustang captains today are Andre Harris,
Brendon Davis, and Gavin Pope." The announcer's voice echoes
across the stadium. "Heads. The Mustangs will be receiving the
ball first."

Gavin Pope. I should've known he was the mystery captain. It
doesn't matter where I am, that ass always summons me.

The crowd bursts into cheers as the Mustang players take their places on the field and the sideline. The energy filling the stadium is so strong, it causes my hair to stand. My heart beats in rhythm with the stomping on the ground, and the scream that rips from the back of my throat harmonizes with the rest of the cheers. The sound builds with perfect momentum as the Raiders' kicker takes a running start and his laces make contact with the football. He sends the ball over Mustang helmets before our returner catches it in the end zone and takes a knee. He hops up after the whistle is blown and tosses the ball to the nearest referee before running off the field.

The crowd stays on their feet as they get their first peek at Gavin Pope leading their Mustang offense. Even though Chris is on the field too, I can't look anywhere but the superfine, super tall quarterback yelling out instructions to his offense.

"Let's get this fuckin' shit done, Pope! Show them why the fuck you play this fuckin' game!" yells a man in the row in front of us, drawing the angry eyes of parents with their young children. Even the woman next to him, who is crazy beautiful, turns to glare.

But whether the language is offensive or not, or if Gavin can even hear him, when Gavin calls for the ball to be snapped, he gets the fuckin' shit done. One of the linemen miss their block, allowing a huge Raiders player to charge straight at Gavin. But Gavin isn't fazed. He spins left with such grace, it's almost as if I'm watching a ballet instead of this brutal and barbaric sport. His long legs guide him with ease to the side of the field where TK is running, and he launches the ball.

I forget how to breathe. The entire crowd goes silent as we watch the football floating into the air, soaring above the defensive line. TK jockeys with the Raiders defender, knocking and dodging, racing to get to the ball when it starts to come down. TK insults gravity and jumps high above the defender, snatching the ball out of the air and securing it tightly against his chest. His pads protect him as he falls back to the field. The crowd goes insane. The ground beneath me starts to shake as everyone loses their minds, jumping up and down, punching the air and hugging their neighbors. I high-five the foulmouthed man in front of me while I'm still screaming, and I laugh when he yells, "Fuck yeah! That's my fuckin' boy!"

One play and Gavin Pope has shown all of Denver he's the player they've been waiting for.

Four

THE MUSTANGS ANNIHILATED THE RAIDERS, BEATING THEM BY more than thirty points. I almost felt bad for them, but then I remembered soldier Marlee shows no mercy. #ThugLife

After games, family and friends of players funnel downstairs and wait for their player to come out of the locker room. After a game like today, the energy buzzes throughout the room. Conversations and laughter fill every nook and cranny . . . except the ones where bitter wives, mad their husbands lost their starting positions, hide.

Old friends discuss plans to celebrate, mothers gush over their son's tackle, kids run around pretending to be big and tough like their daddies. And as the guys come out of the locker room one by one ready to go home and celebrate with their loved ones, the noise dies down, but the energy lingers.

Dre changes faster than Superman and is always one of the first players out of the locker room, which is a bummer for me, because Chris is always last. And because we're buried under 70,000 seats, cell phone coverage is nonexistent. There's one spot in the far corner where, if you balance just right, you can maybe get a bar or two. But otherwise, you're screwed. Do you know how hard it is to avoid conversations when you can't pretend to be checking an important email? Every week, Naomi and Dre offer to wait with me until Chris comes out, but I've never taken them up on the offer. I'm pretty sure some of these women can smell fear—the last thing I need to do is show it to them by calling in the cavalry.

Everyone has left, except for the woman who was sitting in front of us and next to my filthy-mouthed high-five partner. He was down here earlier, but after a few minutes of telling anyone who would listen about the "shitty fuckin' cell coverage," he took off. I'm assuming they're with one of the rookies because I've met a lot of established players over the years, and they don't usually keep people around who attempt at stealing their shine. And whoever these two are? They're the definition of scene stealers. The woman might be quiet, but she's stunning—all pale skin, thick black hair, and legs for days. With a low cut blouse and killer pointy-toe stilettos, she looks like a naughty Snow White. #WhistleWhileYouTwerk

"Dammit," Sexy Snow mutters. She's looking at her phone, and it doesn't take a rocket scientist to figure out she lost her call.

"You have to wedge yourself all the way into the corner, and if you do calf raises while you're on the phone, it helps a lot." I must've been in super stealth mode because what was meant to be a gesture of goodwill causes her to jump back, hit her head, and drop her phone. Oops.

"What?" She doesn't even look at me when she speaks, like I'm not worthy of her attention.

"You're trying to get service, right?" I've been dealing with rude bitches for so many years, her attitude doesn't faze me.

"Oh. Yeah." She almost looks more annoyed now, knowing I'm trying to help her, than she did after she dropped her phone.

"To get service down here, you have to get as close to the wall as you can. Bouncing up and down sometimes helps too."

"How irritating. I'm not bouncing in Louboutins."

Well, excuse me.

"If you go upstairs, service is better there." And you'll be out of my corner so I can use my phone.

"No, it's fine. I'll wait." It doesn't sound like she thinks it's fine. But hey, if she likes it? I love it.

"I'm Marlee, by the way." I extend my hand. If she's new here, we're going to have to get to know each other eventually—might as well get a jump start.

She eyes my hand as if I offered her an old, snotty tissue. She stares at it while, I'm assuming, contemplating if she wants to risk contaminating herself with the millions of germs she seems to think I'm harboring.

That's it. No more Sexy Snow. From now on she's Snobby the Snow Bitch.

I'm about to take my hand away and walk my sparkly ass back to the table when she places her limp hand on mine. "Madison."

I shake her hand, and she lets it flop like a dead fish when I do. Snobby is a special snowflake.

"Yo, Marlee. Let's hit it," Chris calls from behind me right as I pull my hand away. I've never been so happy to see him in my entire life.

"Nice to meet you." I wonder if she's always this miserable or if I'm lucky.

"Mmmh." Her lips pull up into what I think is her trying to smile but really looks like she smells something putrid. I hope it wasn't my hand.

I make no effort in hiding that I want to get away from her and sprint across the room to Chris. When I get to him, his brows are knit together in confusion. I shake my head with as much discretion as possible and pray he'll catch the hint. Thankfully he does and turns on his heel, walking down the long hallway to the elevator.

"Good game, you looked great out there."

"It was okay." He's walking ahead of me, and my short legs in too-high heels are struggling to keep up with his long strides. I knew he was going to be like this. The team won, but he didn't score, and like Lenny told me earlier, my fella is worried about attention. And when he doesn't get it, he gets like this, Pouty McPouterson.

He pushes the elevator button and says no more. I hate the silence. I need there to be noise. Maybe I could sing?

As soon as the thought crosses my mind, the quick clicks of high heels hitting the tile echo through the cold hallway. The quiet hum of conversation grows louder as the footsteps get closer. I sneak a quick glance over my shoulder and when I do, I wonder what in the hell I did in a past life to deserve this. Because coming my way, with her hair floating behind her like she's freaking Beyoncé or something, is Madison the Snow Bitch. And next to her? Gavin. Fuck my life so hard.

I want to start pushing the elevator arrow button over and over again, but before I get the chance, Gavin and Madison stop next to me. I have to do a double take because long gone is the Snow Bitch and in her place is a smiling, giggling supermodel. But I'd probably be smiling and giggling too if Gavin Pope was standing next to me, looking at me like I was the reason the sun rose and set.

Bitch.

I hate her.

The elevator doors open. Because why wouldn't I get trapped in a small space with them?

"Hey, Marlee. Long time no see! You didn't tell me you were married to Chris," Madison says once the doors close behind her.

I look over my shoulder to see if someone else named Marlee got on the elevator without me seeing, because I don't know what the hell just happened. And Chris? Did I miss something? She won't shake my hand, but she's on a first-name basis with my boyfriend? Da fuq?

"Uh . . . yeah. He's my boyfriend, the bedazzled jersey usually gives it away."

If I wasn't so used to seeing it on Courtney, I would've missed the way Madison's eyes narrowed just so and her smile sat frozen. But all's forgotten the second I hear the deep laughter I've been trying to remember for the last four years.

I did *not* do it justice.

"Marlee, nice to meet you." Gavin extends a hand toward me. "Chris is always talking about you. And TK won't shut up about your lasagna, I can't wait to try it."

I take his hand and have to fight to keep my eyes from closing and answering him with a moan instead of words. Even with the extra effort, my voice still comes out strained. "TK will eat anything."

Because after all of these years, he's here. In front of me. *Touching* me. But he's not there. He isn't looking at me the way he does when I dream of his blue eyes watching me. He isn't touching me like he did in his bed before. He's treating me like the stranger I am to him—my only connection to him is being his teammate's girlfriend. I don't know what I wanted to happen. I guess I hoped that even if I was one of many, at least I would've been memorable.

As if hearing my thoughts, Madison wraps her arms around his neck and rests her head on his shoulder. "Do you still want to go to dinner, Gavs? Or are you too tired?"

Gavs? Gross. Why doesn't she pee on him for fuck's sake?

Before he can answer, the elevator doors slide open and yelling fans waiting for autographs fill the small space.

It's like I've stepped into my nightmares. I can't hear my thoughts, just the screeching voices calling for both Chris and Gavin. But truth be told, their names being shouted is the only thing going through my brain lately anyways.

I was wrong, God. I'll take silence over this any day.

Five

"IF THIS STUPID SON OF A BITCH DOESN'T GIVE YOU A RING SOON, I will," TK says from across the table.

He's my favorite. This is his second year in the league, and he's like the little brother I never had. Chris took him under his wing last year, and he's spent every holiday with us. I know for a fact he enjoys my cooking more than Chris, and when he started his nonprofit organization, he hired me to set up his website. When Chris had his website done, he went to a big company that had no interest in him or his cause. He paid triple what I charge and it looks like trash. I'm not bitter either, just smug.

I told TK he didn't have to pay me so long as he recommended me to his friends. The next week I had five new clients and two thousand dollars from "Anonymous" in my PayPal account. He'll always have a special place in my heart.

But by the looks of this dinner, he might not have one with Chris.

I wasn't planning on eating with them. For one, carbs are my frenemy. Second, this is supposed to be a players' bonding dinner and sitting at a table with six football players, listening to them discuss strategy and film, isn't my idea of a good time. Especially when, out of the six, two are feuding quarterbacks, four are competing wide receivers, two have been in my panties, and only one remembers it. Math has never been my strong point and even I can figure out this word problem.

But hey, how could that possibly go wrong?

"Shut up, asshole. You can't come into my house and talk to my girl like that."

Oooh. TK brought out Possessive Chris and it's rare that he makes an appearance. I'm thinking he's regretting inviting all the receivers because this night has backfired on him. He might not agree, but it's pretty comical when you really think about it. Chris was so sure he was going to win Gavin over with his charm and charisma, he didn't realize every other person at the table set out to do the same thing.

Well, except me and Marcus—the rookie wide receiver Chris has taken under his wing this season. We sit together discussing what he should buy his girlfriend for her birthday. She's still finishing her degree back in California. I only met her once, but I'd still wager my gift ideas of an anytime ticket to Denver or a spa day would be better received than his idea of a jersey signed by the Mustangs team.

"All right, guys, while this has been fun, I have a deadline and dishes to do." I clap my hands. I'm so full from dinner, I'm convinced the carbs have already found a permanent home on my ass as I struggle to stand up.

"And we have poker to play and cigars to smoke." Chris rises from the table at the same time I do, but doesn't offer to help clear it like I'd hoped. It's not like I pushed all my work back until later so I could make him enough lasagna to feed an army or anything. Why would he be considerate enough to help clean?

All of the guys follow him after shouting their thanks and farewells my way.

Everyone except Gavin, that is.

"You comin'?" Chris asks.

"You guys go ahead." Gavin holds up his phone. "My agent called while we were eating. I'm going to call him back, and then I'll meet you down there."

"Not a problem, bro." Chris sits back down at the table instead of helping me clear the dishes. "We can wait."

"Please, don't wait for me," Gavin says. "I'll have Marlee show me where you are when I come back in."

Say what now?

Did I miss the portion of the evening where I became the hired help?

"Yeah, why do we have to change everything to cater to him?" Kevin interrupts my thoughts with his whining. No wonder he's married to Courtney. Haters, party of two.

"Shut the fuck up, Kevin." If looks could kill, Kevin would be dead right now. Chris must not have told him this dinner wasn't for Kevin to knock Gavin, it was to get Chris his number one receiver spot back. "If you're sure then. We'll be in the basement. Marlee will show you."

Wait.

"What?" I ask. But I'm too late because Chris is gone and the front door is closing behind Gavin.

I used our good china tonight so it takes me longer to clear the table. Each step is a little more cautious than normal, and the rattling of dishes I usually ignore sounds like alarms wailing in my head. I know I made lasagna for men who wouldn't have blinked if I'd served them on paper plates, but if my nonna taught me anything, it's that presentation matters. Also, I should never leave the house without a little lipstick, but that doesn't apply here.

One by one, I hand wash each dish, dry it off, and stack it on the counter beside me. Dishes might not be my favorite chore, but I'd be lying if I didn't admit to finding a certain peace to it. The constant sound of the water running and the repetitive motions are easy to get lost in. I guess that's the reason I didn't hear Gavin walk back in the house until it was too late.

"Want some help?" His deep voice causes me to jump so high I almost fall and break the dish I'm holding. Lucky for me, Gavin's as good at catching as he is at throwing. He hasn't given any signs he recognizes me, but it's clear my body recognizes him. The touch is innocent, but the feel of his strong hands on my waist causes a shiver to shoot up my spine.

"No." I steady myself on my feet, pull out of his grip, and grab another dish. "Thank you, but I can handle it. Do you want me to show you where the guys are?"

"No. Thank you, but I can handle it." He mimics my words and actions and grabs a dirty plate off the counter, walks around me to the sink, and sets about washing it. "Let's go, Marlee. I'll wash and you dry. It'll be way faster than you doing it alone."

I take the plate out of his hands and dry it with the towel. "You're our guest. Chris would flip if he thought I had you stuck up here doing dishes."

The words come out of my mouth sounding strong and confident, but inside I'm lacking every last morsel of conviction. I don't want him in the kitchen with me, but at the same time, I think I might pull a play out of the Mustangs' playbook and tackle him if he tries to leave . . . and not just because I'm getting tired of the dishes.

"After a dinner like that, I don't mind at all. TK wasn't lying, your lasagna was amazing."

"Thanks, it's my nonna's recipe. She used to make it for my birthday every year growing up. But now that she's getting older, I make it for her." I don't know why I'm telling him this. He makes me nervous and comfortable at the same time.

"You'll have to let me know when her birthday is so I can get in on the next round of pasta."

The idea of Gavin showing up to my family home sets the butterflies in my stomach free. I have to remind myself he doesn't remember me, he's just being friendly to a teammate's girlfriend. End of story.

"Don't you wish. Chris isn't even promised a seat. Quarterback or not, my family doesn't share well when it comes to pasta."

"Well, I'm awesome, and Chris is questionable. Your family would love me."

"Maybe they could find a seat for you, but I'm not sure the room is big enough for your ego to tag along." I ignore the jab at Chris, handing Gavin the final plate.

"Damn. You got jokes?" He acts insulted, but there's a smile on his face when he says it. I shrug it off and give him a hand towel. I tend to forget not everybody knows my sense of humor. Something I should try harder to remember when it concerns my boyfriend's coworkers.

He hands me the last plate to dry, and his fingers graze mine. The contact is so minimal, I shouldn't have noticed it. But when it comes to Gavin, I notice everything. "Thanks for helping, but I really do have work to finish."

I hang the towel from the stove and try to play it cool. I'm not a relationship expert or anything, but I'm pretty sure I've watched enough reality shows to know crushing on your boyfriend's coworker is generally a no-no.

"TK told me you did his website. I checked it out and it looks fantastic. Are you taking on new clients?"

When I turn away from the stove and face him, he's in the same spot, watching me with what I think is either curiosity, mistrust, or kindness.

Yes, I'm aware those are all different, but I've never been very good at reading people.

"Always. It's rare for me to ever turn down a client." I look for something else in the kitchen to keep me busy.

"Good, because my website needs an overhaul since I switched teams."

Oh no. Not gonna happen. Seeing him on occasion is one thing, but working for him is on a whole other level of asking for trouble.

"Your website? Didn't you already have somebody design your website?" I scramble for any excuse to say no. "I doubt you need a new one, just a few tweaks, and I don't like messing with other people's work."

"You just said you rarely turn down a client. I want a new website. I'll have Madison email you some pictures of me in Mustangs gear and shots of my charity events."

Oh lovely, Gavin *and* Madison. This keeps getting better and better.

"Your girlfriend is your secretary? How very old-school."

"Madison isn't my girlfriend. She's an old friend who happens to work in PR." He shakes his head, acting like the idea of him with the leggy beauty is outrageous. "Think about it for me. I'd really appreciate it, and I promise to recommend you to everyone I know."

Dammit. Doing this would be huge for me. I got my degree in graphic design from the Art Institute five years ago and started doing some freelance work to keep me busy. Business has been growing slowly over the past five years . . . which is fine. Chris gets all offended when I offer to pay for anything so I shovel all my money into savings and paying off my student loans.

I graduated with my masters in marketing last spring and have spent all summer (unsuccessfully) trying to find an adult job complete with medical. Unfortunately for me, the closest I got to medical was the marijuana dispensary next door to an interview I went to. So while I wait to find the apparent unicorn job I've spent my entire life preparing for, I might just have to build a website for my ex-fling turned current boyfriend's coworker.

I'm about to agree when the intercom buzzes and Chris's voice booms through the kitchen. "Marlee, can you go find Pope for us?" he asks. He hangs up before I have the chance to answer.

"I guess that's my cue." Gavin starts walking out of the kitchen but stops before he makes it all the way out. "By the way, I think you dropped this." He pulls something small out of his pocket, tosses it to me, and is gone before I even realize what I'm holding.

My grandma's necklace. The one my dad gave me after she passed.

The one I lost four years ago in a Chicago apartment.

Holy shit.

He kept it?

Holy shit.

He remembers me!

Six

"CAN I HAVE TWO ORDERS OF THE GRILLED CHEESE AND TWO MOS-cow mules, please?" I ask the waiter and draw the eyes of everyone at the table.

"Oh sweet lord in heaven, please don't tell me you're eating for two before marriage?"

Before meeting Dixie, I would've never believed that loud could be part of an accent. But it's the only way she ever talks. So when she yells, like she just did, people three blocks over hear her.

"Yes, I'm pregnant. That explains why I ordered two cocktails." Each word drips with sarcasm before I stand up and turn to all of the other patrons. "Vacant uterus, people. Please carry on with your meals."

"Really, Marlee? Why do you always have to cause a scene?" Courtney asks. But by the way her overfilled lips thin and her arms cross, I don't think she actually wants an answer.

I still put as much sugar as I can in my voice when I respond, "The spotlight loves me, Court."

My smile grows even larger when she rolls her eyes to the back of her head and turns her attention to Amber.

"Why did you order so much?" Naomi asks. She must've missed the conversation between me and Courtney because the waiter took her order after mine, and she has so many requests, it always takes her like five minutes. *A Diet Coke with three lime wedges—not two and definitely not four. Salad with olive oil and balsamic vinegar—but only a drizzle of oil and heavy on the vinegar. No! Wait. Bring both to the table. Could you substitute blue cheese for gorgonzola . . . no, blue cheese is fine. No. Definitely gorgonzola.*

Listen, if I didn't love her, I'd throttle her, and I'm sure she's had plenty of extra, undocumented additions to her food over the years.

"One for me, one for you." Her jaw drops, and I know she's going to argue, so I continue before she starts. "No. I want my grilled cheese and if you tried to take half, I was liable to stab your hand with my fork. And since Courtney already gets mad at me for the scenes I don't cause, I can't imagine she'd be thrilled with silverware assault. But I ordered it, not you, so the calories still don't count."

With the last statement, the fight she was about to put up flees. She presses her lips together, nodding her head and clearly wishing I would've swapped the tomato soup for sweet potato fries.

Oh well, still better than dry lettuce.

As soon as the waiter walks away, Courtney pulls the glitter-covered gavel out of her extra large, extra ugly Louis Vuitton bag and starts the meeting.

"So glad everyone could saddle up and gallop on over here for the meeting today." She says the same joke at the start of every meeting. It's not funny the first time you hear it and plain obnoxious the twentieth. The giggles coming from the women around me is proof of the fakeness I already suspected. "I talked to all of the vendors this morning, and they told me everyone had their fittings, so thank you. Everyone's outfits are ready for the fashion show." Her gaze cuts to me. "Except you, Marlee. They said they should have something in your . . . size soon."

Already? Really? Usually she waits until after the food arrives before she starts throwing jabs.

Chris and I went to some little boutique downtown yesterday morning for our fitting. Courtney told the people I was a size fourteen (I'm an eight), and they were left scrambling to get something together for me. They had Chris stuck in a full-on red leather suit with a red turtleneck underneath it. It was absolutely ridiculous and even more so when Chris walked out of the dressing room looking like a black Zoolander. He was so into himself in the mirror, he didn't even realize I didn't try anything on until I told him in the car. The shop said they'd have something for me at the show, but I was hoping they wouldn't.

"Thanks for letting me know." My smile is genuine, and my words have the perfect amount of sugar dusting them for none of the women to pick up on my secret desire to slap the smugness off of Courtney's face.

"Anytime." She smiles at me . . . or at least I think she does. She's gone a little overboard with the Botox over the years. I never realized what a vital part the forehead plays in reading emotions before being around some of these women. "I did hear from some of the other guys who may be bringing dates, and I've made it so the stores will bring extra racks in case girlfriends would like to participate."

Courtney says "girlfriend" like a four letter word. Every time it comes out of her mouth, I envision a battery splitting open and its acid soaking everything surrounding it. It's equal parts fascinating (because I'm pretty sure at some point she was Kevin's girlfriend) and annoying (because I'm pretty sure at some point she was Kevin's girlfriend). The hypocrisy is strong with this one.

"Why can't we just make this one event about us?" Julie, a lineman's wife, asks.

"I'm sorry, Julie, but I didn't see your hand. You know the rules on speaking without being addressed."

Dammit.

I really don't like Courtney, but I can't lie, when it's not me? The pleasure I find in watching her reprimand grown-ass women is endless.

"Sorry," Julie says meekly, melting into her chair.

"It's fine." Courtney says what I guess only I find to be obvious. "We just have to abide by the rules or all we'd be doing is lunching together."

My eyes go wide as I look around the table of women getting ready to eat lunch. I open my mouth to point it out, but before I can get the words out, Naomi's vicelike grip is squeezing my thigh and trapping the words in my throat.

Killjoy.

"Everything for the event looks so great. Amber has picked beautiful floral arrangements. I went to the final tasting last night and it's all delish, and Marlee did a good job with the graphics," Courtney continues, closing the door for me to crack a joke and at the same time, opening another. Because that forced and reluctant compliment she just paid me? It's the reason I volunteer to help with our events. They always say you get more from giving than receiving, and watching Courtney fidget and mumble her way through saying something nice about me?

#Priceless

"It's my pleasure, Court." I know she wasn't giving me an opening to talk, but I'll risk getting scolded like Julie. It's too good of an opportunity to pass up. "Anytime you need anything, Court, I'm here for you." She shakes her head and opens her mouth, but before the words come out, I interject one more time. "No. I'm serious, Court. Anything for the Lady Mustangs."

You know how at Chick-Fil-A they're required to say "my pleasure" every time you tell them thank you? So you say thank you as many times as possible just to hear them say "my pleasure"? No? Well, it's a thing. Trust me.

Anyways, it's pretty much the same concept with calling Courtney "Court." Except she doesn't say "my pleasure." Instead, her eyes reduce to little slits and her body changes from too-much-tanner orange to forgot-sunscreen-at-the-beach red. It's the purest form of entertainment, and it never gets old.

"Thank you, Marlee." Courtney grinds the words out. "I'll keep that in mind."

"Good to hear . . . Court."

Two thank-yous in one meeting?

Best. Day. Ever.

TOWARD THE END of the meeting, my phone starts buzzing with unread emails. Hiding my phone under the table and trying to read them without bending my neck, I see they're from Lauren, a client I'm in the middle of working with.

Now to some bigwig design companies, Lauren's site might not be a top priority. But as a small business, all of my clients are high priority. Plus, I shop at Nordstrom—I know what good customer service looks like. I'll be damned if my clients have anything less than a great experience working with me.

We've been running a soft launch on her site (which looks amazing, by the way) for two or three days now and it came to her attention that her customers aren't getting their confirmations, therefore making it impossible to log in and complete their orders. By the sheer number of emails she's sent over a ten-minute period, it's easy to see she's panicking.

Without uttering a single word, I slide money on the table, give Naomi's shoulder a quick squeeze, and make my exit. I know the wrath of Courtney will fall upon me soon, but I don't care. Work is work and not even she could distract from that.

The meetings are never far from our gated community, so the drive home passes quickly. I park my car on the custom pavement tile driveway (because that wasn't a waste of money), grab my computer from the kitchen, where I left it last night, and make the trek through the marble lined hallways until I reach my office. Except when I sit down and open my computer, I'm met with a background that isn't mine.

Chris and I have the same laptop model, so I'm usually careful about putting it away. But I guess after a certain quarterback threw me a certain necklace, hinting he remembered a certain night together, I totally forgot, and I left mine on the kitchen counter, where Chris usually leaves his.

Luckily, Lauren's problem is a fairly easy fix that I can take care of from any computer. I go to log in to my email, but Chris's computer automatically signs me into his. I'm moving the mouse up to the log out button when the subject line in one email jumps out at me: *Miss you already.*

Now, I'm not normally one to snoop. Chris and I have been together since high school. When he first got into the league, I'd find an earring here or a pair of underwear there, but for the most part, I'd let Chris talk his way out of it. Don't get me wrong, we've broken up many times, but since the last time it happened (four years ago), things have been fantastic. I thought we'd moved on from all of the issues that arose those first few years of Chris's career.

I let the mouse hover for what feels like hours. I know whatever I decide to do next will change my future. I could look, find out he's cheating, and leave like I promised would happen the last time we went through this. Or I could pretend it never happened and try to fight my way back into my rainbow-filled bubble.

I open the email.

Hey baby,

I had so much fun at the game Sunday. I know you had
meetings after, but I was so glad I was able to see you the next
day. This weekend can't come fast enough, when I'll be back
on a plane to see you.

XOXO,
Ava

Oh.
My.
God.
After reading one message, I'm consumed. I sit at the computer, ignoring Lauren and the churning in my stomach, and click
message after message. I find flight itineraries that span the entire
season—home games, away games, even a ticket during the bye
week. And those are just the emails in his inbox. After more obsessing, I check all of his folders and find out the one named
"Confirmations" is filled to the brim with nudes. And like the
glutton-for-punishment fool I am, I look at every single one.

The kicker on it all is while I'm looking at all the different
ways Ava can angle her camera, I notice something disturbingly
familiar sparkling on her right hand. I zoom in and get a crystal
clear view of the ring I thought Chris took to a jeweler to help him
pick *my* engagement ring sitting pretty on this skank's hand.

#OnTheNextEpisodeOfSnapped

I slam the computer shut and navigate my way through the
hallways to the garage. Once there, I pull out every piece of luggage I can find and drag them up the spiral staircase to our room.
All of my shoes. Every dress, skirt, and top. Pictures, yearbooks,
and even my baking supplies all find their way into a suitcase. The
only problem with packing when upset is a few broken picture

frames and more than one gift from Chris hurled across the room and into the professionally painted walls that now need to be professionally patched.

When I have everything I want, I drag them down the stairs one by one, allowing myself to admit how much I loathe this stupid, ugly house.

I pull my last suitcase down the stairs, the sound of my flip flops barely heard over the bang of the wheels every time they hit a marble step. My hair, which I had straightened and left down for our meeting, was getting so frizzy from the sweat I developed going up and down the stairs that it is now in a messy bun on the top of my head. My makeup melted off at some point over the last hour, and mascara is smeared across my cheeks from the traitorous tears I couldn't stop from falling. My tank top is sticking to my chest, and I could really use a re-up on my deodorant. Basically, I'm a hot-ass mess.

So of course this is the moment Chris walks into the house.

He's looking at something behind him and doesn't notice me or my belongings. When I obnoxiously clear my throat, he turns to me with a grin on his face so big, it threatens to take my rage to uncontainable levels. Thankfully, for his safety and my clean record, it flees the second he gets a good look at me and my mountain of luggage filling the space.

"What the fuck, Mars?"

"You took my computer." There's zero emotion in my voice when I speak to him. "I needed to check my email, but yours opened instead."

As I'm speaking, I watch as his face registers what I'm telling him. The range of emotions is fascinating. Confusion, surprise, sadness, until he settles on what looks like anger.

"You went through my shit? I thought we were done with this detective bullshit."

I knew he'd do this. It wouldn't matter if I walked in on him with his dick still inside of another woman, he'd blame me for not knocking. He might get paid from football, but he's a professional fucking gaslighter.

I shrug and walk toward my bags. "Funny, because I thought we were past you fucking groupies and lying to me. Guess we were both wrong."

"Where the fuck do you think you're going?" His temper is steadily rising, but I refuse to give him the reaction he wants.

"My parents' house. I already talked to my dad, he's expecting me."

"Well, you better call him and tell him you need a ride because if you touch my car, I'm calling the cops."

For my birthday two years ago, he woke me up with breakfast in bed and told me he was taking me to pick out my new car. He dragged me to the Cadillac dealership first, then to Mercedes, then to Audi, before I was able to break him down and go to Toyota so I could get my Prius. I love my car, but Chris hates it. The only time he ever rode in it was for the test drive the day he bought it. But you better believe he made sure his name was the only one on the title.

"Really, Chris? You're going to be that petty? You hate my car."

"*My* car," he says.

I guess I'll take that as a yes.

"You're such an asshole. I'll call my dad, but you might want to make yourself scarce. I told him about the pictures of Ava wearing my ring, and he wants to kill you." I throw it out there casually while I'm looking for my phone in my purse. Chris might be a big bad NFL player, but around my dad he's still the same skinny, stuttering kid he was eleven years ago. Actually, having my dad come makes this even better. The thought causes the first hint of a smile since I found out about Ava . . . and Rachelle and Monique and Livvy and . . . well, you get the picture.

"I can take you if you need a ride," says a new, deep voice. And with one short sentence, the smile is long gone.

Chris told me last night that Gavin was coming over to go over some plays with him, but I guess discovering years of betrayal caused me to forget. Clenching my eyes shut, I send up a silent prayer Gavin cancelled and it's another person witnessing this personal low point in my life. My hands stay frozen in my bag, like maybe if I make no sudden movements I'll be able to vanish into thin air. I turn as slowly as I can to identify our new guest.

When I manage to convince myself to open my eyes, my gaze is met with Gavin's hard, angry one before he shifts it to Chris. Even though I'm standing still, I can't get my breathing to slow down.

"No. She's not going to burden my boys with her shit."

"You're not my boy, Alexander. And this shit you're pulling right now is why you never will be."

Welp, that gets my attention.

Chris sucks in a breath so deep, it's a wonder he doesn't pass out.

"You can go to my truck, Marlee," Gavin says. "I'll get your bags." Locked tight in a glare-off with Chris, Gavin doesn't even look at me when he offers.

"Thanks." My answer is quick and quiet, and I'm out the front door before Chris can even register that I've left.

Or before I realize I'm leaving with Gavin.

That escalated quickly.

Seven

"EVERYTHING YOU NEEDED WAS BY THE DOOR, RIGHT?" GAVIN asks.

I've been sitting in the nice air-conditioned cab of his pickup truck—yes! An actual pickup truck!—while he loaded all of my bags from the house in the bed. When he'd first said "truck" I'd figured an SUV.

I didn't want to be stuck in the house with Chris while I waited for my dad to drive all the way out here, but sitting on the leather seats while Gavin climbs in next to me? Well, maybe I would've been better off waiting.

"Yeah, thank you for doing that." I can't look at him. It's embarrassing enough to realize you've invested a third of your life to a total fucking dirtbag, but doing it in front of the man who has managed to sneak his way into your fantasies for the last four years takes it to a whole other level.

I'm not sure what takes up more room in the car, his presence or my shame.

"Not a problem. I'm glad I was here." That makes one of us, I guess.

"Yeah, lucky you."

"Marlee." The way he says my name is almost my undoing. I was prepared for Chris's reaction. I was ready to listen to my dad rant. What I did not brace for was the gentle way Gavin whispers my name. I promised myself no more tears, and he's about to make me break my promise only minutes after making it.

"What?" I hate that I can't even say one word without my voice breaking.

"Can you look at me?"

"Can we please go?" I'm not doing this on my—nope, not mine—Chris's driveway.

"We can, but first I need you—"

"Fine!" I cut him off, narrowing my red, puffy eyes his way. "Is this what you want to see? Listen, I really appreciate you doing this, but I don't want to talk right now. I. Want. To. Go." I take a deep breath, reminding myself that Gavin isn't the person I'm mad at. "Can you please just drive?"

"Yeah, I can drive." He leans over the center console, his face mere inches from mine, and tucks a stray curl behind my ear. His hand lingers next to my face, but he doesn't touch me again. He doesn't retreat back to his space either. "But I'm gonna need you to put the address in my navigation so I know where I'm going."

My address. Of course he needs my address.

My cheeks start to heat, but I can't tell if it's from embarrassment or lust. The tiniest hint of contact—I mean, does touching my hair even count as contact?—has my body humming. Like I've been in sleep mode for the last four years and with a graze across my ear, a whiff of his cologne, the heat of his breath against my cheek, he has woken me up.

"Oh. My address. Yeah . . . of course." I lean in and start tapping on the screen, but Gavin never moves. He just sits there, invading my space while I'm praying my hands stop shaking so I can stop pushing the wrong letters.

Only once I hit enter and a voice comes through the speakers informing us a route is being created does he sit back in his seat. The little bit of space sets my nerves at ease, and I'm able to buckle my seatbelt on the first try.

Gavin shifts the truck into reverse, and I pull my attention from him to the monstrosity I've called home for the last three years of my life. Chris is standing in the doorway, back straight, shoulders back, with his phone to his ear, eyes to the truck as we start to pull away. For a hot second, I wonder if Ava or one of my other replacements is on the other end of the phone. I force those thoughts out of my head.

As the distance grows between me and the house, the reason I've always hated this place hits me. Nothing in there was for me. Every single thing Chris brought into that house was to impress other people. Whether it was his dad, teammates, or women I'd pretended not to know existed, Chris didn't try to make it a home for us. He didn't care if I felt comfortable. If he did, I wouldn't have been able to fit everything important to me in the back of a pickup. If I would've opened my eyes at all, I would've seen what Chris was practically screaming in my face. He was never going to marry me, and if he ever did, that would've been as fake as everything else he gave me. Our entire relationship was an act. I was a showpiece he wanted to be able to dispose of whenever he felt like it.

And that realization freaking sucks.

My chest tightens, my breathing comes quicker, more painful, and I'm trying to find anything to distract me from the volcano bubbling inside of me. So when I think I hear Gavin mutter something under his breath, I latch on to it like a life raft.

"What did you say?" It comes across panicked, almost accusatory.

"Nothing." He stays focused on the road, turning up the music with the controls on the steering wheel.

"No. You said something. What did you say?" I turn the music back down.

"It was nothing."

"If it was nothing, then why won't you tell me?" I'm a dog with a bone, and I'm not letting this go. Nothing he could've said could be worse than the thoughts bouncing around my head.

"I said Chris is a fucking idiot."

"Oh. Okay." I got the idea he wasn't Chris's biggest fan, but I still wasn't expecting that. I reach my hand to the radio to turn the music back up, but Gavin turns the radio off before I get the chance.

"You wanted to hear what I was going to say, Marlee, so let me say it."

Well, crap. Can I call take backs?

"Chris is a dick. Everyone on the team knows—hell, everyone on other teams know. You didn't want to waste your life away with a guy like him. When TK said he'd marry you? You laughed, but you were the only one because every other person at the table knew he was serious. None of the guys can figure out how a fuck-off like Alexander got you, and we ask him about it often. So yeah, sucks you found out the way you did. But it doesn't suck, you finding out."

While a poet he is not, the sentiment's there. And it's there at the time I need it the most. If I hadn't made a blood oath to myself to never date another athlete in the event that Chris and I ever broke up for real, for real, there's a good chance I'd be climbing across the front seat and onto his lap. Highway be damned. #ClickItOrStickIt

"I think that was sweet." The shakiness has left my voice and for the first time in a long time, I feel like a giant, 215-pound man-baby weight has been lifted off my shoulders. "Thank you."

Gavin glances my way, taking his eyes off the road for what's on the verge of being a second too long, and squeezes my hand before turning the radio back on. The music fills the car seconds before Future tells me all about never apologizing for cheating.

I can't hold it in.

My eyes, still sore from crying, crinkle. My lips, bruised from how hard I was biting them, curl up. And a laugh slips out at the irony of "Low Life" being the first song I hear after leaving Chris.

Even the universe knows what's up.

Or it's mocking me . . .

Eight

PULLING INTO MY CHILDHOOD HOME, A SENSE OF PEACE SETTLES over me. The flowers my mom obsesses over every spring until fall brings their demise are the perfect accessory to my dad's flawless, manicured lawn. The bright buds line the walkway and hang from every corner of the quaint front porch. The turquoise rocking chairs we painted when I was a freshman in high school are still sitting in the same place, though they have faded and chipped over the years.

But before I can reminisce any further, the screen door swings open and my dad comes out, already in the middle of a full-blown, on-the-verge-of-gloaty rant.

"I told you, Marlee. I told you when you came home with hearts in your eyes at sixteen I didn't like that damn kid. He was a squirmy little fucker then and he's still a squirmy son of a bitch today. Flying girls out here like he didn't already have the prize in that ugly-ass palace he stuck you in."

I love how my dad goes all papa bear for me. "I know, I know. You were right."

"Damn straight I was." He says the words, but it's clear he

takes no joy in this as he walks to me and wraps me up in a tight hug. "You all right, baby girl?"

"I'm fine. It's been a long time coming. I'm just grateful I found out before I wasted more of my life on him." It's the truth. Crazy how fast perspective can shift over the course of a car ride. "Where's Mom?"

"She went to the store to get some of that healthy crap you like to eat." His lip curls up in disgust.

"It's not like I'm juicing kale all day, but margarine isn't real food."

"You say tomato, I say ketchup." He's totally where I get my elegance from.

We're both laughing when he looks over my shoulder and almost as fast as he grabbed me, he lets me go, straightening to his full, six-foot-three-inch height (how I'm only five foot two is still a family mystery). He growls at somebody behind me. "Who the hell are you?"

"Gavin Pope, sir." Gavin, more swoon worthy than ever, holds his hand out to shake my dad's. "I happened to be there when Marlee was ready to leave and offered her a ride."

"The new quarterback, huh? Good first game. Everyone around here was glad to find out Jacobs still has some sense, bringing you in."

What in the fresh hell is this?

Never, not once in my twenty-seven years on Earth, has my Dad ever straight-up complimented a person. Not even me!

"Thank you, sir. Hopefully he'll get a new receiver I can throw to."

"My man." My dad slaps him on the back and laughs. Laughs! "Call me Jarod."

Okay. What is this trickery?

"Nice to meet you, Jarod. I'm going to grab Marlee's bags, where should I put them?"

"I'll help—dropping them by the front door will be fine." They start down the stairs, laughing and talking and going on their merry way together. I stand in the same place my dad left me, watching them, catching a few flies with my open mouth, and decide that of all the not okay things that happened today, this is the most not okay.

My dad and Gavin are not allowed to be buddies.

They're walking back together, the perfect yin to the other's yang. Gavin's olive skin and blue eyes are the direct opposite of my dad's chocolate on chocolate features. They're both about the same height, but Gavin's broad shoulders and defined arms make him look larger than my dad.

"Why didn't you just drive your car, Mars?" Dad asks.

"Ummm . . ." Crap. Gavin and I started talking about the merits of country music verse hip-hop in the car and I forgot to figure out a game plan for when this question inevitably came up.

My non-answer gives away more information than I hoped. I know this because the happy-go-lucky guy who laughs and tells people to call him Jarod is long gone. His nostrils flare, and his lips are pulled in a thin, straight line. I instantly revert to my fourteen-year-old self who got caught sneaking Old Lady Jenkins's cigarettes. My palms are sweaty, and I'm desperately searching for any plausible reason I wouldn't have a car when Gavin decides to speak up.

"Chris told her she had to leave it."

My nerves disappear, and I turn my hard eyes to him. He must not feel my anger—or know about my boxing skills—because he just shrugs a shoulder my way.

Traitor.

And that's the moment my Dad loses his ever-lovin' mind.

"He what?" He's so loud, I swear I can feel his words. I look around to see if our neighbors rush to stand in their door frames, mistaking Jarod Harper's wrath for an earthquake.

"It's not a big deal, Dad. I didn't want anything he bought me anyways." Except my shoes. I might not care about many material items, but shoes are like mini sculptures. And what kind of designer (graphic still counts!) would I be to deny such an art form?

"I'm gonna kill him." His volume has decreased, but the low, menacing tone manages to make the words come out ten times scarier. I think the only reason he lowered his voice is so the neighbors can't tell the police what they heard.

I shoot a glare Gavin's way, trying my best to say *look what you did now* without having to say it. Again, he just shrugs. Jerk.

"Dad, really. It's okay."

"It's not okay. You had a car. One you bought yourself and were almost finished paying off. That fuckin' scumbag convinced you to sell it when he gave you that ugly thing."

"Whoa now. No need to insult Honey-Blossom. She's innocent in all of this." I try and pull the anger away from my car, who's a victim just as much as I am.

"Honey-Blossom?" Gavin asks.

"Her hippy-dippy Prius," Dad says at the same time I tell him, "My Prius."

With this new bit of information, I can't tell if Gavin is going to laugh at me or join my dad in his quest for blood.

"You named your car Honey-Blossom?" Gavin's eyebrows reach his hairline, and his jaw comes dangerously close to the pavement.

"Yeah . . ."

"Why?" he asks.

"Because it's an awesome name for an awesome car." Am I missing the real question here? Why would anybody *not* want to name their car a name they found on a list for "Top Hippy Baby Names"?

"Alexander is *such* a fuckin' idiot," Gavin mumbles.

I'm not really following how he got there after asking about my car.

Dad seems to get it though. He turns his wide, brown eyes on him and says, "You get it!"

"Of course I do. The only one who didn't is Alexander. Everything around her and all she wanted was a Prius she named Honey-Blossom."

Ugh. And men say women are confusing?

"You guys are so strange." I ignore the weird tingly feeling I have watching these two get along so well. I won't be going to games anymore, and there's not a chance I'd ever move back toward where the players live, so the chances of running into Gavin after this day are slim to none. But I still think about it.

"You wanna ride with me to go get it?" That is Gavin . . . Gavin asking to give my Dad a ride to Chris's.

"Yup. Let me grab my bat first." That's Dad agreeing to go, but only after he gets a potential weapon.

Oh sweet lord, where is Dixie when you need someone to pray for you?

"Oh no. It's really not that serious, you two." Not as serious as five to ten, that is. "I have money in savings. I'm not loaded or anything, but I'll have enough for an apartment and lightly loved car. I'm thinking I'll name this one Bluebell Sparkle."

"Bluebell Sparkle?" Gavin asks incredulously.

"This damn girl. You see, Gavin, you see what she does to me?" My dad sounds defeated. Like he's accepted I'm the reason he will have a heart attack one day.

"Yes, Bluebell Sparkle, and you're going to love her, Dad. So stop whining and let's get the rest of my bags. And, Gavin." I get his attention, my voice changing to a conspiratorial whisper. "If you stop encouraging my Dad, you can see my room. And if you're really good, maybe I'll even let you sit on my twin bed."

"What'd I tell you? This damn girl's gonna put me in an early grave," Dad says to nobody and everybody.

Then the three of us get busy grabbing the rest of my bags. After we drop them in our entryway, Gavin says he has to leave, even after my Dad's multiple attempts to keep him around for longer. I'm okay with him going, but I think I see my dad wipe a few tears as Gavin's taillights disappear through our neighborhood.

He might've been a good guy today, but I've been around this life for too long to be tricked.

No more athletes, and definitely no quarterbacks.

Nine

SO, I MIGHT'VE EXAGGERATED THE AMOUNT I HAD IN SAVINGS. IT wasn't enough for an apartment and a gently used car.

I mean, technically, it was. But the design work I do isn't a consistent, reliable income yet, and the thought of draining so much of it on a car when Denver has invested so much into their public transportation seemed like a waste.

And rent.

Don't get me started on rent.

My mom warned me that ever since Denver legalized marijuana, the cost of living here skyrocketed. But like a typical daughter, I brushed her off and ignored her warnings.

She was not wrong.

When I first started looking—as in the day after I moved in; living with my parents was not an option—I was hoping for a little apartment in a super trendy area downtown. But when I realized I wasn't willing—or able—to spend $2,500 a month on a studio, my search had to move. I ended up in Denver's historic Five Points neighborhood. Just on the outskirts of downtown, it's in the middle of revitalization. So while one block was covered with million-dollar condos . . . some were not. My one bedroom, one bathroom, five hundred square foot apartment fell somewhere in the middle. A little classy, a little hood, a lot Marlee. I fell in love with it immediately.

Since I'm lacking transportation, the fact that my apartment's right around the corner from the light rail was a huge selling point. More importantly, it's only two blocks away from a hipsters' paradise complete with an organic coffee shop, a restaurant filled to the brim with ping-pong tables, men with beards and skinny jeans, and my new favorite place ever: HERS.

HERS is the most badass twist on an old gentleman's club. Instead of a shoe shine, there's a paint touch-up for manicures. Instead of sports playing on TVs, it's a different city of housewives. Beer on tap? Nope. But there is a never ending selection of Skinny Girl.

A free photo booth is outside of the bathrooms to take pictures with the friends you made inside. Next to it is a wall where you can tape your pictures and scribble a note on one of the many Post-its declaring your new, lifelong, just-for-the-night bestie.

The moment I walked in, I knew I wanted to be a part of it. I found the owner that night and offered to help build her website, do designs for ads—anything she needed, I was her girl. I left HERS that night equal parts buzzed on Skinny Girl and high on life because not only was I the new part-time bartender, I was also head of the newly (as in that night) formed marketing department.

#KickingAss&TakingNames

I love my tiny-apartment-renting, public-transportation-taking, multiple-job-having new life, and even though my walls are bare and my coffee table is an unpacked box, I couldn't wait any longer for Naomi to come see.

I called her last night and bribed her with the promise of my company.

Kidding.

I promised her booze and homemade cookies. So, she came . . .
obviously.

"But what happened, Marlee? Everything was fine last week
and now you're living here." The way she looks around my little
apartment, her lip curled up like she smells feet, is hilarious.
"Stop laughing! I'm serious. Wednesday we go to a meeting together, then that night you tell me you moved back home, which
I thought was a joke until I ended up sitting next to a redheaded
Courtney Junior at the game. What the hell is going on?"

I doubt she was supposed to tell me about Chris's new flavor
of the week going to the game, but once it's out, it can't be shoved
back in.

"He already has her going to the games? What an asshole!
What's next? Is she going to be driving Honey-Blossom?"

"Oh sweetie." She squeezes my leg. A stranger would think she
was being sincere, but I know better, and her sweet voice isn't fooling me. "Nobody, and I mean *nobody*, wants Honey-Blossom."

"Oh, I'm sorry. What was I thinking? Why would anybody
want to help the environment and save money?" I set my wineglass on the table—I mean box—so I can have the full use of my
hands to get my point across. It's a weird thing to get worked up
over, but insulting my car is the equivalent of insulting the children I may have one day in the very distant future. "Enjoy driving
around in your giant earth killer, but don't come complaining to
me when gas shoots back up to five dollars a gallon and I'm just
chillin' with my fifty-eight miles per gallon."

"Hey now. I drive a hybrid too."

"An Escalade hybrid," I correct her. "What's the fucking point
of that?"

"You're the strangest person I know," she says without a hint
of a smile.

"You love me." I blow her a kiss from the opposite end of my
Ikea couch.

"Whatever you say. Anyways . . ." She sets her glass next to mine in the most awkward transition ever. "You're still coming to the fashion show, right?"

I mean . . . is she for real?

"Can you pass me the remote?" I ask.

"Sure . . ." She gives me my remote, and I start flipping through the channels until I find the station I'm looking for. "The Weather Channel?"

"Yeah, I'm just checking to see if it's going to be a cold day in hell on Monday." The words come out so seriously, it takes a minute for Naomi to register what I said, but I know when she does because my bright yellow throw pillow hits me in the head.

"Can you be serious for one minute, please?" she asks, and I can tell by her tone she means it.

"Fine." I'll do this, but not happily.

"You have to go," she says plainly. Like those four words change everything.

"Ummm. . . . no. I don't. Half of those women didn't want me there when I was dating Chris. Now, I'm not even a girlfriend, and I'm not letting them stick a groupie label on my head."

"Screw them all. You worked harder than all of those bitches combined. All Courtney did was use the same caterer we've always used. Amber literally called the florist and told them to do what they wanted. You're the only one who did any actual work."

"You speak the truth, continue." I wave her on.

"You designed the site to buy tickets. You went out and brought in all of the new designers. You made and sent out invitations. You're the reason ticket sales are up thirty percent. So it will be a cold day in hell if you think I'll let you stay at home while Courtney steals all of your credit!"

Naomi's the most even tempered person I've ever known, so to see her all worked up on my behalf has me feeling weirdly honored.

"It's not that I don't appreciate your passion, because trust me, I'm totally living for it right now. I'm just not sure I want to go. I'm doing really well. I have a new job. I have my own place. I'm relearning who I am. I don't know if I want to throw a wrench in what I'm doing by going to the fashion show." I reach out and grab her hand because for some reason, her eyes are shimmering with tears while she listens to me. "I know what you have with Dre is real and good. But that's not what I had with Chris. Chris was every bad athlete stereotype rolled into one, and I sat there, oblivious for *years*. I'm not ready to see him."

"Forget Chris. What about me? You cannot just move across town, throw me to the wolves, and disappear. Last week's meeting was akin to torture. I cannot deal with those bitches without you there calling Courtney 'Court' and ordering food I can steal. The least you could do after abandoning me is come to the fashion show."

I wonder how much she paid for my ticket when she booked this guilt trip.

"How about this? We go shopping tomorrow and if I can find something to wear, I'll go." Compromise is the key to life. Plus, she's so pathetic when she's sad, only a monster—or Courtney—could flat-out deny her.

"Oooh . . . a shopping challenge." She wiggles her eyebrows. "I'm always on board for that!"

"You're going to be the best mom because you give a fantastic freaking guilt trip."

"I know. How do you think I got Dre to give in to redecorating the living room?" she asks. And she's smiling! What a sneaky—but talented—asshole.

"I really don't like you right now. But even so, I feel obligated to compliment you on your ability to fake cry." I throw the pillow back at her, but instead of it hitting her in the face like it did to me, she grabs it out of the air and catches it.

So unsatisfying.

"Thank you. I was the lead in my high school's plays four years in a row. I also played softball." She waves the pillow in my face with a triumphant smile on her face.

"Way to keep that card hidden in your back pocket. Well played, Mrs. Harris."

"Appreciated." She stands and walks the three feet to my kitchen and grabs a pop out of the fridge. "So after we find your smokin' outfit, are you gonna ride with us?"

"*If* we find an outfit, I'll just Uber it. No need for you guys to drive all the way down here to go right back. But I'm *not* walking in alone. If you get there before me, keep your tight little asses in your car and wait for me."

"Fine with me. I don't want to go in there without you anyways. I'll tell Dre he's got two dates. He thinks you're a hottie, so he'll be thrilled."

I won't lie, finding out Chris was cheating on me with the red-headed human version of Jessica Rabbit was quite the knock to my confidence. And by knock, I mean getting in the ring with Mayweather, Tyson, and Ali. So hearing Naomi say her smokin' hot superstar hubby thinks I'm a hottie doesn't go unappreciated.

But I suck at accepting compliments, so I joke it off. "He should. I mean, according to some of the women, I'm your twin. Remember?"

"You're ridiculous." She rolls her eyes. "But since we have the fashion show squared away, are you gonna show me these bartender skills of yours or what?"

"If by skills you mean pouring tequila shots and glasses of wine? You got it." I grab my keys and turn to her before we reach the door. "Oh! I can practice on you! Experiment with my talents."

"Shit. Then let me call Dre now and warn him that he'll be driving to the hood later to get me."

"Excuse me, ma'am. I do not live in the hood. I live in a historical part of Denver, surrounded by original architecture, character, and history."

"And the homeless man set up on the corner? What's he?" she asks.

"You mean James? He's part of the character."

"You know his name? Please tell me you're being careful. I know you think your boxing classes have made you invincible, but they haven't."

"Yes, I know his name. Some days I'm able to bribe him with a latte to keep me company on my walk to get coffee, and he tells me all about what it was like living here in the eighties." I imagine we have matching expressions, both eyes wide and mouths dropped open. Except her face is filled with horror and mine with excitement. "Did you know a house only a few blocks west was where the biggest dealer in Denver lived, and before these apartments were here, there was a nightclub he owned solely to deal cocaine out of?"

"Why would I know that, and why are you excited learning it?"

"It's cool! Knowing these places were here years ago, unsavory characters and all. Can't you just see them on the street with Kangol hats and a boom box on their shoulder?" Clearly she can't or she just doesn't try because her horrified expression never falters. "Whatever. You enjoy the cookie-cutter mansions and the wicked wives. I'd take James, his stories, and my little place any day of the week."

"Can't I have my house without the wicked wives?" Her bottom lip pouts, and she looks so adorable, I almost pinch her cheeks.

"You know as well as I do, they go hand in hand." An unfortunate truth. It seems as though having the big house and fancy cars aren't enough for some people. The only way they can feel good about themselves is if they squash others around them.

"I hate it when you're right." She throws her phone back in her purse and opens my front door. "Now I need to get drunk since you've made me jealous of your friend James while I'm stuck with Courtney and Amber."

I lock my door and follow her down the staircase.

"If drunk is what you want, drunk is what you'll be. You're going to love HERS so much, I wouldn't be surprised if you and Dre are my neighbors soon."

I was happy to wash my hands of just about everything I had in my life with Chris, but my friendship with Nay wasn't one of them. Having her next to me, embracing me, encouraging me, means more than she'll ever know. But I'm going to try and show her how much with the best night ever.

At least, I hope it will be.

Because tomorrow I might see Chris . . . and let's face it, it's going to be a complete shit show.

Jen

NAOMI IS SLOSHED.

We drank a little bit at my place, but the second Brynn—the owner of HERS—saw us walk in, I was summoned behind the bar with her, and Naomi was placed front and center, serving as our unofficial taste-tester. Naomi ingested copious amounts of alcohol and expelled all my business.

So now, instead of serving her more drinks, we are leaning against each other, preventing the other from tumbling off the barstool and onto the floor.

"Fuck men, you know?" I slur. "Especially athletes."

"Heeeeyyyy," Naomi whines from behind me or next to me. I'm not sure. After the last tequila shot, my entire body started to become numb. "Dre plays football, and he's aaaaamazingg."

"And I'm so happy for you." I swivel around on the barstool and send both of us stumbling in different directions. Once we've found our footing, we take long, slow, crooked steps back to each other, and I wrap her up in a bear hug. "Because you're just, like, so amazing and you deserve to be happy."

Naomi squeezes me tighter. "You deserve to be happy too."

She's crying now. Naomi always cries when she gets drunk. "Chris was never ever good enough for you."

"Now that we know how much y'all love each other and what Marlee deserves, what's the plan for tomorrow?" A stone-cold sober Brynn interrupts us. "You're searching for something to wear? I'll have my pops watch HERS and go with you guys. At the very least, a night with your ex calls for a new dress, shoes, and lipstick."

"And new panties!" Naomi shouts what I'm pretty sure in her head was meant to be a whisper.

"Why would I need new underwear?" I ask. "I can't see into the future and even I know nobody will be seeing those."

"I dunno. I just like shopping for lingerie. Plus, pretty undies make you feel sexy even if nobody else sees them." She locks her eyes with mine and places her hand on my shoulder. "And I say this with love, girl, if Chris brings Ava, you're gonna wanna feel sexy. I hate her, but I'd be a liar if I said she wasn't super freakin' hot."

"I'm well aware." I'm also in the know about her waxing style, but I decide to keep that little tidbit of gossip to myself.

I hate Naomi for bringing Ava up and at the same time I want to kiss her. I was a mess enough at the thought of seeing Chris, Ava hadn't even crossed my mind.

Okay.

Lying to myself again.

Ever since I stumbled across Chris's personal porn gallery, I've been trying my hardest to convince myself this had nothing to do with me and Chris is just a pig. Some days I even believe it. But others? Well, those days I think about all the times I didn't order a salad or go to the gym like I should've. I think of the sweats I've had since high school that I wear for pajamas and not something silk and lacy like Chris was always trying to get me to wear. I ask myself if I tried harder, if I lost those pesky fifteen—FINE!—

twenty pounds I've been holding on to for years if he wouldn't have strayed.

Naomi's right. I'm going to need every little bit of sexiness I can manage.

SIPPING MY ICED coffee and tapping my foot at the Nordstrom entrance, I check the time on my phone again. This is why I'm always late. Waiting for other people sucks.

Brynn shows up first. Her blonde hair is pulled into a topknot on the crown of her head, and she's wearing a fitted tee, skinny jeans that are ripped at the knee, and a pair of Converse, and she still manages to look as if she spent all her life roaming the streets of Paris and Milan. She's one of those effortless beauties you hate because if you walked down the street like that, people would probably give you their change and leftovers.

Naomi, on the other hand, looks a hot-ass mess. She shows up twenty minutes late with oversized sunglasses, a large coffee, and Advil on hand to help with the hangover she's nursing. If we weren't here to get me around my ex tonight, I would've felt bad for her. But as it is? I stick my tongue out at her and point and laugh.

Maturity isn't my strong point.

"First we find the dress, then shoes, unless of course we need to hit lingerie for a special bra." Brynn looks to her phone where she no doubt has a note written with today's schedule on it.

"We should probably look for a bra . . . or Spanx, first. I'm gonna need some armor to brave fluorescent lights and extra-large mirrors."

"Let's just get this show on the road and lower our voices while we do it." Naomi grabs her head.

"Every party has a pooper, that's why we invited you, party pooper," I sing much too loud. Naomi cringes, Brynn laughs, and the old man holding his wife's bags glares. You can't win them all.

"Oh my god. If you never sing again, I'll buy whatever shoes you want today," Naomi says.

"Are you kidding me?" Brynn asks. "If you sing everything like we are living in a musical, I'll double your pay."

Suffice to say, I'm not the most talented singer in the world. But what I lack in talent, I make up for in volume and chutzpah.

I don't go full on *Rent*, but I have to buy my own shoes.

Three hours, one dress, one matching bra and panty set, two pairs of shoes, three shades of red lipstick, and a necklace later, I'm broke.

I'm also going to the fashion show.

Curse you, Nordstrom, and your wide selection.

We're also ordering lunch.

"Naomi, we aren't at a Lady Mustangs meeting. I swear if you order a side salad and reach for anything on my plate, I'll shank you."

"Are you kidding me? I'm getting the bacon burger and fries. Hangovers are a valid excuse to break your diet. Lettuce doesn't absorb booze; you can only count on carbs to get that job done. Speaking of Mustangs meetings"—Naomi closes the menu and looks to me with a sparkle only good gossip can put in her eyes—"did I tell you what happened on Wednesday?"

"Oh lord." I settle on the chicken sandwich and put my menu down. "You didn't, but I'm not having a hard time imagining it."

"Wait, wait, wait." Brynn slams her hand on the table. "What the hell is a Lady Mustang?"

Sweet girl, so innocent from the horrors and cattiness of NFL wives.

"The charity group run by the Mustang players' wives. The cause is good, but somewhere it went a little haywire." Naomi fills her in.

"By somewhere, she means Courtney Matthews. The evil other half of Kevin Matthews," I whisper across the table in case any Nosy Nelly's are sitting nearby.

"Got it . . . start talking." Brynn motions for Naomi to start her story. I mean, the girl owns a bar; she's not one to shy away from juicy gossip.

"Okay. So Courtney starts the meeting with the bang of her stupid glitter gavel. Yeah, she has a gavel," she says to Brynn, whose eyes have already doubled in size. "And she goes, 'Welcome Lady Mustangs. My fellow *wives*.' She stressed 'wives' like that. '*Wives*, if you haven't already heard, we're finally back to the way we're meant to be. I think Dorothy said it best, but I'll give it a go: ding-dong, the girlfriend's dumped!'"

I laugh at the same time Brynn lets out a horrified gasp.

"Can you believe it? And everyone's laughing at her like she's on *Saturday Night Live* or something. I'm sitting there looking at them like they're crazy and say, 'Pretty sure Dorothy never said that, maybe it was the brainless scarecrow.' Like freaking *Mean Girls* robots, they all stop laughing at the exact same time and aim their red, glowing eyes my way. It was terrifying. I thought they might all attack me, remove my brain, and put it in a jar for Courtney to put next to the rest of theirs that are no doubt hidden somewhere in her house."

The waiter stops at our table to take our order, but before he gets a chance to speak, Brynn turns to him and says, "She's in the middle of the best story I've ever heard, we need another minute . . . or fifteen. Please."

Good news for us, he's had heart eyes for Brynn since the second we walked in, and he not-so-discreetly whispered to the hostess to seat us in his section, so instead of being insulted and maybe spitting in our food, he's just happy he heard Brynn's voice.

"Okay." Brynn looks back to Naomi when he walks away. "Continue and don't lose any of your enthusiasm."

"Girl, I know you're new, so I'll clue you in." Naomi sits a little taller and zooms in on Brynn. I've already been clued in, so I mouth the words along with her. "I tell the best stories . . . all the time."

I can't take these girls anywhere.

"Naomi 'The Best Storyteller' Harris, got it." Brynn draws a checkmark in the air in front of her.

"Got that right." Naomi takes a deep sip of her Diet Coke. "Where was I? Oh yeah. So they're all staring at me like I'm the enemy intruder until Courtney bangs that stupid glitter gavel on the table and all at once their heads swivel toward her like good little soldiers, and she starts the meeting. Throughout the entire meeting, every time she'd mention anything about the advertising or funds raised, I'd call out, 'Marlee got so many donations,' or, 'Didn't Marlee do a great job on the design?' Basically, I just mentioned your name at every opportunity I could find.

"And then . . ." She bounces in the seat so hard, it sends my chest into the metal edging of the table. "As soon as she hit the gavel for the final time, I paid my bill, stood up, and said, 'See you next Tuesday, Court. Oops. I mean Wednesday,' winked at her, and walked away."

"Shut up!" Brynn and I shout at the same time and startle the two women chatting at the table next to us.

"I know, right! It was so good!" Naomi falls back into her seat as if she just finished running a marathon. But, to give her proper credit, she talks so fast and gives such exaggerated hand movements, it really is like she's leading a mini Zumba class.

"I'm not sure if I've told you lately, but I love you," I say. Because when your girl drops a not-so-subtle see (C) you (U) next (N) Tuesday (T) to a group of women talking shit about you, you're obligated to divulge your feelings. #FriendshipRule183

"I know." She looks at me. "But as many times as you've had my back, I figured it was about time I had yours."

"Shit." Brynn's gaze flickers between me and Naomi. "I need to hang with you guys more often."

"Ain't that right, boo?" I ask the question I've asked Naomi hundreds of times.

"True." She raises her glass in the air and we cheers just as our waiter returns.

Nobody orders a salad.

Eleven

THE ROAD TO HELL IS PAVED WITH GOOD INTENTIONS.

I'd really do well to remember that in the future.

Grayson, my Uber driver with an awesome knit hat and glasses with no glass, drops me off in front of Naomi and Dre, who I texted a few minutes ago letting them know I was almost there. We walk in together, like proud polygamists, while Dre, under the extreme pressure of Naomi, tells me I look beautiful.

The second we enter the building, I run smack-dab into Mrs. Mahler, the over-Botoxed, slightly eccentric wife of the Mustangs' owner. She's one of the lucky few who get a free pass out of the meetings, but a front-of-the-line pass to the events.

"Marlee, my love! Courtney told me you wouldn't be coming tonight," she says, her voice laced with the rasp that never leaves because of the cigarettes she's always smoking out of her long, gold cigarette holder.

"She must've heard wrong, because here I am." I frame my face with my hands and curtsy.

"And I'm thrilled you are, darling," she says. She takes a long pull from her cigarette, even though there's signage everywhere saying the venue is smoke free. "You did such a phenomenal job putting this all together. You know, even Mr. Mahler came to me discussing this year's fashion show. Your marketing skills have been so effective, one of the boys from marketing thought he was being replaced."

She's leaning in conspiratorially, which would normally make me cringe—I can't deal with close talkers—but she's telling me gossip that's wrapped with compliments for my work, and I spotted Courtney watching us in the corner. Since Courtney wants to be Mrs. Mahler and she hates me, every time I laugh at something Mrs. Mahler says, I direct my smile and gaze Courtney's way. She's redder than a tomato and working so hard on scowling, she might just succeed. I bet Chris's dad will be on the receiving end of a phone call requesting more Botox tomorrow.

"Oh you're kidding! That's so funny and good to hear. I'm so glad you like my work and that the crowd is even bigger than I anticipated," I say, and I'm not lying. I might not be as desperate as Courtney to be in Mrs. Mahler's good graces, but I'd be insane if I said I'm not over-the-moon thrilled for her to like me and my work. Between her and her husband, they have connections I could never even dream of.

"Yes, darling. You did a wonderful job. I know that Courtney girl is trying to take credit for your work, but I wanted you to know that we all know who's really behind tonight's success." She throws a wink my way before she waltzes across to the room to one of her friends.

I look to where Courtney was standing, only to see she's been joined by a few of the other wives. And if I'm not mistaken, which I'm not, they have flipped the script on me and all the sly looks and evil laughter are now being sent my way. They must not realize they conditioned me for this treatment during the meetings. I smile, then turn on my heel to go search for Naomi . . . and booze.

I find Naomi and Dre by the bar, guarding an empty barstool I'm assuming is for me, and try to make it there as fast as I can without running. I'm so close, I can almost feel the leather barstools sticking to my thighs under my too-short dress, when a cold, strong hand grabs my wrist and stops me in my tracks. I turn around slowly, praying I'm wrong, but knowing I'm right, and look into the eyes of the last person I wanted to see.

Well, the last two people I wanted to see.

And so now, instead of being snuggled next to a bottle of tequila, I'm face-to-face with Chris and Ava, who's wearing my ring and making my slutty-to-me dress look conservative.

"Chris." I try to sound like a bitch, but bitchy has never been my thing and instead I just sound kind of constipated. "Ava. Nice to see you outside of emails and with clothes on."

Correction, kind of with clothes on. I'll never understand these see-through dresses women wear. What's the point of the fabric if I can still see your underwear?

"What are you doing here, Marlee? And why were you talking to Mahler's wife? You better not try to fucking sabotage me because I won't take you back."

Pretty boy say what?

"I'm sorry. You must have me confused with another girlfriend who dumped you, because the one you're talking to right now has no interest in *ever* getting back together with you." I turn to Ava and look to her hand. "Nice ring. I remember when Chris gave it to me for Valentine's Day a couple years back. It looks great on you though."

So maybe I'm catching on to this bitchy thing after all.

The smile she was wearing starts to fade at the same time her cheeks brighten, but instead of directing her angry gaze at Chris, she aims it at me. Like I'm the one who gave her stolen jewelry. Don't shoot the messenger.

"Bitter doesn't look good on you, sweetie." Her voice is so high-pitched I wouldn't be surprised if she has been solicited to lend her voice to a dog-calling app.

"Oh, sweetie," I mimic her. "Trust me, I'm not bitter. You saved me from making a big mistake. Actually, you know what? Find me later, I'll buy you a drink."

When Brynn was doing my makeup before I came, we ran over lots of different scenarios in my head. This was the third one. I bitched and moaned when we started, but now I owe her a huge apology. Because without our practice, there's no way I would've been able to come up with that comeback and sound as genuine as I did. And the look on Ava's face when she doesn't get the reaction she wants out of me is so satisfying.

"You're so full of shit. I'm the only reason you're here and you know it," Chris cuts in, putting the spotlight back on himself. Typical.

"I've missed your overinflated ego, but now that you've refreshed my memory, I should be fine without you for a little while. But I'll come find you later if I need another reminder." I turn and make my final steps to the bar. My confident, bitchy facade fades with every step, and when I reach Naomi and Dre, they already have a tequila shot waiting.

Without a word to either of them, I bring the tequila to my lips and throw it back, savoring the burn as it travels down my throat and warms my stomach. Good thing I like it because before I can reach for the lime, another punch is thrown.

"Marlee. We didn't know if you'd come tonight. I was so sad to hear about you and Chris," Courtney says from behind me. I know she said she was sad, but it sounds a lot like gloating to me.

I make sure my bright smile is secure on my face before turning to her. "And miss a night with you, Court? Never! Besides, Mrs. Mahler was so happy *I* made this event such a huge success. I would've hated to disappoint her."

Beside me, I hear Naomi snort and see Dre shaking with laughter. Courtney aims her narrowed eyes at them before shifting them back my way.

"This was a group effort. I know you aren't a part of the Lady Mustangs anymore, but no individual takes credit for a group effort."

"Trust me, Court, I know. Nobody in the Lady Mustangs would dare steal the spotlight by, say, using a glittered gavel or making sure they're the only one to talk at events or for publicity interviews." I glance at the time on my phone. "Which, speaking of, isn't it almost time for you to go onstage to welcome everyone?"

Never mind.

I'm the queen of bitchiness.

"This is why you were never welcomed into the group, Marlee. Because we could all see who you really are. A groupie." She flips her long blonde curls over her shoulder. "Who shows up at a team event a week after they were dumped in a dress two sizes too small and more makeup than a stripper on a Saturday night?"

I know I should be offended, but I can only focus on one part of her evil villain speech.

"Strippers wear a lot of makeup? I knew about glitter and stuff, but not the makeup. And why more on Saturday nights? I'd think Mondays and Fridays would be just as busy." I look to Naomi and Dre for their opinion. "Right? Don't you think they'd get a lot of action at the beginning and end of the work week?"

"Play obtuse if you want. It's obvious why Chris left you, and just know every single person in this room thinks you look desperate and pathetic tonight."

Damn. Obtuse, desperate, and pathetic? I wonder if she's hiding a mean girl's thesaurus in her clutch?

I'm trying to think of any kind of comeback when someone else beats me to the punch.

"Not everyone. I think she looks gorgeous." The hairs on the back of my neck stand in recognition, and I don't even have to turn around to know who is talking. Which, as it would turn out, is something I'll be forever grateful for. Instead of looking over my shoulder, I get to watch as the color drains from Courtney's face, and her jaw almost hits the floor. "Kevin's looking for you, Court."

At the mention of her nickname, the shock disappears so quickly, and if I hadn't witnessed it with my own two eyes, I would've never believed it happened. Her narrowed eyes focus back on me for a second, like I'm the one who called her the name. Then, like watching an ugly caterpillar transform into a beautiful butterfly, her snarl turns into a million-dollar smile, and her posture improves so much, I'm worried I might get taken out by her nipples. "Thanks, Gavin." Even her voice is different! Like a bad imitation of Marilyn Monroe, and although I definitely don't like her, even I cringe with embarrassment for her.

She turns to walk away, and for some reason I might never know, I yell after her, "Finish talking later, Court?" Her faltering steps as she sets out to find Kevin is the only clue she heard me.

"Mr. Pope to the rescue again—" I turn to offer him a drink, but when I face him, the only thing going through my head are thoughts about how fine this man is. Because sweet lawd, he's *fine*.

His hair is short on the sides but longer and combed back on the top. He could maybe do with a shave, but the scruff on his chin looks so delicious, all I want to do is lick him to see what it feels like under my tongue. His bright blue eyes are watching me as I try to remember what I was going to say, and the crooked smile that crosses his face as seconds pass by without me saying anything tells me he knows what I'm thinking. But all that smile does is draw my attention to the deep V at the top of his full lips, which acts as an arrow to the almost hidden dimple in his chin.

Are sexy chins even a thing? Or is Gavin just that hot?

He's super fucking hot.

"You all right there?" His voice snaps me out of my trance.

"Yup. Fine, I'm totally, one hundred percent fine. Totally, completely A-okay." When I'm finished rambling, his grin is no longer crooked, now it's full-blown cocky . . . and still hot.

Dammit.

"Got it. You're fine."

"Whatever, Pope. I was going to ask if you wanted a shot with me, but now I'm just asking Naomi and Dre." And like the mind readers they are—or friends aware of the tequila crutch I use in uncomfortable situations—when I turn to them, Dre hands me a lime and points to the shots lined up on the bar.

But instead of three, there are four.

For a second, I think they might've been genius enough to order two for me, but my dream is squashed when I see Dre hand Gavin a lime. Which is really too bad, because if this is just the beginning of my night, I'm going to need a lot more liquid courage than I had anticipated.

Twelve

ONE OTHER SMALL DETAIL NAOMI FAILED TO TELL ME WHEN SHE convinced me to come to this godforsaken event: I still have to walk in the show.

Here's something not many people know about me—I have terrible stage fright. The only reason I agreed to do this before was because Chris was going to be next to me, being his normal, obnoxious, spotlight-loving self, and I was going to float down the runway beside him and nobody was going to notice me. But, seeing as Chris and I aren't together anymore, my plan has been shot to hell. Now, not only do I have to walk alone, but Courtney put Chris and Ava right in front of me. Guess who loves girlfriends now?

Waiting backstage, the feeling in my feet comes and goes from the absurd/bordering-on-dangerous number of shots I've consumed over the last hour. My breathing is ragged, partly from nerves about walking in the spotlight, partly from how tight the leftover dress Courtney handed me is. And, of course, I'm stuck staring at my ex-boyfriend's hand plastered on the ass of the woman he cheated on me with.

I'm starting to think I should've stayed home.

But then, I get the most brilliant—or the worst ever—idea.

When Courtney's voice comes over the speakers as she welcomes everyone to the fashion show, I run to the back of the line where the single players are paired together and find Gavin.

I don't have to look hard—he's so gorgeous, I swear a little angel follows him around, shining a light over his head. And also, he's super tall and easy to spot.

"Gavin!" I poke his arm, startling him out of the conversation he's having with TK. "Will you walk with me? I was supposed to walk with Chris, but you know what happened there. Then I thought I wouldn't have to walk at all. But because I'm in the program and there's music timing or some shit, I do have to walk, and Courtney hates me, and I'm in this." I motion to the skintight atrocity I got stuck in—literally. I might never be able to get it off. "And she has me alone and—"

"Marlee," Gavin cuts me off. "I'd love to."

"Damn, Marlee," TK says. "How're you gonna ask this scrub when I'm right here?"

"Sorry, TK, but you're too pretty to walk down the runway with. You'll upstage me." I wink.

"Oh shit, girl. You're right. This ugly motherfucker was definitely the better choice." He laughs as he dodges a punch from Gavin.

"Where are you in line?" Gavin asks.

"Where do you think?"

His eyebrows go up and his head shoots back. "She wouldn't."

"She would, and she did." I point down the line to the empty spot behind Chris and Ava.

"Damn. That's cold." He reaches for my hand and intertwines our fingers. "Well, let's show everyone how it's done."

When we get back to my spot, Courtney is finishing up talking about all of the work she put into the event and thanking the Lady

Mustangs for assisting her. She touches on the charities benefiting from this event for a brief moment and finishes by having all of the designers and donors who made this night possible stand up and take a bow.

Everyone around me is buzzing with anticipation, thrilled with the prospect of having all eyes on them, even if only for a short time. The guys are laughing and having fun while the women are practicing their model walks in the open space. And me? Well, I'm just hoping I don't throw up.

Oblivious that I've found a partner, Chris turns around, his mouth already open, preparing to, at least I assume, say something to get under my skin. He's known me forever. We might not be dating, but I doubt he forgot about my fear of being in front of large crowds.

But when he sees Gavin next to me, his eyes go wide, and the words die on his lips.

"Make sure you stop and watch us when you get off the stage, Alexander," Gavin says.

Chris doesn't respond. Instead, he pulls a play out of Ava's playbook and gives me a dirty look instead of Gavin.

Ugh. What did I ever see in him?

The curtains open, and Courtney comes flying through, her blonde hair bouncing, eyes wide as she directs people to start walking. The line is creeping forward, and every inch causes my stomach to turn a little more. When I feel the breeze from the curtain as the couple in front of Chris and Ava walk through it, I contemplate running. My fear of crowds is no joke. The first time I had to present in a college lecture room, I ran out of the room to throw up . . . I had to repeat that class. But lucky for me, I have something—or someone—I didn't have in my freshman public speaking course.

Gavin squeezes my hand and whispers in my ear. "Relax. You look gorgeous."

I have too many knots in my stomach to respond, but I look up to him and give him the best smile I can manage.

Chris and Ava step through the curtain in front of us, and I try to focus on the feel of my hand in Gavin's instead of the cheering crowd and flashing lights.

I'm not successful.

"Ready, Marlee?" Courtney asks as she's peeking through the curtains watching Chris and Ava go.

"We are," Gavin says.

Thank god, because I still can't talk.

His deep voice stole her attention, and she spins around.

"Gavin! No! You're supposed to go at the end, and she's supposed to be alone!"

I can't tell if she's more pissed I'm not facing public humiliation alone or that he's messing up her order.

But either way, she's pissed, and it's just the distraction I need before Gavin shrugs and pulls me onto the runway with him.

Before I know what's happening, the bright lights hit me. The loud music slightly masks the gasps and growls the women make when they see me with Gavin. We walk side by side until we reach the stairs and Gavin motions for me to go in front of him. Once we reach the bottom, we circle around to the back so we can return the clothes to the designers we borrowed them from. After we're back in the clothes we came in, we're guided to the front of the stage where a group of empty seats is waiting for us to watch the fashion show with the real models.

Gavin is waiting for me as we head for the seats in a single file line. The cherry on top of this delicious (rotten) evening is after Gavin and I sit down, Chris plops down into the seat next to me. Gavin must sense my urge to run and before I can go anywhere, my small hand is wrapped up in his large one again.

"Hey." He leans in close. "Are you good? We can go somewhere else if you want."

Le sigh. He's so dreamy.

"I'm fine." I don't know if it's his proximity or the shots I took earlier, but I forget everything—and everyone—else. I sit next to him, watching the fashion and feeling giddy, regardless of all of the death glares being sent my way.

That is . . . until Chris makes it impossible to ignore. His long arm reaches in front of me, pushing my back flush against my chair, and grabs Gavin's shoulder. "What the fuck is your problem, Pope?"

The Gavin who was just with me, laughing and having fun, is no longer next to me. His warm eyes have gone cold, and the comfortable grip he had on my hand now feels like a vise. "You want to get your hand off me and your arm out of Marlee's face?"

"No. I don't. I want to know why the fuck you're touching my girl, inserting yourself into matters that don't concern you."

His girl? Is he insane?

"She's not your girl, Alexander. First, because she got rid of your sorry ass and second, because she's not property, you lowlife piece of shit." Glad to know at least Gavin and I are on the same page.

"Oh. I'm the fuckin' lowlife?" Of course he only heard the part about him. "You walk into the locker room like you're god's gift, changing plays, cutting my routes. Then I invite you into my fucking home and you make a move on my old lady. It doesn't get lower than that."

"I'm only twenty-seven. I don't think that qualifies me for an AARP membership." I speak up even though it's clear I'm only being talked about, not talked to.

I say it to Chris since he's the one who said it, but I'm looking at Gavin when I do. And when he turns to me, eyes soft and his lips curving up, my insides turn to jelly.

"Goddamn, Marlee. Can't you ever shut the fuck up?" Chris's arm is back in my face, and his voice has raised high enough to draw the attention of a few people around us. "You want me to notice you so bad, you'd act like a fuckin' slut with my teammate you already know I'm having problems with? Fine. Let's talk."

Say what now? #BetterCallBeckyWiththeRedHair

"I'm acting like a slut. For what? Sitting here?" I can't believe what's happening. I look to Gavin to see if he's witnessing this too, or if I'm in a tequila-induced hallucination. But when the same cold grip that grabbed me earlier strikes again, I know this is just the latest chapter in Marlee's Great Misadventure.

I'm about to tell him where he can shove his hand, but Gavin beats me to the punch.

Literally.

One second Chris is sitting next to me, grabbing my arm, and the next I'm free, and he's standing several feet away from me, nose to nose with Gavin.

"Do. Not. Touch. Her." Gavin whispers so low, it's a miracle I can hear him over the music.

"You Captain Save-A-Ho now, Pope?" Chris was never too smart, and he's an idiot when it comes to reading people. Like right now? If I were him, I'd shut up because Gavin looks about ready to explode. But he keeps going. "She's not worth the effort."

I mean, come on now. I'm right here! Is this stomp on Marlee night? Because I know I didn't include that in any of the promotions I designed.

"You should stop talking." Gavin speaks for everyone watching, which, unfortunately for me, is everyone in the player section.

Chris doesn't listen.

"She's a boring fuck. I only kept her around for appearances, but if you really want a go at her, we can compare notes later."

First? Rude.

Second? Screw you, Alexander.

I get he's having some weird testosterone showdown in front of the rest of their gang, but I can't believe Chris would say something so vulgar. Did all of these years mean so little to him he doesn't care about me at all? He cheated on me. I did nothing to deserve to be on the receiving end of his vile behavior.

All of the anger I've been suppressing these past two weeks makes a sudden reappearance. I shoot to my feet, fully intending to give Chris a piece of my mind. But before I reach him, Gavin's fist lands square into Chris's nose with a sickening crunch. Chris, not one to stay sober at an event like this and always one for dramatics, falls to the ground upon impact and holds his nose as blood leaks from the sides of his hands. He rolls around on the floor, moaning so loud I wouldn't be surprised if the valet attendant could hear him.

Gavin, on the other hand, is calm as ever as he pulls his sleeves and turns to find me in the crowd. When he spots me, he walks toward me until he's few feet in front of me. He looks a little nervous, which in turn makes me really nervous.

"Did you come with Dre and Naomi?"

I was expecting something between a friendly farewell and stay the hell away from me, but not that. "Umm . . . Uber?"

"Are you asking me or telling me?"

How he's so proper in the middle of pure chaos is throwing me off. I want to answer him, but I can't stop looking behind him at Chris's hunched figure on the floor, or the accusatory eyes of just about every woman watching.

"Telling," I manage to respond.

"Okay." He nods. "I don't know if you want to stay and leave with them later, but I'm heading out now. I can give you a ride or sit with you until your Uber driver gets here."

"I can Uber it. I live downtown, I'd hate for you to have to drive out of your way." I was planning on leaving with Dre and Naomi, but after the scene that just played out, I'd rather leave sooner than later.

"I live downtown too. Why don't you ride with me so I'll know you made it home okay?"

"You do? I figured you lived in Parker with all of—" Courtney cuts me off, grabbing my shoulder and spinning me around to face her. Because my encounter with Chris wasn't painful enough.

"Are you happy, Marlee? We're going to lose sponsors and money because you couldn't just stay at home and mind your own business." She stops and moves her narrowed eyes toward Gavin. "And I'm so disappointed in you, Gavin. I don't expect much from her, but you should know better. I can't believe Coach Jacobs replaced Kevin with someone who would fight a teammate. Kevin would never behave the way you have tonight."

"You're right," Gavin says. Courtney's eyes widen with surprise—her forehead still doesn't move—and it's clear to anyone around us she approached us looking for another fight. "Kevin would never stick up for a woman who's being harassed. Which is the reason I was brought in. Your husband lacks the integrity and leadership it takes to have a winning team." He turns his back on her and completely blocks her from my vision. "So are you riding with me?" he asks, like Courtney never happened.

"Dear god. I need wine." I ignore his question. I clearly do not share his ability to ignore everything going on around us.

"Is that a yes?" he asks.

I nod, watching the smile cross his face before he reaches for my hand and guides me to the bar.

"White or red?" he asks me when the bartender approaches us.

"With alcohol." Because after the way this night has played out, I have no right to be picky.

"Can she have a bottle of your most popular wine, please?" Gavin asks the bartender, who happily agrees. Both men are looking at me with huge grins on their faces, and the bartender is laughing! Apparently he was one of the unlucky few who didn't see what just happened. If he had, he'd be looking much more sympathetic and handing me a bottle of Patron.

He's walking away when I remember one very important detail and yell after him, "Make sure it's a twist lid!"

"A twist lid bottle of wine? Really?" Gavin says beside me.

"Yes, really. Do you have a corkscrew in your truck?"

He's full on laughing at me when Mr. Bartender comes back with a bottle in his hand, its metal lid gleaming under the lights.

"It's not our most popular, but it's the only one I could find that didn't have a cork."

"Do I seem like my standards are sky-high right now? This is perfect." I start looking through my clutch trying to find my card, because I'm guessing unopened bottles of wine aren't covered by the open bar. "How much?"

"It's covered," he says at the same moment I pull out my card. I look to the bartender and the smile on his face has grown tenfold, something I understand when I see the hundred-dollar bill in front of him.

"You really didn't need to do that, I can pay." Which might be a lie. I stretched my budget to the max at the mall today, and there's a good chance my card might be declined.

"I know, but I wanted to." His fingers find their way between mine again, and he gives my hand a comforting squeeze. "Grab your wine, boozer. Let's go."

I go.

But not because he said so. Because with an ass like his? I can't imagine there's any place I wouldn't follow him.

#HisAssMadeMeDoIt

Thirteen

"YOU'RE REALLY NICE," I SLUR. WE'RE WAITING FOR THE VALET TO bring Gavin's truck around, and it feels like the fresh Colorado air has increased my alcohol level from drunk to trashed . . . and I still haven't cracked open my wine.

"You're pretty nice too." He's watching me closely, and I'm *trying* to watch him closely. His eyes are crinkled with amusement; mine are struggling to focus.

"I really wish you were an investment banker."

Oh no. The loose lips part of the night has arrived.

"Besides my mom, you're probably the only person in the world who does."

"Because everyone else would miss their superstar quarterback in his super-hot pants throwing the ball every Sunday?" Sober me hates drunk me so hard right now.

"Because I'm terrible with numbers. I had three different tutors trying to get me to pass my math courses in college. And I'm not sure most of the fans focus on my pants, but I'm glad you do." His body is shaking with laughter as he nudges me with his shoulder.

Now, any other time in my life this would be fine. But at this moment? Not so much. You know that feeling when you're standing on a bus or train and it starts moving before you are prepared? The sensation of the ground being pulled from under your feet while you're left scrambling to find anything to grab on to before your ass meets the floor in the most embarrassing way? Well, that's me right now. After all of my work to get all dolled up and fancy, I'm going to end my night with my ass on the pavement.

Nope.

I'm not ripping this dress and only wearing it once.

I spin and dance like an ungraceful ballerina back to my feet. I'm a little dizzy and still wobbling a bit when Gavin's hands reach for my waist to help stabilize me.

"Sorry about that. You okay?" He's looking down at me, watching me with warm eyes and a wide, genuine smile.

"Uh-huh," is my well-thought-out response.

"You sure?" he asks, still smiling.

"Positive." How could I not be? I'm standing across from Gavin while he's resting his hands on my waist and revealing his dimple, right?

"Good." He glances to the street. "Where's this kiss?"

Wow! I wasn't prepared for that! And I have no idea why he's asking, but who am I to deny him?

As much as possible in my heels, I roll onto my toes, trying my hardest to get closer to him—or more specifically, his lips. When I can't get all the way there, I bring my hands to the back of his head, feeling the softness of his hair beneath my fingers, and pull his head to mine.

The kiss starts out gentle . . . reluctant even. I'm not usually the forward one, but he asked for a kiss, so a kiss I'll give him. When I part my mouth and I suck at his bottom lip, the hesitation he was showing disappears. He nips at my lips and then takes full advantage of my mouth opening with the gasp I let out. Our tentative tongues join in this wild, wonderful dance. Slowly, the kiss becomes more urgent, more demanding. Our tongues are tasting. The hands that were satisfied only with touching are now grabbing and pulling at the other. It consumes me. I forget we're standing on the sidewalk outside of a building with my ex inside until the gentle clearing of a throat snaps me back to reality.

"Umm . . . sorry, Mr. Pope, here are your keys," the valet attendant says. He doesn't look either of us in the eye as he opens the truck door and thanks Gavin for—I'm assuming—a very generous tip.

Once we're both in the truck, Gavin focuses on the road, as the silence settles around us.

"Damn. I was not expecting that," Gavin says, finally breaking the silence.

"You weren't expecting what?" I ask, confused.

"That kiss," he says matter-of-factly.

He didn't expect the kiss he asked for? What?

"You said you wanted me to kiss you!"

"No I didn't. I mean, I wanted you to kiss me, of course. But I didn't ask you to." The cab of his truck is too dark, and his face is only lit by the lights of his dashboard, so I can't tell if he's joking or not.

"You did! You said, 'Where's this kiss?' and I kissed you." I might be drunk, but I'm not crazy.

"I said, 'Where's this kid?' I was looking for the valet!" He starts laughing.

Oh.

My.

God.

Kill me now.

"Please tell me you're joking." I close my eyes, thankful for the darkness hiding the furious blush that's taken over my entire body.

"I can't tell you that." He reaches his hand across the center console and squeezes my knee. "But if it makes you feel better, I thought you taking charge was really fucking hot."

"It helps a little." I pout beside him, but kind of revel in him calling my kiss hot.

"Really, you kissing me was hot. You want embarrassing? When I was a college freshman, my mom surprised me for a visit and ended up walking in on me with a girl," he says.

"You're lying to me."

"I wish. I thought it was my roommate fucking with me and answered the door butt naked only to find my mom on the other side holding a tin of homemade cookies." The sun has long since set, but even so, I can see his cheeks heat as he tells me. "And instead of turning and leaving, she came inside and questioned me and the girl on our relationship status and whether or not we were practicing safe sex."

"No she did not! I love your mom!" I hear it after I say it. "I mean, obviously I don't know your mom so I can't love her, but I love—no. Like. Stop saying love, Marlee. I like the story about your mom. There. Was that too weird?" Holy hell.

Oh dear god. Why, tequila? We've always been such great friends, I treated you well. Why would you turn on me like this?

"You're my favorite drunk person." We're at a red light, and even though there's laughter in his voice, all I hear is I'm his favorite person ever. Most people just lose their filter when they're drunk, I guess I lose my hearing too.

"You're my favorite person too." The full weight of the alcohol is starting to settle. Between the soft R&B coming through the speakers and the gentle bouncing of the truck, my eyelids are becoming heavier and heavier. "Why do you have to be a football player? I hate football players."

"You don't hate football players. You hate Alexander, but everybody hates him."

"He's the worst. He cheated on me. Like a lot a lot a lot. And stupid me had noooooo idea. Well, maybe I knew, but pretended not to." My eyes won't open, and my mouth won't close. In the back of my mind, I know I'm going to regret this in the morning, but it still doesn't prevent me from saying what I'm going to say next. "But he didn't know I slept with you, or that I thought about my night with you almost every time I slept with him since. So joke's on him."

"You got that right, babe," Gavin whispers. "Joke's definitely on him."

And thankfully, before I can say anything else, I fall asleep in the passenger's seat of Gavin Pope's truck.

Fingers crossed I didn't snore . . . or drool.

Fourteen

I'M NOT SURE WHAT WAKES ME UP.

It could be the way my head pounds with so much force, it feels like somebody is punching me. It might be my tongue sticking to the roof of my mouth because it's so dry. Or the sun beaming so brightly through the giant window next to my bed, my entire body is sweating.

Never mind. I know.

It's number three.

My tiny shoebox apartment doesn't have a window this big and that realization is definitely the one to get me up.

I spring out of the bed like a jack-in-the-box and instantly regret it. My eyes slam shut, and I slowly lay back down, hoping the banging in my head will slow down too. And after a few minutes, it does. Not all the way, but enough so I can crack open one of my eyes again.

Big mistake.

The source of the sunlight is a huge floor-to-ceiling window lacking any form of window treatment. The football memorabilia that outed Gavin as a football player years ago is scattered around the room. Framed jerseys, pictures of him throughout his entire career—spanning from high school until now—are littered on the dresser and hung haphazardly on the aqua walls. It's undeniable that I'm in Gavin Pope's house.

But I'm not in his bedroom. At least, I don't think. There's a soft lace comforter and the furniture is white and carved with floral designs. If I had to guess, it's an older woman's guest room, maybe his mom decorated it for herself.

But as I calm down, memories from the night before rush into my mind. Going to the fashion show. Chris with Ava. Courtney openly hating me. Gavin sticking up for me . . . the kiss. Holy moly. The kiss that was so good, just thinking about it makes my toes curl. But, he'd asked for the valet, not a kiss, and then the more embarrassing moments start to flow. Like me telling him I hate football players and how much Chris cheated on me. How I passed out in the front seat of his truck holding an open bottle of wine.

I'm still cringing when there's a quiet knock at the door. I look around the room again searching for an escape route. Maybe I could wiggle through the ceiling vents? Shimmy down a drainpipe? No, those would never work in last night's dress and this morning's tequila bloat. Out of realistic, non-superhero options, I call for him to come in.

"You're awake." He smiles, walking through the doorway. "I thought for sure you were going to be sleeping for a long time after last night."

I wish.

"My head feels like it might explode, and your giant window was trying to roast me, otherwise I would be." I regret my snarkiness because, from what I can remember, he was amazing to me, but I don't know what to say. I wanted to be over him, I wanted to be over Chris, but if these past few weeks have proven anything, it's that I have a long way to go.

I'm still pissed about our night all those years ago. I'm mad at Chris for saying he wanted a break and space instead of just ending it. I'm mad Gavin lied to me about who he was and how he wasn't there in the morning to tell me the truth. I'm pissed as hell he just showed up here, tossing a necklace when the last thing I need is to try and figure out anybody besides myself.

I try to let my emotions simmer. "How do you not have curtains or anything? These windows are gigantic. Fans are going to park their creepy butts outside and watch you walk around."

"They're like one-way mirrors. You can see outside, but people can't see in. Half the reason I bought this place was for the windows. Why would I cover them?" He walks over and sits at the foot of the bed.

"Makes sense, even though it does get super freaking hot. You have the bed perfectly in line with the morning sun."

He smiles a sly grin. "I know. My mom claimed this room as hers, and I needed a way that wasn't too obvious to keep her from getting too comfortable."

"I don't know if I think you're a horrible son or an evil genius. How long did it take you to figure out the exact location the bed needs to be in for maximum discomfort?"

If he was a real genius, he would've moved into a shoebox like mine and there would be no room for visitors. But then again, I don't make a bazillion dollars, and my mom has never expected anything other than eating dinner with me at least once a month. I hate cooking and if I wasn't pretending so hard to be an adult, I'd go over there every night.

"I slept in here for a week getting it just right. Now when she comes she's always saying how the elevation makes it seem so much hotter." His smile never changes when he talks about his mom. He obviously really loves her . . . even if he's a terrible son.

"Your mom is amazing." The second the words fall out of my mouth, I'm there with a spoon trying to shovel them back in. I flash back to talking about loving her. "You know, as amazing as a person I've never met could be. Not that I want to know her or anything because I barely know you and that would be creepy."

Smooth.

"Marlee, I got it." He rests his hand on my leg beneath the comforter, a very effective stop to the onslaught of rambling coming out of my mouth. "I was coming to drop off some Advil and give you water for later." He takes a bottle of water out of his pants' pocket with the same finesse as a magician pulling a rabbit out of his hat.

"Oh. Thanks." Why is he thoughtful? There should be a limit on the charm one could possess. Like Chris, for example. He's hot, but a giant douchelord, so the balance of the world is in check. Gavin, however, is unbelievably handsome, a gentleman, kind, a fantastic kisser and those skills do not diminish in bed, and he's one of the highest-paid quarterbacks in the NFL. What the hell, universe?

I lean forward to grab the water from his hands, but as I do, the down comforter (which is so amazing I'm trying to figure out how to smuggle it in my clutch) falls from my shoulders. The ridiculously low cut, metallic gold dress Naomi and Brynn forced me into is barely in place. Good news for me though, my nipples decided to remain in hiding. Gavin's face followed the blanket, and his gaze hasn't moved since.

"Hey now, Pope. Eyes up here," I call to him at the same time I pull the blanket up.

"Face. Yeah. My bad." He looks at me and shocks me when his olive skin flushes scarlet.

Add adorable to his list of charming traits.

Dammit.

"So . . . can I have the water?" I ask.

"No." The blush was fading, but at his answer, it returns full force.

"No?" My eyebrows rise. What's going on with him?

"I mean, of course you can. It's just that . . . since you're . . ." He stops himself and takes a deep breath. "Sorry. Since you're awake, do you wanna grab breakfast?"

Do I want to eat breakfast with this perfect specimen? Short answer? YES! Long answer? Oh my god! A million times YES!

"I'm not sure. I have a deadline coming up for a client I'm working with and I still have a ton to do." Way to play it cool, Marlee. And it's not a complete lie, I do have a lot of work to do, but the deadline isn't for couple of weeks. It's just Gavin seems to disarm me more and more every second I'm around him. I know after today I probably won't see him anymore, and I don't need to find anything else to add to my list of reasons I want to love him forever. I wonder if this is the struggle all of Chris's girls felt? The struggle is real.

"I almost forgot you have two jobs. I'll get my keys and take you home then." The disappointed smile on his face weakens my resolve. It's not every day I wake up in Gavin Pope's house. Shouldn't I make it last?

"Maybe coffee?" I almost scream at him.

"Coffee sounds good." His lips curve up and pull my heartstrings along with them. I swear to god, him looking at me and smiling like that? I feel it in my chest. "There's a great little place a few blocks over. I'll go find my keys."

"We can walk. Let me wash my face first." I climb out of bed, checking to make sure all my goodies are still tucked away, which makes me think of one thing. "Oh! Do you have sweatshirt I can borrow?"

He was almost out of the room and when he turns back to me, he lets his gaze slowly travel from my pedicured toes all the way to what I'm sure is a mascara smudged, hair-resembles-a-bird's-nest head. "Yeah, I think I can find you something," he says like he's in on some joke I'm not aware of. "I'll be right back."

"Thanks." I walk as fast as I can without it looking like I'm running. I open the door to what I'm praying is the bathroom and for once it seems like G-O-D is listening to me. Well . . . until I look in the mirror, then I think He's apologizing.

Rough is an understatement. I took on tequila last night and it's obvious it kicked my ass. Because if the memories weren't enough to taunt me, now I have a physical reminder.

Booze: 1. Marlee: 0.

I wash my face the best I can with hot water and a washcloth. It does a fine job at removing the mascara, but leaves red, irritated skin in its wake. I try my hardest to wrangle my wild hair into a bun and when I look at the finished product, I finally understand what Churchill meant when he said, "Sometimes your best isn't good enough."

After Gavin yells that he found a sweatshirt and a pair of flip-flops his mom left behind, I take one last glance in the mirror and the sound of a train's horn blares in my head.

All aboard, ladies and gentlemen.

#HotMessExpress

Fifteen

EVEN THOUGH I DON'T HAVE SUNGLASSES ON AND THE SUN IS close to burning a hole through my retinas, I can't stop staring up at Gavin's sick freaking condo.

"I can't believe you live here." I slap Gavin's arm.

"Why are you hitting me?" he asks even though he sounds more amused than curious.

"I love these places! They're waaaay out of my price range, but so effing cool. If I would've known I was in one, I would've paid more attention."

When Gavin said he lived downtown, I figured he meant one of the swanky high-rises in the heart of downtown. I pictured him sharing an elevator with the old lady who wore excessive amounts of jewelry and always had her yappy dog on either a bedazzled leash or in a dog stroller. I never thought he'd live in one of the newly built, glass-front condos I've walked by dozens of times.

Which, thinking about it, means I'm going to have to find a new route. I can't walk past his house now that I know he lives there. Sucks, but can you say stalker?

"I'll have to give you an official tour sometime."

"I'd love that." In all fairness, I'd love a tour of the sewer if he was the one giving it.

"Me too." He slides his hand around mine and gives it a gentle squeeze.

Two words, five letters, one million butterflies. I have to bite the inside of my cheek to prevent my smile from overtaking my entire face. He turns me into the giddy little girl I was in high school, before I fell for the hot football player who led me down a road of lies and betrayal. Dammit, do I never learn?

We walk the rest of the way to Fresh—the organic-only coffee shop—in total silence, and for the first time in a very long time, I don't hate it. Actually, the opposite—I love it. Once I force Chris out of my head, I'm able to appreciate the simple moment. The clean, brisk air against my face in contrast to the warmth of Gavin's hand encasing mine; constant chatter of businessmen and women on their phones before they start their nine-hour work shift; the hum of the light rail as it passes and the bored faces looking out of the windows.

Walking into the coffee shop, the strong smell of coffee is equal parts repulsing and enticing. I order my usual, a vanilla latte, Gavin gets a *caffè Americano*, and we both choose the huge, flaky croissants.

"If you want, we can eat at my place, it's only a couple of blocks over. Or we can eat here, whatever you like." The effort I put forth for the question to come out casually is a massive fail.

"Your place sounds great."

"Yeah?" Shit. I wanted him to say yes, but I thought he'd say no. Now that he agreed, I'm trying to remember what state I left my apartment in after Brynn wreaked havoc on it with her on-slaught of beauty products.

He takes our food and coffees from the barista and gestures toward the door. "You lead the way."

The walk is more of the same from before, minus the hand-holding. I think that's only because his hands are already filled with caffeine and carbs, and I'd never endanger either of those things.

We make it back to my place in under ten minutes. The smell of coffee was enough to put a little extra pep in my step . . . and so was the idea of Gavin in my space.

Because yum.

Obviously.

"I just moved in, and yesterday was a little insane, so you'll have to excuse the mess," I warn him before I open the door.

"I'm sure it's fine."

I walk in, flip on the light switch, and as luck would have it, he's right. It's not as bad as I feared, still not good . . . but it for sure could've been worse.

"Home sweet home." I gesture with open arms and for some reason do jazz hands.

I shouldn't be allowed around attractive humans of the opposite sex. Someone please kill me now.

"This place is really great, Marlee," he says, looking around the room.

He sounds genuine, and I have to admit, I'm surprised. Chris would've hated this place. It's too small. The furniture is cheap. The neighborhood is awful. The list would never end. I was expecting Gavin to have the same reaction and give me something to not like about him.

"Thanks. It's small, but I love it so far." I grab the coffees from him and bring them to the tiny, two-person Ikea table I (fine! My dad) put together the other day. It's the perfect size for me, but now, with Gavin on the other side, I feel like I bought dollhouse furniture and Gavin's a giant about to crush it all.

"It's perfect," he tells me after he's situated on the tiny stool.

We sit across from each other, eating our croissants and drinking our coffee. Where we were okay with the silence as we walked, it doesn't reappear here.

"So . . ." I start. My conversation skills are on point. "How are you liking Denver?"

"I love it." He takes another sip of coffee and places his cup on the table. "I wasn't sure how I felt about it when the trade happened, and I'd be lying if I said I was welcomed into the locker room with open arms. A few guys are starting to warm up to me now that we're winning. I'm happy to be here . . . for more than one reason." He never drops eye contact and his foot taps mine under the table. It's such an innocent gesture for the big quarterback across from me and it's disarming.

Which sucks.

I need all the arming I can get around him.

"That's good. Denver's a good place to live." I shove a bite of croissant in my mouth. Not because I'm hungry or lacking basic table manners, but because I need a minute to compose myself. "How's the weather compared to Chicago?"

Good, Marlee. Weather is a safe topic. Mindless small talk, you got this!

Gavin's lips curve at the corners the tiniest little bit, and I'm pretty sure he knows the game I'm trying to play here. Fingers crossed he goes with it.

"It's great. You know Chicago. When it's hot, the humidity chokes you, and when it's cold, it chokes you. It's nice and dry here, I like it." He humors me. Thank god. "How's your dad doing? He said his back was bothering him?"

Never mind.

The alarms are ringing in my head to get the heck out of dodge. *Don't answer. Discussing family is way out of small-talk zone.*

"He's okay. His back's still bothering him a bit, but he said it's getting better." When Gavin leaves, I'm calling my mom and yelling at her for ingraining me with such superb manners.

"Give him my number. I found the best chiropractor; I'll bring him with me next time." He sips his coffee. You know, like he didn't just casually offer to hang out with my FRICKIN' DAD!

"I don't know if he's the chiropractor type." This is true. I can already imagine my dad yelling about some quack trying to break his back. But even if he was an Eastern medicine junkie, I'd still say no. Jarod/Gavin (Javin) time isn't going to be a thing. #StopTryingToMakeJavinHappen

#ItsNeverGoingToHappen

"Well, the offer's on the table if he wants to try." He takes the lid off his coffee and shoves his croissant wrapper inside. "Where's your trash can?"

"I got it." I reach across the table to grab his cup, but his large hand covers mine before I can reach it. The innocent touch causes goose bumps to spread across my arms.

"No, finish your food. I have two legs. I can throw it away myself. Where's the garbage?"

"Under the sink." I point into the kitchen.

"Thanks." He winks and turns with his trash in hand.

I watch as his long legs make quick work of my small space; it only takes him about three steps to make it. I'm watching him in awe, like he's some sort of chivalrous alien because he's throwing away his own cup. That's how fucked up my relationship experience is. I'm awed by a grown man cleaning up after himself.

"Marlee." Gavin pulls me back to the present.

"Yeah." My head snaps his way.

"Where'd you go?" He approaches, but instead of sitting down across from me, he stops beside me.

"Sorry." I take a deep breath and paste my best faux smile on my face before looking up. "I'm still waiting for this coffee to kick in, last night kicked my butt."

"It was a crazy night." The words are right, but the tone is all wrong. He pulls me in for a hug that lasts a second longer than it should.

I know what this is. It's the same way I'd talk to some of my girlfriends when they'd tell me about their cheating husband. It's pity.

I pull out of his arms and put my coffee cup to my lips, not taking it away until I've finished it. I grab my scraps off of the table and follow the same path Gavin took to my trash can.

After I drop the cup in my tiny can, I close the cabinet door with more force than necessary. It pops back out and the edge nails me in the shin.

"Son of a!" I shout and grab my leg.

"Are you okay?" Gavin opens my freezer and then kneels, examining my life-threatening injury.

"I'm fine. It just—" My sentence falls away and a gasp takes its place.

With one hand on my hip, he holds the bag of frozen corn to my leg.

If you haven't had it before—a big, tough, bearded football player on his knees, tending to your tiny scratch like it's the most serious situation he's ever encountered—you should try it. It's sweet. It's naughty. Even though the bag is cold against my skin, it doesn't prevent heat from filling my core.

When he lifts the plastic pouch and grazes his finger near the scratch, I don't even attempt to hide the full body shiver that takes over. Fingers crossed he'll blame it on the corn.

"Better?" he asks, still on his knees.

"Y-yes," I stutter. I move my focus to my floor beneath him instead of him . . . *still on his knees*. "I'm gonna go get out of this dress." I pull back so fast, I almost go tumbling into the wall behind me. Smooth. "Make yourself comfortable or go. You know. Whatever you want."

Smoother.

What can I say? When I'm on a roll, I'm on a freakin' roll.

"Thanks," he says to my back as I speed walk to my room.

Sixteen

I SLAM THE DOOR SHUT BEHIND ME AND COLLAPSE ONTO MY UN-
made bed.

I know it's rude to keep a guest waiting, but it's also rude for
said guest to get me all worked up in my frickin' kitchen.

I mean, how dare he. Right? It's not like we haven't had sex
before and I don't vividly remember every last detail about what
he can do with his fingers. And I know I kissed him last night, but
I was drunk! My armor is made of a special material that loses all
hardness when doused in alcohol.

I roll around in my comforter and smother my face with my
pillow until a few of my wits have returned. Once I feel a little
better, I stand up and peel myself out of the dress clinging to my
bloated midsection under Gavin's sweatshirt and toss on some
yoga pants and a tank top. I run to the bathroom to brush my
teeth, apply some face lotion . . . brush my teeth again. I stare at
my reflection in the mirror long enough to give myself a reassur-
ing nod, but not long enough to harp on the dark circles surrounding eyes.

I walk back into the room with his mom's folded sweatshirt

and flip-flops, but I stop short at the sight of him lounging on my couch with my remote in his hand. The casualness of his basketball shorts and T-shirt is the polar opposite from the Gavin I spent last night with. His hair, which was gelled and combed to perfection, is falling carelessly in front of his face. The scruff on his face is a little bit thicker and a whole lot sexier. Chris never grew a beard. He was a pretty boy and spent double what I did on beauty products. Gavin looks like a sporty lumberjack and I can't lie, I'm not mad at *any* of it.

I wonder what his beard would feel like against my thighs. I mean, it's not like I remember him being clean shaven four years ago, or anything.

Trying to shake those dreamy thoughts out of my head, I word vomit all over my living room.

"Thanks for the sweatshirt," I say a little bit too loud. "I wish I would've grabbed one last time I left your place looking like a call girl."

Gavin's relaxed body tenses, and he sits up. With the exception of him throwing my necklace at me—which is a pretty big freaking exception—we've barely discussed that night. And we *definitely* haven't mentioned what came after.

I'm positive he's about to run his tight ass out of my front door, but he holds still.

"Since you brought it up. What happened that night?"

Curse your big, careless mouth, Marlee Harper!

"What do you mean?"

"I thought we had a great time. I know I did. Then the next morning, I grab us coffee and when I come back, you're gone without a trace." He stands up. "I searched through scraps of papers for days hoping you at least left a number."

Uh . . . what?

"I'm sorry, but come again?" My cheeks start heating along with the rapid rise of my heartbeat.

"You just . . . disappeared. And four years later, I see you again and you're with that jackass, Alexander—and have been for years! It's fucked up, Marlee."

" 'It's fucked up, Marlee'? Are you serious right now?" I hiss.

"Why wouldn't I be serious?"

"You lied to me. You told me you were an investment banker. I woke up the next morning to an empty bed. I went to find my clothes that were scattered all over your apartment." We started undressing by his front door, I had to go into four rooms to gather all of my clothes before I gave up on finding my missing accessories. "And then I got punched in the freaking face when I saw the picture of you with the commissioner."

He goes to speak, but I cut him off before he can say anything.

"Besides Chris, I have only slept with one person. You." I pause to let that sink in. "Can you please try to understand what I felt like in your apartment that morning? I was so damn happy to have taken a huge step in moving on from Chris only to wake up alone and find out the guy I was with lied to me."

"Fuck." The accusing tone he was using with me is gone and in its place is one filled with regret. "I didn't think you would wake up before I got back. I swear, I was only gone for thirty minutes. You must've woken up right after I left."

"But you still lied to me. If I would've known you were a football player, I wouldn't have gone home with you."

"Maybe you wouldn't have, but from my experience, me playing football is the only reason women *do* want to come home with me. I was trying to protect myself as much as you were."

"Have you looked in a mirror lately?" I narrow my eyes and purse my lips. Even mad I can't deny the glory that is Gavin Pope. With his full lips, sharp cheekbones, large arms, and washboard abs? Homeboy's a sculpture. "Trust me, that's not the only reason."

"Marlee." He says my name like I'm supposed to know what he means.

"Marlee what? I don't speak macho man shorthand." Chris did that condescending shit all the time. Nothing pisses me off more.

"You just complimented me while yelling at me. Now I don't know if we're still fighting or if I get to kiss you yet."

Wait . . . what?

"Kiss me? Did you really say that or am I hearing you wrong again?"

#NotMakingThatMistakeTwice

"Yes. Kiss you." He closes the distance separating us in two quick strides.

"But I'm not done yet."

"Yeah you are."

"No, I'm not." I fold my arms across my chest and stick out my hip.

He puts his hands on my back and pulls me close. "I fucked up. I should've let you know I was getting coffee. I should've told you who I was before you found out from those pictures. You were right to be pissed. But I'm not sorry I lied to you, and knowing you would've shot me down makes me even surer of it. Because if you did that, I wouldn't be standing in front of you right now."

Was that an apology?

No matter what Chris did, I always ended up being the person who apologized.

"You don't fight fair, Pope." I can't prevent the way my bottom lip pokes out.

"Me? You coming to the fashion show dressed like you were dressed, walking the way you were walking, showing every single one of those women up and rubbing Alexander's face in what he

lost? Then kissing me the way you kissed me? You're the one playing dirty, babe." The way his voice gets even deeper and his eyes
get darker as he talks? Game. Set. Match.

"I'm done now."

He smiles again, the corner of his eyes creasing and the dimple
on his left cheek deepening. He slides his hands down to my hips
and tightens his grip before pulling me so close, my chest presses
against his abs.

"But I'm just starting," he whispers.

I have no time to respond before his teeth are nipping at my
pouty lip and my instincts take over. I open my mouth, giving him
full access, and let my hands roam his strong back.

I still intend to keep my no-more-athletes promise, but you
know what? I deserve a little fun. And what's wrong with a small
indulgence before I turn my apartment into a Jesus-only convent?
Not a damn thing.

I pull back, both of us breathing like we finished running a
race, and I push him onto my couch. He watches me, hands
clenched by his sides, as if my yoga pants and tank are the sexiest
thing he's ever seen. I climb onto him, my legs straddling his body,
my hands tangled in his hair, and do what I've been wanting to
do all morning. I trace a path from the base of his neck up to his
chin. Each whisker against my tongue sends shivers through my
body. When I get to his mouth, he loses control.

#FirstDown

His hands are off of the couch and on me before I even know
what's happened. The bun I threw my hair in this morning has
started to unravel and Gavin takes full advantage, wrapping the
loose strands around his hand and pulling to give himself full access to my neck. The slight ache on my scalp only intensifies the
yearning between my legs. His mouth follows the opposite path
mine made and he grasps the top of my tank with his teeth, pull-

ing each side beneath the lacy bra that's doing nothing to conceal my hardened nipples.

"Fuckin' gorgeous," he whispers against my cleavage, the heat from his breath somehow causing goose bumps to cover my arms.

When his tongue starts tracing the scalloped lace edges against my breasts, my back arches, pushing my heavy breasts impossibly closer to him and causing my ass to rise just enough for his hand to slip beneath it. If my mind was capable of thinking about anything other than how to get closer to him without physically climbing inside of him, I might worry about where his hand is heading. Instead, the only thing I'm worried about is why it's taking so long to get there.

"Please." I manage to say as I roll my hips against him. Usually this is the point where I close my eyes and let my mind present me with a better, more exciting reality. But for the first time since my drunken night in Chicago, reality is so much better than anything I could dream up. Gavin doesn't pull back. He doesn't even answer, he just looks at me from beneath his lashes and unclasps my bra at the very same moment his fingers find proof of how turned on I am.

I try to keep my eyes open, I really do, but then Gavin bites down on my nipple that has been begging for attention and his thumb starts moving in delicious circles between my legs. I have no control over the way my jaw goes slack as every other inch of my body tightens until an orgasm so intense—I'm positive no other woman on the planet has felt anything like it—rips through my body and my eyes slam shut. But I think that just before they closed, I saw Gavin still watching me with a smile on his lips.

LATER THAT NIGHT, my phone lights up with a text while I'm catching up on the latest *Real Housewives*.

Had a great time last night and this morning. You looked
beautiful and made a night I wasn't looking forward to
fun. Let's make plans soon.

I start to type out a response, but before I hit send I remember
my promise and delete it, hoping he's not watching the bubbles of
a response disappear into never-never land. Today was fun. I deserved a little pleasure after years of mediocracy and the possibil-
ity of an STD, but that was it. I did the athlete thing for ten years
too long and I'm not going to go back on my promise to leave
them behind because of one slightly—whatever, majorly—mind-
blowing orgasm. I'm a grown-ass woman, I know that a little
hand action on the couch doesn't equal love or any kind of com-
mitment.

And if I always respond the way I did to him this morning, I
know even a friendly series of text messages could get way out of
hand.

I can't go down that road . . . not again. No more athletes.

I shut it down there and turn off my phone, wishing I had a
voodoo doll so I could poke Chris in the eye for ruining yet another thing in my life.

Seventeen

THE PROBLEM WITH BEING AN ADULT IS ABSOLUTELY EVERYTHING.

Bills. Work. The bone-crushing disappointment that comes from knowing the guy you want isn't right for you. A slowed metabolism.

The only perk is being old enough to purchase wine to numb the pain while paying said bills. Except after I paid the bills, I realized I couldn't afford any more wine. Then I made a spreadsheet to determine which bills I could cut in order to provide the necessary amount of wine and in the end, wondered if shelter is really necessary.

There's a good chance I need a therapist. Maybe I should add a column in the budget for insurance? Or maybe not.

It's been four weeks since I've talked to Gavin. Four weeks from the fashion show. Four weeks from coffee and croissants. Four weeks since we made out like teenagers and dry humped on my couch.

It hasn't been four weeks since I've heard from Gavin, though.

I don't know why I exchanged numbers with him. It just seemed like the polite thing to do. That's my story and I'm sticking to it.

The first week, he called or texted every day. The next week he texted a few times. The following week he called once. Now I haven't heard from him at all.

I'm glad. Really, I am. I've got work, Brynn has entrusted me to take over all of her marketing, and I took on one final freelance client. Also, for the first time since high school (besides those stupid breaks), I'm single. And I need to stay that way.

For some reason I haven't figured out, I can't seem to stop thinking about Gavin, or more accurately, about the way Gavin kisses . . . and tastes . . . and feels.

But thankfully for me, I'm so busy making sure I don't end up back home with my parents, I can only think of him when I'm not working . . . like I should be doing at HERS right now.

"Are you heading out?" Brynn calls from behind the bar.

"I was, but I can stay if you need anything." I offer because I love my job so much and not at all because I'm avoiding my quiet apartment and empty couch.

"No, you don't need to stay for long. I just need to show you something before you leave." She tosses the rag she was cleaning the bar with into a bucket and turns toward Paisley, the newest hire at HERS. "You good on your own for a sec?"

"I'll be fine." Paisley smiles from behind the clipboard. "See ya tomorrow, Marlee."

"Later, Paisley." I wave to her as I follow Brynn to the office.

"Miss Harper, please take a seat." Brynn points to the chair in front of her desk. "We need to talk."

Brynn is never serious about anything, and the longer she goes without smiling, the more I freak out. She's not saying a word and I'm going over every promotion, every email, hell, every drink I've made in the last few weeks, trying to figure out what I could've done wrong.

"We need to talk about the promotions and advertising you've implemented recently." She's not even looking at me. My stomach drops to the floor, and my mouth goes dry. We've grown close over the last couple of months, but this is her business, and I'd never expect her to sacrifice one for the other. I'm just so screwed if I lose this job.

"Yes." I'm holding back my tears with a single thread. If she doesn't tell me the bad news fast, there's a high probability I'll be a puddle of tears all over the brand-new rug under her desk.

"I want you to look at these." She turns her computer screen toward me and my entire body tightens. I look at the bright, number-covered screen in front of me for seconds, but for the life of me, I have no idea what it means. Creative is my thing—or was my thing if I end up getting sacked today. Numbers have always eluded me, and right now I feel like I'm looking at Russian.

"I have no idea what I'm supposed to be seeing." My voice is thick from unshed tears.

"Those are the numbers from HERS for the last month. The profits, the traffic to our website, number of reviews, everything since you took charge of marketing." She turns her computer back toward her and focuses on the screen again. "Want to know what I see?"

Not particularly, but if she draws this out much longer, tears on her rug would be the least of her worries.

"I'm thinking you're going to tell me." I sit on my hands to prevent them from fidgeting anymore.

"You're right, I am." She pauses for what feels like an eternity, and I have to remember that even though she might be firing me, she's still my friend, and strangling people is generally frowned upon. "All of our numbers, since I gave you free range of marketing, have . . ." Oh my god! What is this? A result show for some singing competition? "Gone up."

The tough-as-nails boss facade disappears from her face and she jumps out of her seat, clapping her hands and laughing.

I, on the other hand, take a minute to process this news. I'm so relieved I didn't sink my friend's business to the ground, all of my bones seem to evaporate and I'm a pile of sludge. Then the news that not only am I not fired, but I'm kicking ass at my job replaces the missing bones with springs and I shoot out of the chair and start jumping along with Brynn.

"Oh my god!" I slap her shoulder when we're out of breath from bouncing and screaming. "I can't believe you did that to me! I thought you were going to fire me!"

"Wasn't I good? Naomi's been giving me acting classes the last couple of days so I could pull this off."

Snakes. I'm friends with sneaky snakes.

"That's so mean. I'm still shaking!" I show her my hands for proof. "But really good." Because let's be honest, we're friends for a reason, and I would've done the exact same thing if I was in her position.

"I know." She looks at me with a smug smile and pulls an envelope out of her back pocket. "For you, Marketing Master."

I snatch it out of her hand and rip open the seal.

Could I have played it a little cooler? Yeah. But when you know you aren't fired and your boss hands you an envelope while bowing, you get excited. Especially if you're as broke as I am.

I pull out the check and almost cry when I see five hundred dollars written on it.

Brynn shifts from foot to foot and struggles to maintain eye contact. "I know it's not much, but I wanted to show you how much I appreciate all of the work you've put into HERS."

"Are you kidding me? This isn't much? I'll be able to pay my electric bill *and* buy wine *and* have extra to put in my savings thanks to this!" I wrap her up in a giant bear hug.

"You know you work at a bar, right? We have wine here. You can have a glass before you leave." She pulls out of my embrace. She hates hugs, something I have a tendency to forget until she acts like I'm trying to start a wrestling death match. And she might look skinny, but my girl is ripped. I've been dropped on my ass more times than I'd like to admit.

"If I took the product as much as I'd like, you would've been giving me an intervention, not a bonus check."

"You're so strange." She rolls her eyes and walks to the door. "Get out of here. Go call Nay and tell her how convincing my performance was."

"Ten-four, Boss-Lady." I salute. "Thanks again for my moola!"

"Yeah, yeah. Whatever." She tries to sound uninterested. I might not be able to see her face, but it doesn't stop me from hearing her smile.

I put my envelope in my purse and walk out of the room with a little pep in my step.

This.

This is why I left Chris.

Okay. So technically I left him because he's a lying, cheating dirtbag. But I like to think I would've left him eventually anyways. I wasn't my best with him. I dulled myself in order to let him shine.

In the words of the infamous Ice Cube, today was a good day. #GangstaRapInspiration

Eighteen

YOU KNOW WHEN PEOPLE SAY DON'T COUNT YOUR CHICKENS BE-
fore they hatch?

I hate the saying. I'm terrified of birds and their evil, beady eyes and razor-sharp beaks waiting to peck me to death. But that's not the point. The point is someone should've repeated this to me before I skipped down the street, whistling rap songs.

It's the end of October, but we're having an unusually warm fall, and I'm enjoying it before the inevitable return of snow sends me running to my parka.

I turn onto my street and for the first time in a couple of weeks, James is back outside of my building. I have mixed emotions seeing him. Part of me is relieved to know nothing terrible happened to him, but the other part is sad because I really hoped he'd found a better, warmer sleeping arrangement.

"Hey, James," I say when I get closer to him.

"Miss Marlee." I don't know why he calls me Miss Marlee. He's thirty years older than me, and I've asked him to stop too many times to count, but he never listens. "How's you doing tonight?"

"I'm good. How are you?" I wish these streets were better lit and I could get a better look at him. I don't know if it's because it's been a little while since I've seen him, but something seems off.

"Oh . . . I'm okay." He's talking so slow, it's almost as if he's about to fall asleep.

"James," I say when I see his head bob and his body sway.

"Miss Marlee. How are you?" he asks again.

Crap. This isn't good.

"Have you eaten today?" I watch him as he shakes his head and uses his sleeve as a tissue. "I got a bonus at work today. I was thinking some tacos from El Señor sounded like a good way to celebrate. Want to come with?"

"Ooooh, girl." He whistles even though his eyes are still closed. "You know I love tacos."

"Great! I didn't want to go alone." He refuses to except charity, so I always let him know he's the one doing me a favor by coming with. "Would you mind waiting here a few minutes so I can change first?"

"Does it look like I have places to go, Miss Marlee?" He walks to the bench a few feet away and sits on the unforgiving metal seat with zero grace, but I flinch more than he does. "I'll be here when you're finished."

"Okay. I'll go fast." I turn on my heel and run into my building. I don't know what's going on with him, but I don't want to keep him waiting long.

When I come out in my leggings and running shoes, James isn't alone anymore. A man I've never seen before sits next to him on the bench. In most instances, I'd be thrilled to see somebody giving James attention, treating him like he exists instead of ignoring what they don't want to acknowledge. But something about this guy has the hairs on the back of my neck raised high. He looks to be about my age, his blonde hair cut down to a low buzz cut, and he's wearing a gray, short-sleeve button up shirt that, if I had to guess, I'd say was a nice shade of blue in its prime.

"James!" I wave, letting him know I'm ready. I'm the person who pushes her instincts to the side to be kind, but this guy is setting off warning signals left and right, and I'm not trying to get any closer. Too bad for me, not even distance can protect me from the silver-toothed smile and disgusting way his gaze trails my body when he sees me.

"You must be Marlee," he says from his spot beside James. "Nice of you to take our boy out tonight. Getting your good deeds in for the day?"

Even his voice makes me want to retreat. I wonder if this is how Harry Potter felt the first time he heard Voldemort?

"Nope. He's doing me the favor. I didn't want to eat alone, and he's good company." I keep my voice strong and casual. I've watched enough Lifetime movies to know guys like him get a kick out of scaring people. "Ready to go, James?"

James struggles to stand and I want to go help him up, but the guy I'm pretty sure might moonlight as a serial killer is in my way.

"What? No invite for me?"

Hell no.

"Not this time." I avoid eye contact and watch James as he makes his way to me at a turtle's pace.

"That's okay. Maybe if I'm lucky, I'll see you around," he says right before I turn around. "I mean, I know where you live now."

"Ready, James?" I pretend to ignore him, but my back goes straight at the laughter. If I wasn't so worried about James right now, I'd run straight into my apartment, lock the doors, and call my dad.

"Yup, Miss Marlee." He hobbles beside me. "Let's go."

EL SEÑOR'S TACO truck sits on the edge of Lincoln Park. During the day, it's filled with urban yuppie moms pushing their babies in strollers that look like they were designed by NASA and wearing yoga pants that cost more than my electric bill. But at night, the crowd becomes less savory. The kind that makes you keep your eyes straight ahead, and you don't look twice at what's being exchanged during handshakes. I usually try to stay away after sunset, but sometimes the need for tacos surpasses self-preservation. Tacos are life.

It's only a fifteen-minute walk from my house . . . and a five-minute one from Gavin's. Not that I knew that. Why would I? We're not friends. Gavin who?

Walking with James tonight though, it takes thirty.

Not that I mind, because even though he's pretty out of it, he still tells killer stories about the neighborhood. Tonight he told me about this woman who pretended to be a prostitute to get close to the other girls on the corners and when they'd get in trouble, she showed up like fuckin' Wonder Woman (his words, not mine) and hid them in the basement of her Five Points bungalow. Until one day she trusted someone she shouldn't have and they ended up shootin' up her house and killing her.

"The moral of the story," he says, "is not to trust everybody. You might be doin' right by them, but some people ain't strong enough to do right by you. And that's as much yo fault as theirs."

Kind of a downer story during tacos, but . . . beggars can't be choosers.

I give him the change from the tacos, only about ten dollars, but his eyes light up when I hand it to him. I'm not sure what he does with the money, but I figure it's not my place to ask. I give him the money from my heart, it doesn't come with strings. Of course I hope he saves it for food tomorrow in case I'm not around, but it's up to him.

Just as we're taking our final bites, James asks me to walk with him in the park. We meander around the paths—him talking and me listening—but he bails on me halfway through—right around the fountain currently being used as a drug exchange headquarter. He seems more alert after getting some food, so I'm not worried as I watch him head in the opposite direction we came from. And since I'm alone, it gives me the opportunity to do something I haven't done in weeks . . . four weeks to be exact. Walk past Gavin's house.

I keep my head down and pull my headphones out of my crossbody purse I threw on before I left the house, and blast my country playlist. I find my way out of the park, focusing on making myself small. I keep my eyes to my feet, and I walk fast, but not so fast I would draw much attention. As the park exit near Gavin's house comes into view, the knots in my stomach ease and I stand a little taller. I know I should speed up and get the hell out, but I do the opposite. I come to a stop and contemplate whether or not I really want to do this or not.

The entrance by El Señor's is flanked by old houses in desperate need of paint updates and housing projects, whereas the exit I'm taking is surrounded by million-dollar condos lining the streets. They're all stunning—some kept the integrity of the neighborhood in mind and simply remodeled, others are Mediterranean with clay roof tiles, but my favorites have always been the modern ones.

Gavin's modern one, to be exact.

It's crazy to think of all the times I walked by, blissfully unaware of its occupant, and would stop and stare. I used to wonder what kind of countertops were in the kitchen, what the light fixtures looked like, but now I spend more time than I'd ever admit wondering what his bedroom furniture looks like. I think about how his sheets would feel against my skin or, if, when I get off of his bed, my feet would hit cold wood floors or soft carpet.

The flickering streetlight draws my gaze from the empty path in front of me up to the orange light when a glare off of something pulls my attention back down.

The glare came off a silver tooth.

I'd always thought if I found myself in a situation like this, I'd run. No thinking, no second guessing. I'd turn and run.

Not so.

He leans toward me and pulls my headphones out of my ears.

"Didn't anyone teach you it's not safe to listen to music while you walk, especially for someone with a sweet little ass like yours?" he asks, his hot breath warming my ear. "They should also tell you not to trust junkies like James. They'll sell you out every time if it means they can get their next fix."

Fuck.

James. His story makes so much more sense now. If I make it out of this alive, Naomi's gonna freak.

If I make it out alive.

The thought goes through my head again . . . and again. My feet feel like they're glued to the pavement beneath me. I already knew this guy was dangerous, but with him this close, the strong scent of alcohol and body odor mixing with my fear causes my stomach to turn. My eyes widen, and I can't seem to get enough oxygen. His mouth twists into a sardonic smile as he watches my fear turn into panic. I knew this sick fuck got a kick out of this shit.

He must see my stance change from one of a scared, frozen girl to one preparing to run, because before I'm able to release the scream building in the back of my throat, he throws and lands a hard punch to my jaw.

My fight-or-flight instincts finally kick in. I clench my sweaty palms into a fist and throw a quick cross, catching him, and myself, off guard. His eyes widen with either shock or respect, I'm not sure which, and I don't wait around to see. I turn on my heel and will my shaky legs to help me run as hard and fast as I can.

I don't get too far when he grabs the purse wrapped around me and jerks me backward, causing me to stumble to the ground. The beat of whatever song is playing on my phone and his sick laughter form a sickening melody. I take a deep breath, trying to calm myself for what I know is about to come, and when he gets close enough, I snap my leg up and nail him right between the legs. He groans and before he even hits the ground, I'm back on my feet running.

I can't hear anything other than the sound of blood rushing through my ears as I'm darting down the street. Not my breathing, not the frantic rhythm of my Nikes hitting the pavement, not the sound of my lipstick and phone as they fly out of my purse and onto the sidewalk. Hell, I don't even know where I'm running until I reach Gavin's house. I don't slow to make the turn into his walkway and my feet slip from beneath me, causing my hip to collide full force with the cement. I push the pain to the back of my mind, focus on his door in front of me, and scramble back to my feet.

My chest is on fire. From what? I'm not sure. Maybe the cold air I'm swallowing with every inhale of breath or it could be from the powerful, throbbing heartbeat threatening to crack my sternum in order to escape.

"Gavin! Help!" I try to yell, but I can't seem to get the words as I near his door. "Gavin!"

The adrenaline starts to leave my system and hysteria is quickly replacing it.

When I reach his door, my hands move at their own accord, slamming against the door with so much force, I know they're going to be black and blue in a few days.

"Open the door, Gavin!" My voice is unlike I have ever heard it—scratchy like I've swallowed glass, more frightened than a wild dog. Each second I stand there, shaking and throwing myself at his door, feels like an eternity. I had managed to keep my eyes ahead, but the thought that Gavin might not be home makes me turn to see if my attacker is still there.

Icy terror grips my throat when I see him standing on the corner. Still as can be.

Watching me.

When he sees I've turned to him, he waves and walks away. It's at that moment I remember what he said earlier. He knows where I live.

He wasn't waving to say good-bye. He was telling me he'll see me later.

"Gavin!" My shrill voice disrupts the calm night once more. My hands, sore from the punch and fall and hitting the door, try once again and at last, it works.

The solid oak door swings open and Gavin's large form fills the doorway. I don't say anything before I'm inside his house, slamming the door shut and turning the deadbolts.

"Marlee?" he asks, probably confused to see me at his door at all, let alone the state I arrive in.

"The guy with James. He followed me. He knows where I live. How do I go home?" I shout a bunch of broken sentences at him. I wrap my arms around my midsection to try and comfort myself against the shaking taking over my body.

"What guy, Marlee?" I hear him, but I'm not listening.

"I knew it. I knew he was no good. But I froze and holy shit, he hit me so hard." My hand absently touches my jaw where the pain is starting to make itself noticeable.

"Marlee. What guy? What the fuck happened?"

I've been so focused on myself, I didn't even notice how his posture has changed from relaxed to tight and alert.

"The guy with James. He . . . he . . . I was listening to music and the light got crazy when I was almost out of the park. He came out of nowhere. I don't know what he wanted. I dropped my phone while I was running, but when I got to your door, he was still standing there watching me and then—"

I don't even finish the sentence before Gavin has the door open and is stalking down the walkway to the sidewalk.

"No! Gavin, come back!" I saw the guy walk away, but for some reason, I can't convince myself he's not still out there. Maybe with a weapon, ready to hurt me . . . hurt Gavin. I stumble back into the wall behind me and flinch with the painful reminder of slamming into the concrete outside. I lose the strength to hold my body up and melt down onto Gavin's hard, cold floor.

I don't yell for Gavin. I don't look out of the window to make sure he's okay. That would all take energy I no longer have. I don't even have the strength to let out a sigh of relief when he walks back through his front door, safe and with my phone in his hand.

"I don't know where he went, but he's not out there." He hands me my phone, still crack free under its rhinestone covered case.

"He's probably waiting for me," I whisper, unable to look Gavin in the eyes.

"Marlee." He says my name gently as he closes the distance between the two of us. "Are you all right?"

He sits down on the floor a couple of feet away from me, watching closely, like I might snap at any second—which, if I'm honest, I think I already did—so he doesn't miss the way I flinch and retreat when he reaches for my aching hands.

"Come sit down." He stands and helps me off of the floor. He walks slightly in front of me, enough to where he's close if I need him, but not so near that I feel overpowered, and guides me into the living room.

"Thank you," I say after we've been sitting on his couch for minutes . . . hours? Who knows.

"You're welcome. I'm sorry I took so long to answer the door."

"I wouldn't have opened the door at all if somebody was banging on my door like that this late at night." I try to reassure him, but my words come out weak and unconvincing.

"Do you want water or coffee or anything?" The change of topic is kind. "I can get something while you call the police."

Shit. The police.

"I forgot about them." I try to pull myself back together. "Coffee would be great." Wine would be better, but a clear head is probably necessary for this part. I guess caffeine is going to have to do the trick.

Freaking James.

The road to hell is paved with good intentions.

When will I learn?

Nineteen

AFTER GAVIN MENTIONED THE POLICE, I CALLED RIGHT AWAY. I didn't want to forget details, but mainly, I wanted it over with. And when Officer Green walked in, I wanted it even more.

Officer Green, aka Brian Green of the Denver Police Department, is a jackass. He went to high school with me and Chris. He was full of himself back then, but give him a friend in a Mustangs jersey and a badge? His asshole-ness increased at warp speed. Every time I see him, he throws out some crude comment about my ass or how much fun I must be to have kept Chris around for so long. And today's no exception.

I mean, come on, Universe. I just got punched in the face. You can't give me a break on this?

"Damn, Marlee. When they said your name and gave this address, I thought there had to be another Marlee Harper in Denver because why would you ever leave your golden tower in Parker," he says with a whistle. "But now I see not much has changed since high school."

"What are you talking about, Brian?" I'm not in the mood to engage with him tonight, so I cut straight to the point.

"Oh, you know. Still sinking your claws into any athlete you can find." He laughs at his stupid insult. I'm used to his idiocy, but I can sense Gavin's anger rising with each word coming out of Brian's mouth. "I thought once Chris got to the big leagues, you'd give it a rest. But the quarterback? Even I'm impressed. I didn't figure you'd be his type."

You'd think being a cop, he would be more attuned to the environment around him and do his job. But he keeps going, watching me, oblivious to the storm brewing beside him.

"Be honest, did anything even happen tonight or did you make it all up in order to weasel your way in here?" He gives me the same cocky smirk he's been aiming my way for years. He doesn't seem to realize my opinion of him is so low, nothing he could ever say would bother me.

Unfortunately, the same can't be said for Gavin.

"Are you fuckin' kidding me right now?" he whispers, but it somehow echoes in the room. "She was attacked an hour ago and you're standing here accusing her of what, exactly?"

"It's not a big deal, Gavin. Marlee and I go way back. She doesn't mind," he answers.

"First, you don't know me. You can call me Mr. Pope. Second, I don't give a flying fuck if Marlee's your damn sister. You don't walk into my home, imply she's not only a liar but a groupie, and joke around after *she was fucking attacked*!" Gavin stops and takes a deep breath.

While good old Brian makes the first wise decision he's made in his entire life and shuts the hell up, I stay in my spot on the couch enjoying Brian getting his ass handed to him.

"So here's what's going to happen. You're going to ask Marlee what you need to ask her to get the report. Nothing else. No jokes. No mentions of the past. Nothing outside of the reason you're here tonight. And if you can do that, then maybe I won't report you to your boss. Maybe I won't mention your name in a live broadcast on ESPN discussing the terrible experience I had with an Officer Brian Green of the DPD."

Mic drop.

The shit-eating grin Brian walked in with has taken flight and headed south for the winter. His eyes drift between me and Gavin, while his mouth sputters like a fish out of water. The look on his face is one I'll treasure forever. I try to hide my laughter in a failed attempt of cough cover-up. When Brian hears it, his mouth snaps shut and he directs his angry gaze my way.

"You won't do that shit either, Officer Green," Gavin says, gaining his attention back. "Can you do your job and speak with a victim properly or do I need to call and request a new officer?"

"You don't need to call, Mr. Pope. I can speak with Marl—"

"Miss Harper," Gavin corrects him, and this time I don't even attempt to hide my laughter.

"Of course." Brian turns back to me, his gentle tone a stark contrast to his pursed lips and narrowed eyes. "Miss Harper, can you please tell me what happened tonight?"

"Well . . . since you asked so politely." I smirk at him and live for Gavin's deep chuckle next to Brian.

"I'M SORRY YOU had to go through this, Marlee." The sincerity in Brian's voice takes me by surprise. Sometime over the past hour, he stopped being the d-bag I knew in high school and transformed into a really good police officer. "I have your information, and I'm going to give your number to the victim's advocate. You don't have to use their services, but I want you to have the option."

"Thank you, Brian. I really appreciate it." I never would've thought I would say those words to him and it sucks it's under these circumstances, but I'm happy there's a good guy hiding underneath his douchebag exterior.

"My job." He brushes me off as he walks to the door.

"Have a good night, Officer Green." The formality of our meeting never faded in Gavin's eyes . . . or his tone.

"Mr. Pope." Brian nods and walks past him.

I think tonight made it clear Brian will never be a Gavin Pope fan. Also made clear, Gavin has about as many fucks to give as I do when it comes to people liking me.

#FreshOuttaFucks

Gavin closes and locks the door behind Brian. His walks toward me, his bare feet padding quietly across the dark hardwood floors while his gaze never leaves me, even as he stretches out beside me on the chaise part of his couch.

"Are you okay?" He was quiet as Brian questioned me, but by the way he went ramrod straight when I got to the part about the guy's cheap shot to my face, I know he was bothered by it.

"I think so. It could've been so much worse. I'm glad he came out where he did and didn't wait until I was farther from some place to run." I don't mention the little detail where I go out of the park the wrong way so I could look at his place.

"Me too." He reaches for my hand, but instead of lacing our fingers the way I love so much, he traces his fingers lightly over the darkening bruises. His soft touch is the complete opposite of what I would expect from hands so large and calloused. "Do you want more ice?"

"I'm okay. Thank you, though."

It's getting late, but there's no way I can go home. After I described the guy's silver tooth to Brian, he knew exactly who I was talking about—Gregory Thomas, lowlife extraordinaire.

Gregory Thomas. Such a simple, normal name. His parents probably thought he'd grow up to be an accountant, maybe dreamt of a lawyer. But instead they got a sociopath with silver teeth. Life is so weird.

I'm sure Gavin would take me to my parents' house if I asked, but I don't want to tell the story again tonight. I want to ask him if I can stay, but after ignoring all of his calls and texts for the last month, I'm nervous.

He's been wonderful tonight, but that's what sucks about him—he's just all-around a fantastic guy. I mean, he oversteps a little bit and if my jaw wasn't so sore and I didn't dislike Brian so much, I would've told him to back up tonight. But he always means well.

"Stay the night." He startles me out of my thoughts by speaking them out loud.

"I don't think that's a good idea."

Just say yes and get this over with, Marlee!

"I'll take you home if you want or to your parents, but I'd feel better knowing you're safe and with me." His fingers leave my hand and his thumb brushes under my jaw.

"Are you sure? I don't want to be a burden."

"Positive. You're never a burden." He lifts my chin and kisses me.

Soft and sweet—nothing like our last kiss. The only thing they have in common is they're so addictive, I might need rehab.

"I'll stay," I whisper even though there's no reason to be quiet . . . unless fighting the urge to moan against his mouth counts.

"Good." He punctuates the word with a kiss and drapes his free arm across my stomach, resting his hand on my hip. Just that small gesture causes lightning to zap my core awake. "Come on, let's get you some clothes."

He removes his hand and my body instantly mourns the loss of his touch. I follow him up a familiar staircase, but this time, instead of turning to the right where I slept last time, I follow him to the left and into his room. He walks to his dresser and pulls out a T-shirt and boxers.

"Shit!" he says when he sees me. "I didn't know you were there. Here are some things for you to sleep in and if you wait a second, I'll grab some towels. Or if you want, I can bring them to your room."

"Can I sleep with you tonight?" I throw it out there. Quick, like ripping off a bandage. "I'll understand if you say no, I just . . . never mind. Sorry. I'll be in the other room." I want to turn and run, but my entire body aches and instead of being the hare, I'm for sure the tortoise.

"Where are you going?" Gavin's hand on my shoulder causes me to stop. "Of course you can sleep with me."

Tortoise wins again, slow and steady.

"Are you sure? I've already invaded your house, now I'm taking over your bed. And my nose is stuffy from crying so I'll probably snore."

Stop while you're ahead, Marlee.

#TMI

"I'm positive." He leans down and kisses my forehead before straightening and guiding me to his bathroom. "The towels are here." He points to the bottom cabinet. "I don't know if you'll like it, but my soap's in the shower and my lotions are here." He points to the top cabinet. "If you need anything else, just ask."

"Thank you," I say as he leaves.

I make quick work of showering. Showers aren't much fun when the water pressure hurts your bruised back, face, and ass. When I walk back out, he's lying in bed, staring at the empty ceiling.

With no shirt on.

Oh my god.

"Hey," he says. "Everything okay?"

"Everything's great." I make my way toward the bed and climb in beside him. My brain shouts at me to haul my black and purple ass to the guest room, but my body puts up a pretty convincing argument to give Gavin a chance.

I know I've been in his bed, but this is different. When we were together before, everything we did was covered in lies. It was fun, but it wasn't real.

But now, next to him, under his comforter, wearing his clothes and smelling of his soap, it's different. I feel more vulnerable with him than I ever did with Chris. Maybe because with Gavin, I feel like for the first time in my life, the person across from me sees through the pretend front I put up.

The way he watches me, the way he touches me? He makes me feel beautiful in a way Chris never did. That I'm beautiful not in spite of the flaws I work so hard to hide, but because of them.

"You even manage to look gorgeous in my old clothes." He's so quiet, I doubt he even realizes the words came out.

"Thank you." I almost laugh off the compliment, but I feel the bed shift and him moving closer. The only thing I manage to do is sigh.

"I'm glad you stayed." His lips graze my ear. He wraps his arms around me, pulling me toward him until my back is flush against his chest. Each time he exhales, his breath caresses my neck, sending chills down my spine and making my thighs clench.

"I'm sorry I ignored you." I close my eyes, thankful he can only see the back of my head. "I really like you, Gavin. It scares me how much, because I did the football thing already, and we all know how it ended. You're this huge presence, even bigger than Chris. And I don't want to lose myself in another person again. And every time I'm around you, I catch myself falling into the same trap. Even tonight, I could've stuck up for myself with Brian . . . I *should've* stuck up for myself. But with you next to me, I let you take over. You scare me."

"I really like you too, Marlee." He pulls the hair from my neck and moves it over my shoulder. "I know you don't need me to fight your battles for you. Now that I know you need to, I'll step back. You don't have to be afraid of me. I'm not Chris and I never will be."

"Thank you for saying those things."

"I only said them because they're the truth." He kisses the top of my head. "It's hard enough to maintain my willpower with you pressed against me. The rasp in your voice is making it even harder."

His words make me hyperaware of the bulge pressed against me and I unintentionally . . . intentionally? Either way, I wiggle my way closer to him.

"Marlee." The way he says my name, I'm not sure if it's a plea for me to keep going or stop.

"What?" I fake innocence and repeat the movement.

"Too much happened tonight and both of our emotions are running high." It's clear he's hanging on to his restraint by a thread and if I really wanted to break it, I'd be able to . . . easily. "It's not like last time. We'll both be here in the morning. We have time."

"Okay." I give in but only because time with Gavin might be the only thing better than being in bed with him.

Also, because as entertaining as his reaction to my wiggling is, my whole body hurts. When I have Gavin Pope again, I'm going to want it in prime working condition.

Twenty

UNLIKE THE GUEST ROOM, GAVIN'S WINDOWS ARE TREATED WITH fancy electronic blackout blinds. Tuesdays are Gavin's day off, and when I called Brynn last night to let her know what happened, she banned me from coming in. So I take full advantage of the dark room and comfy bed. Gavin, however, still wakes up at the ass crack of dawn.

When I manage to climb out of bed and join him in the living room, it's almost noon, and Gavin has my Fresh's coffee order and croissants waiting for me.

I fall back into the corner of the couch and snatch the remote out of Gavin's hand. Not a chance in hell I'm gonna watch ESPN all day.

Chris's remote was off-limits. It sounds ridiculous (because it was) but one day I took the remote and turned on *Ellen* and he didn't talk to me for a week. Gavin doesn't care though.

"Go for it, but if you turn on a soap opera, I'm out." Lucky for him, I stopped watching soaps years ago.

I open Gavin's DVR and come across a butt load of unwatched *Jeopardy!*'s and almost lose my shit. I'm a trivia freak. I buy little kids' yogurt instead of grown-up ones just for the little trivia on the side . . . and maybe because cotton candy yogurt is amazing. #NotAshamed

"You watch *Jeopardy!*?" I toss a throw pillow at his head.

"I try to, but if the number of unwatched episodes tells you anything, I don't get around to it much."

"Well at least I know what we're doing today." I stand, giving him my best elderly woman impression, and find my purse. When I come back to the couch, he's sitting there looking both amused and curious.

"What's going on?" He watches me as I lower my sore self back into my spot, and I don't miss the way his jaw tightens.

"We're playing *Jeopardy!*" I state the obvious. "Get your phone. For each question, we bet like they do. Except, I'm not a baller like you, so the first round, we do it in cents. Two cents for two hundred, four cents for four hundred. You get it. Then for the second round, we move to dollars. Twenty dollars for two thousand." I point to the calculator on my phone. "Keep track of your total on your phone." I stop and look at him. "Honor system, Pope. Then at the end, we bet for final *Jeopardy!* and the winner has to pay the loser."

"Are you serious?" He grins and drums his fingers against his coffee table. "How have I never played this?"

I press my lips together and shrug. "You know, Pope, you might be the big football player in the room"—I point both of my index fingers at myself—"but I'm the *Jeopardy!* queen. Be prepared to go down." I push play on the first unwatched episode I come across. "Oh. And also, if somehow you do manage to win? I'm broke, so don't expect me to pay you."

"IN YOUR FUCKIN' face, Pope!" I yell at his back as he walks to the kitchen to grab another pop. "Who doesn't know that Italy is the second most used setting in Shakespeare? And you call yourself a competitor."

What? I never claimed to be a gracious winner. #NaNanaNaNa #BamWHAT

"I didn't call myself a competitor. I think the term I used was 'aficionado,' you're the one who wanted to bet real money."

"Tomato, potato," I toss at him while picking the next episode to watch.

"You know the final *Jeopardy!* question, but you don't know it's tomato, tomato?"

I'm about to answer him when Gavin's picture behind a news anchor draws my attention. I exit out of his DVR and fight back the onslaught of nausea that takes over as I hear the news story.

"A mugging and assault brought the police to Denver Mustangs' quarterback Gavin Pope's home late last night," the news anchor says robotically, imposing the right inflections at certain points, tilting his head, creasing his eyes with the skill of a practiced reporter. "The victim, Marlee Harper, was attacked in Lincoln Park walking home from dinner. She managed to escape and run to Pope's downtown residence for help. We were told that after Harper arrived at Pope's downtown Denver residence, he went outside looking for the attacker. Police have named Gregory Thomas and James Walters as the suspects for the attack."

I know James set me up, but my heart clenches knowing he's getting in trouble for this. He needs help, not jail.

"Wow, Mark. Not only is Gavin Pope saving the day every Sunday, now he's proving to be a hero off the field too," the perfect redhead next to him says.

"He really is, Andrea. And you may remember, Marlee Harper is the longtime girlfriend of Mustangs receiver Chris Alexander. Bet he's going to be very thankful his teammate was around when she needed him."

"So true. We'll be right back with the weather," she says to the camera, her pearly whites gleaming beneath her tan.

Oh no. No. No. No! This is bad.

I was so wrapped up in the report, I didn't even realize Gavin had come back from the kitchen until his hand touches me.

"You okay?" His quiet voice holds unhidden concern.

"How'd they even find out? And why would they report my name? Isn't that illegal or something?" I ask, very much not okay.

"The media is full of vultures. If they think it will bring in viewers, they will broadcast your pain loud and clear."

"This isn't good." And as if to confirm my words, both of our phones ring. Gavin squeezes my knee and gives me a quick peck on the forehead before going to his phone. It's so sweet, so dreamy, if I wasn't in the middle of a breakdown supreme, I might've melted into a puddle of contented goo on his couch.

Thankfully, I called my mom and dad and filled them in this morning before Channel 7 was able to, but there are many people I didn't tell and I have a feeling they will all be much more interested in a certain blue-eyed, bearded quarterback than my brush with danger. I'm expecting to see Naomi's name on the screen, but as luck would have it (because I have no luck) Chris's name flashes on my phone.

Not in the mood to hear his mouth, I hit ignore, but before I can even put the phone down, he's calling again. We play the ignore and call again game ten more times before I give up and answer.

"What do you want, Chris?" I sound as defeated as I feel, which is to say, really freaking defeated.

"So you're fucking Pope?"

What a well-thought-out, meaningful greeting.

"I'm fine, thank you. He only landed one punch before I was able to run," I respond, my voice shooting up an unnatural octave. "So nice of you to check on me."

"Don't play coy, Marlee. That shit's not cute."

"But I'm fucking Gavin, Chris. Isn't that what you just said? So why would I try to be cute for you?" I can picture the color rising in his cheeks as he paces the floor, the way he always does when he gets angry.

"Shut up, Marlee!" His loud, angry voice rings in my ear. "You leave me and run to that arrogant bastard? What the fuck? Are you trying to ruin my career?"

"Chris," I say gently, "I don't think about you anymore. I know you think you hang the stars and the moon and are god's gift to women, but you aren't. I'm living my life and you won't believe this, but my decisions have nothing to do with you. We broke up. I'm moving on. And whether or not I'm with Gavin while I do is frankly none of your concern."

"So you're fucking him." Dense as ever. Really, how did I stay with him for so long?

"Maybe I am, maybe I'm not. Either way? It's none of your business."

"I swear to god, Marlee. Do you not see how embarrassing this is for me? I fought to get you involved. I paraded you around my teammates and their families and look at you. You're the same as these groupie sluts. Spreading your legs for anyone who looks your direction." The acid soaking his words makes me aware that he really believes what he's saying.

"You're delusional if you think after the way you treated me, embarrassed me, that I'd dedicate a single thought to your image or your comfort."

"Whatever, slut. Tell Gavin I said fuck him too. He's just as foul as—" The phone's out of my hand and Gavin's moving across the room, listening to Chris's rant.

"I already told you I'm not your fuckin' boy, Alexander. You treated Marlee like shit and now she wants to spend her time with someone who can appreciate her. If you ever want a ball thrown your way again, I suggest you lose her number, because if I ever hear you say the shit you said to her again, I will end your fucking career."

Are you kidding me?

I know I had quite a few aspirins last night, but I'm still pretty positive I didn't imagine the conversation we had where I asked him to step down. And here he is, twelve hours later, doing it again.

"It's not a threat, it's a promise. When you see her at the games with me, don't even look her way." He pauses and even from this far away, I can vaguely hear Chris yelling on the other end. "Yeah, it's like that. Last warning, leave Marlee the fuck alone, Alexander." He ends the phone call and stares at me for a moment before he moves back toward me.

Gavin's long strides make quick work of closing the distance between us and when he reaches me, his right hand runs through his hair, and he avoids making eye contact.

Good.

"Are you okay?" he asks.

"Why wouldn't I be?"

"Because you asked me last night to let you fight your own battles and I just did it again." He's quiet when he answers, and I can tell he regrets what he did, but I'm having a hard time caring.

"Oh, so you do remember? I wasn't sure if you forgot, but now I know you just disregarded me." I walk to where he left my phone and find my dad's contact. "Hey, Dad," I say into the phone when he answers. "Can you come grab me from Gavin's? Great, I'll send you the address."

Sure, it's not like he's cheating on me—we're not even an official couple—but he still disrespected me. I had one request for him last night and already it doesn't matter. And for the cherry on top, since I don't have a car and Gregory is at large, I had to call my dad to come pick me up! Like I'm in freaking middle school again.

"I'm sorry," he says. "I shouldn't have taken your phone from you. It wasn't my place to step in. But I couldn't sit next to you and listen to what he was saying to you anymore."

"Yes, you could've!" I close my eyes and take a deep breath to try and regain my composure. "You could've," I repeat when I'm calm again. "You just didn't."

"Marlee—" he starts, but I don't want to listen.

"Not now, Gavin. I'm just not in the right mind-set to deal with this." I turn and walk toward his floating staircase. "My dad's going to be here soon. I'm going to change."

When he doesn't try to call me back, I hurry upstairs and stay there until I hear the doorbell ring and my dad's unmistakable voice carry through the house.

"Bye, Gavin," I say without looking at him.

Twenty-one

THE FIRST BOUQUET SHOWS UP AT MY PARENTS' HOUSE THE DAY after I leave Gavin's.

The second one shows up at HERS two days after that, on a Friday. The third, fourth, fifth, and sixth arrive at my parents' house during the Mustangs game on Sunday. I didn't even know they delivered on Sundays.

My mom thinks it's romantic.

My Dad and Brynn think it's obnoxious.

I fall somewhere in the middle.

Monday at work, the seventh and eighth bouquets arrive.

"If he moves to singing telegrams, I'm going to walk over to his house and kick him in the balls," Brynn tells me ever so elegantly.

"Nice. I thought I was supposed to be the irritated one." I try to look at her, but even though I want to hate them, I can't stop staring at the flowers.

"You were, but I can see your resolve weakening with every stupid flower, so I'm taking over for you."

"So does that mean I should run?" a deep voice calls from the front door.

Gavin.

I twirl around so fast, the vase full of pink and purple blooms flies out of my hands and just misses Brynn's head before it crashes into the wall behind her.

"Oops," I say at the same time Paisley shouts, "I'll get the broom." I look at the sparkling shattered glass mixed with the flowers around Brynn's feet. It might be dangerous, but it's really pretty. #ArtImitatingLife

"Are you okay, Brynn?" Gavin asks. He's no longer in the doorway, and he's carefully collecting shards of glass off the floor.

"Get away from the glass, Pope!" I yell. All I need is him injuring his hand and the entire city turning on me.

He does as I ask and unfolds from his crouched position to his full height. "So it takes a potential injury to get you to talk to me again?"

"I was going to talk to you," I say, and he throws me major side-eye. "I was . . . eventually." What? I'm a crappy liar. "Why are you here?"

"I wanted to see if you'd go out with me." He rubs his hand down the back of his neck and shifts from foot to foot. "I know you're mad at me and you have every right to be. But I've been thinking this last week that we've spent a lot of time together, but never gone on a proper date."

"Aww! That's so sweet, and he's super handsome," says Paisley. Yeah, she's supposed to be sweeping Brynn out of the danger zone and into safety. "You can't say no."

"Yeah." Gavin sticks his bottom lip out. "You can't say no."

"Oh brother." Brynn rolls her eyes so hard, they almost get stuck behind her head. "If she goes out with you will you stop sending these damn flowers?"

"Hey!" I glare at Brynn. I like getting the flowers. After being with a man who never apologized, it's nice to be on the receiving end of a little groveling.

"What?" She glares back. "It's not like I don't already know your answer."

"I don't know your answer though," Gavin cuts in. "You wanna fill me in?"

"Before I answer, where would we go?"

"I have one date planned if you want it to be a surprise or you could choose." He leans toward me, his eyebrows up. Even with his beard, he looks so young.

"Thank you for offering, but . . ." I pause and watch his body slump over. "I hate planning dates. I'll take the surprise."

"Is that a yes?" His head pops back up, and he's got the dimple-revealing grin plastered to his face.

"Yes, it is," I say right before he punches the air above his head and picks me up off the floor.

"Yes!" He hugs me tight and kisses me on the cheek before putting me back on the ground. "You won't regret this."

I know I won't.

What he doesn't know is I was going to call him tonight anyway.

Ha. Sucker.

"Are you free tomorrow?" he asks but starts talking again before I can answer. "What time do you get off?"

"I get off at three."

"Then I'll pick you up at five, if that's okay with you." He's bouncing on his toes and still smiling his wide grin. Who needs flowers when their man acts like you hang the moon? Not I.

"Five is perfect." I try to bite back my smile, but I'm not successful. His excitement is contagious and it's impossible for me not to catch it.

THE ONLY HINT Gavin gave me for our date was to dress in comfortable clothes.

I'm sure there are women who'd be disappointed not to go on some fancy, expensive date with an NFL quarterback, but I'm not one of them. And his knowing that made me feel even more secure in saying yes to tonight.

With Gregory still on the loose, I haven't felt comfortable going back to my apartment, so Gavin gets to pick me up from my parents'. He knocks on the door at five on the button. Punctuality isn't one of my strong points, but I can appreciate when it is for others. Unlike the first time he met my dad, there are no bro-hugs or nicknames today. By making me mad, interrupting the Mustangs game with flowers, and taking me on a date, Gavin has been removed from my dad's friend list and placed on his "Guys Who Date My Daughter" list.

Gavin hates it, but I like it much better. Seeing them interact was like watching a dog who only walks on its hind legs. It's just weird.

"I want you back by nine," my dad says before we leave.

"Yes, s—" Gavin is in the middle of agreeing when I cut him off.

"He's messing with you, Gavin." I turn to my dad, who isn't doing a very good job hiding his amusement. "Bye, Dad."

I push Gavin out of the front door and slam it behind me before I hear my mom and dad bust out laughing. Immaturity runs in the family.

"Damn," Gavin says as he opens my door to his truck. "Is it weird that I already miss your dad liking me?"

I climb into the seat. "Yes. Very weird. But if it makes you feel better, he still likes you. He just likes to mess with you more."

Dad never messed with Chris. He just shot him dirty looks

from wherever he was standing when he came around. This thing he has with Gavin is actually pretty adorable . . . even though I'll never admit it.

When Gavin starts his truck, he already has the country station playing, and I feel a little breathless. I don't try to hide my smile when my favorite song comes on and I belt the lyrics out right along with Luke Bryan.

I'm a terrible singer. Chris used to try and turn up the music until it drowned me out or he would get pissed because I "ruined another good fuckin' song." Gavin doesn't do either. Instead, he laughs right along with me, singing just as out of tune and butchering the lyrics. He threads his fingers through mine while he's driving and brings my hand to his lips during the drive. Each sweet, quick touch of his mouth while he's laughing causes warmth to radiate through my chest until I worry I might explode.

"We're here." Gavin motions to the arcade in front of us.

"Shut up!" I hit his arm a little harder than I meant to, but he still doesn't flinch. "I've wanted to come here forever! I thought it was closed on Tuesdays though?"

"Not for us." His chest puffs out. "It's just you, me, and Pac-Man in there tonight."

Gavin's so laid-back and easygoing, it's not hard for me to forget he's loaded, and a date with him could include renting out Denver's most popular hipster arcade.

We're walking to the door when it swings open and a forty-something man in a plaid shirt, skinny jeans, and a knit beanie walks out, giving Gavin a very enthusiastic welcome.

Gavin and I listen to him for a few minutes before Gavin gives him a polite, yet very effective, brush-off.

"That was real smooth, Mr. Pope," I whisper when we've put enough distance between us and our hipster host.

"Oh. You liked that, did you?" He bends over and brushes his lips against mine. "Don't try and pick up my techniques to use on me."

"Please." I roll my eyes. "I hope your ego's not so bruised from me kicking your ass all night long that you don't try them on me."

"Yeah right, Harper. You're going down tonight."

#ThatsWhatSheSaid

Pinball machines and retro video games fill the room—Donkey Kong, Centipede, and some Michael Jackson dance game I will definitely return to later. I'm halfway down the row when the perfect game comes into view.

"What do you say, Pope?" I point to the giant, four-player game. "Pac-Man or bust?"

I skip toward the game in the corner of the arcade, unable to prevent my hands from clapping like a child.

"Damn, girl, you must not know you're standing next to the Pac-Man king," Gavin says from close behind. "They don't call me the cherry-busting master for nothing."

"Oh my god!" I stop mid skip and turn into his chest. "Please tell me you did not just say that!"

"Yeah . . . I heard it after I said it." Gavin's face flames red. "My friends started and stopped calling me that in second grade, it didn't have the same meaning to our seven-year-old minds."

"Well, there will be no cherry busting, and you're going to lose." I pat his chest two times and walk toward the game. "I hope you still have fun tonight."

"You don't stand a chance! Did you forget who I am?"

#InfamousLastWords

Twenty-two

"STOP POUTING." I SLAP GAVIN'S THIGH WHEN HE GETS SETTLED IN the driver's seat. "I told you a million times. The football field's the only place you'll ever beat me. Learn to accept it."

"You're a sore winner," Gavin says.

I give him a crisp nod. Duh.

"The only thing I heard you say was I'm a winner."

At first, Gavin was letting me win, but he has not taken Naomi's acting classes. He's as bad of a liar as I am. After a little whining and taunting on my behalf, he finally gave it his all.

I still won, and I didn't ever ease up.

Obviously. I'm a beast.

"I'll get you next time." He stops talking and checks his rear-view mirror as he reverses out of the parking spot. "And when I do, I'm going to gloat all night."

"I'm just happy to hear you still have dreams, babe." Oops. My eyes widen, and I freeze. We had so much fun tonight, and I got so comfortable with him, it just slipped out.

I can't look away as every last trace of his pouty loser face (yes, that's what I call it) disappears and a shit-eating grin takes its place.

"Aw snap!" He glances at me from behind the wheel. "My master plan worked! Let you beat me, steal your heart."

I snort. "You're so full of shit! I beat you fair and square and you know it."

"I do not." He shakes his head. "You fell into my trap!"

We're laughing so hard, my cheeks are sore from smiling and we can barely hear the radio. So much so, I almost don't notice it when the DJ says a familiar—and unwelcome—name.

"What's wrong?" Gavin asks, staring.

"Turn that up." I point to the radio. I don't mean to whisper, but I can't speak any louder.

"Okay?" Gavin turns up the volume.

"And if you don't remember, this Gregory Thomas guy—who has quite the record, by the way—attacked the girlfriend of Denver Mustangs player Chris Alexander. She managed to escape to quarterback Gavin Pope's house. Thankfully, she's fine and hopefully, with Thomas now in custody, she'll be able to rest a little better tonight."

Holy shit.

Gavin turns the radio down when the music starts playing again, but doesn't say anything and neither do I. I don't know how long I stare at the illuminated station numbers before my brain starts to function again. But the second it does, I reach to the floor and snatch my phone out of my purse. Sure enough, I have five missed calls and one new message.

I unlock it and push play, letting the message play on the speaker. I'm gonna tell Gavin all about it anyways, so it's easier for me if he hears it now.

"Good evening, Miss Harper, this is Detective Long. I hoped I'd be able to talk to you rather than leaving this in a message, but since I've called four times without an answer and this is bound to get out in the press shortly, I guess this will have to do. We apprehended Mr. Thomas at around seven o'clock this evening. He's being processed and with all of the other priors and women who have come forward since your report, the DA will press for him to be held without bail. If you have any questions, feel free to give me a call."

I play the message one more time to make sure I've heard him right, and after I'm sure I have, I take my first deep breath since the attack.

"Are you all right over there?" Gavin asks.

Only then do I notice we've pulled over on the side of the road.

I turn to him with a smile so big my cheeks ache again, unbuckle my seatbelt, and crawl on top of the center console.

"I'm better than all right. Take me home, Pope," I say. "And I don't mean my parents' house."

It's a demand, not a request. One I punctuate with a kiss.

"OH MY GOD!" I run through my apartment and jump on my bed. "I missed you so much."

"Are you talking to your mattress?" Gavin asks from my doorway.

"No. That'd be stupid." I grab my pillow from under my head. "I was talking to my pillows. Here, come test them out. It's like laying on a cloud."

He shakes his head but starts walking over, dropping his jacket on my floor along the way. When he gets to my bed, instead of climbing in nice and slow like I thought he would, he jumps in next to me, and I'm almost sent flying off the side.

"Damn. These are amazing!" I think he says, but his face is shoved into my pillow, and I can barely understand him.

"They're amazing?" I repeat when he rolls back over to make sure I heard him right.

"Yeah." He's a little out of breath from almost smothering himself. "Where'd you get them?"

"Furniture Warehouse." I turn toward him and toss one of my legs over his. "They're the only thing in the apartment I splurged on."

"You're gonna have to take me there sometime." His hand finds its way to the back of my thigh and starts moving up and down. After a fun but eventful night, the simple touch is so relaxing, I struggle to keep my eyes open.

"Next date," I mumble, right on the cusp of sleep.

"So there will be more dates, you're saying. Want to make this official and be my girlfriend?"

"I'm not sure yet." I hook my ankle behind his knee and pull him on top of me. "What are the benefits like?"

"Is this how you want to play it?" he asks, and his crooked smile changes to a full-blown, teeth showing, eye crinkling, one dimple–revealing *smile*.

It. Is. Glorious.

"Well, it's been a while."

"It has, four years." His eyes never leave mine as he inches his way closer.

"Four years . . ." I repeat, watching his eyes change from bright blue to navy.

"Are you sure?" he asks before he drops his mouth the last inches.

In answer, I wrap my arms around his neck and pull him closer. "I've never been so sure about something." I lift my head off the pillow that started all this and press my lips to his.

It's the only thing I need to do to make Gavin's restraint snap.

He brings his mouth to mine. His soft, full lips steal all of my breath.

My back arches off the bed and pushes my soft breasts into his hard chest. The kiss becomes more insistent, more demanding. My hands travel down to his strong shoulders, pulling him even closer. I'm aware of every part of my body he's touching, but even more so of those parts he isn't.

It's not at all what I remembered.

It's so much better.

He pulls his face back and watches as his fingers grab on to the hem of my shirt and slowly raises it up and over my head. My skin is so sensitive, even the small feel of the cotton—of his fingertips— gliding up my stomach causes me to shiver.

"God. You're so fucking beautiful." The words come out so rough, so raw, I swear I can feel them across my skin.

"Come here," I whisper, feeling a confidence and a boldness I've never felt before. My hands find their favorite position at the back of his head, his hair like silk under my fingers, and pull his face to mine.

The small gesture is like a bolt of lightning. Both of us feel it. The charge of electricity shooting through our bodies, the crack- ling energy surrounding us, the sparks that fly with every look, every touch, every kiss after.

He pulls his mouth away from mine, and I almost whine in protest. But then he reaches for the bottom of his shirt and he pulls it up, revealing the V cuts peeking out of his jeans and his toned abs one magnificent inch at a time.

No words.

But when a shirtless Adonis is on his knees between your legs, words aren't necessary.

"How about we get the rest of these clothes off?" he whispers. His tongue glides down my neck, and my legs clench together.

"No more clothes is good," I say. My voice is unrecognizable. I'm sure it's the exact voice phone sex operators shoot for.

#Dial69ForYeeeesssssss

"Glad you agree." One second he's whispering in my ear, the next he's at my feet and my jeans are nowhere to be seen.

His fingertips skate up my legs, dancing and twirling around my thighs, causing goose bumps to follow in their path. He *just* brushes over the fabric of my thong, but it's enough to make my already arched back lift even higher. I don't even get the chance to beg for more before he's taking advantage of my position and making easy work of undoing the clasp of my bra. I hold my breath as he slides the straps off my shoulders ever . . . so . . . slowly . . . and by the time the room stops spinning, my bra and thong have joined the rest of our clothes piling up somewhere in my room.

He takes a deep breath and sits back on his heels while his gaze travels over every inch of my body. The urge to cover up I always felt with Chris never comes. I lay there unflinchingly, feeling the heat of his gaze as it moves up my legs. Goose bumps break out all over my body as I wait for any hint of contact.

"Holy shit, Marlee. You're what dreams are made of." The words are quiet but forceful, like he's never meant anything more in his entire life.

I'm soaking up his compliment when his hands are back on me and they aren't the whisper they were before.

His tongue traces a pattern down my throat as his calloused hands drag over my hips, up to my waist, and grab on to my rib cage. His thumbs and forefingers brush across my chest, my nipples hardening under their touch when his tongue reaches the curve of my breast. I'm trembling so hard I twist the sheet around my fist to anchor myself to the bed.

"Please, Gavin." Between the moans and my heavy breathing, I might as well be speaking a foreign language.

"Tell me what you want, Marlee."

I try to answer, but every time I find the words, he takes my nipple into his mouth, and I lose the ability to speak.

"Tell me what you want," he says again.

"Touch me, please," I beg, my body crying out for more.

"With pleasure." He drops his head back to my nipple and before I know what's happening, his free hand is between my legs.

"Oh my god." I moan when his finger dips inside of me.

"Fuck, babe." Gavin kisses his way up to my face. "You're so fuckin' wet, I have to taste you."

I'm in such a lust-covered haze, I can't even comprehend what he says before his warm body is no longer covering me and his mouth is on my mound.

I might be well into my twenties, but I've never felt this good before.

"What are you . . ." I try to ask him, but when his tongue flicks at the same time his finger moves, my head flies back onto my pillow, and I tangle my hands in Gavin's hair. I don't know if I want to pull him away or never let him move, but before I can decide, heat starts to radiate from my core and from my toes to my head, everything insides me tenses.

"Oh . . . my . . . GAVIN!" My eyes clench shut, and a light so bright explodes from behind my eyelids, I worry I might be dead.

Death by orgasm? I could think of worse ways to go.

After minutes . . . or hours, my breathing slows, and my body stops trembling. I gather the strength to open my eyes and when I do, I'm met with Gavin's dark eyes and bright smile.

"You taste even better than I dreamed." He kisses me.

Even while I'm laying naked on my bed, he can still make me blush.

"That was amazing," I tell him, because after a performance like that, the man deserves to know.

"It was." He peppers my breasts with kisses.

"Is it time for more?" I ask, really wanting more.

"Oh yeah," he responds while reaching in his pants' pocket and pulling a condom out of his wallet.

"In your pocket? Pretty sure of yourself there, Pope." I lay on the bed, totally satisfied but still craving more, watching as he takes off his jeans, pulling his boxer briefs down with them until he's left standing naked in front of me.

"Just hopeful." He winks before ripping the condom wrapper with his teeth.

I thought he looked good in his jeans? I didn't have a clue. These past four years have been *very* kind to him. I immediately focus on his V cuts. I try to keep my gaze there, but the V is a giant arrow pointing to his very impressive, bordering on scary, manhood. I watch, enamored, as he stands at the edge of the bed, rolling on the condom.

He finishes and looks to me, and a cocky smile—no pun intended—crosses his face as he makes his way back to me. I see the way his quads and hamstrings flex with every step he takes and nearly have to wipe the drool from my face. I didn't even know sexy hamstrings were a thing!

He climbs onto the bed and settles between my legs. He softly touches his lips to mine and looks directly in my eyes. "I've been waiting for this for the last four years."

I wrap my legs tightly around his back, pulling him to me so he's nestled to the edge of my entrance. "Then stop waiting," I tell him, my voice never wavering, my eyes never leaving his as he moves his hips forward and connects us.

#Touchdown

With every movement, every moan, every deep kiss, it becomes clear this is where I'm supposed to be. I'm not comparing Gavin to Chris, not only because there is no comparison, but because Chris is a long forgotten memory. It's scary how much I feel for Gavin. How right it feels to be in bed with him, feeling his bare skin against mine, running my hands down his back. It almost causes me to mourn the last four years of my life that I could've spent with him, reveling under his touch, blossoming under his words. But I don't.

"Yes, Marlee." His becomes voice even deeper, gravelly even, and I know he's on the edge right next to me, waiting for me to fall so he can follow. "Give it to me. Let me watch."

And this time, I listen to him. I let go and my body, still loose from earlier, rewards me with an orgasm so powerful that when I scream out, there is no sound. My eyes slam shut, my back curves off of the bed, and my arms fly around his neck, pulling him toward me. Gavin's hands are firmly pressed against my thighs, holding them in place as he drags out my orgasm to uncharted lengths before a guttural moan comes from him, and he collapses on top of me.

Then we lay there with his weight pushing me into the bed, my fingers drawing circles on his back, saying nothing while our heart rates return to normal and our breathing calms. When he does roll off of me, it's not before he gives me one more kiss and breaks the silence.

"Did I pass the test? Are you my girlfriend now?"

"You did pretty good. If I'm your girlfriend, can I wear your ring?" I attempt to joke, but as soon as the words leave my mouth, I panic. "I mean, you know what I mean. Not a ring, ring. Like no diamonds. A class ring like from *Happy Days* when they did that kind of stuff . . . of course I don't need a ring from you. That'd be crazy, and I'm not crazy. Totally sane. Totally."

Being awkward isn't new for me, but being awkward and naked? New heights. And it's the worst because I'm pretty sure my entire body might be blushing right now and Gavin can see my entire body! The only thing I can hide under is Gavin, which is *so* not optimal, but I go for it anyway because . . . desperate times.

I try to use his chest for cover, but it's shaking too hard to get a firm grip on.

"I got it, babe." And I can hear the smile in the jerk's voice. "I just like listening to you ramble when you get nervous."

"You're such an asshole. Next time, can you at least do it when I have clothes on or, at the bare minimum, am under a blanket?"

"I can't make any promises." He climbs out of the bed and stops to let his gaze travel down the length of my body once more. "But I do like that you said there will be a next time."

"Don't be all sexy and sweet when I'm trying to be irritated with you!" I call to his back as he walks into the bathroom.

"Keyword was 'trying.'" He reappears in the doorway, still naked, only missing the condom I'm assuming he flushed. "So, what do you say, Miss Harper? Are we going steady now?"

"Yes, Mr. Pope, we're going steady."

He doesn't say anything to my answer. Instead, he saunters across the room, his gorgeous manhood swaying between his legs with every step until his gets to the edge of the bed and climbs over me.

"What are you doing?" I ask when he starts moving down the bed.

"Giving *my* girl a kiss."

"But my head is up here." I pop up on my elbows, watching as he pulls the comforter from my stomach.

"I'm kissing a different set of lips," he says and punctuates it with his tongue dipping into my core.

Damn.

"Holy shit," I whisper to the ceiling. "I love being your girlfriend."

And the vibrations from his quiet laughter between my legs only make me like it that much more.

#Bliss

Twenty-three

IT WASN'T WHAT EITHER OF US WANTED, BUT GAVIN WENT HOME later that night. I was finishing up on one of my final freelance projects before I focused entirely on HERS. Plus, I had to get all of my stuff from my parents' house before I even went into work.

Adulting sucks.

The next morning, I wake up to knocking on my door. When I open it, on the other side is Gavin, standing there in his Mustangs sweatpants and sweatshirt, holding a large vanilla latte and a croissant.

Swoon.

My boyfriend is so dreamy.

He gives me my goodies and a quick kiss—which turns into a long kiss—before swatting me on the butt and leaving to go to practice.

I go back inside, and even though I technically still have thirty minutes to sleep before I need to be up, I get an early start on the day.

When I walk into HERS an hour later, not only am I early, I'm grinning so wide it's a wonder I don't have bugs stuck in my teeth.

"Well, well, well," Brynn says when she sees me. "Looks like somebody's date was a success."

"If me being Gavin's girlfriend means it went well, then yeah. You could say that."

"Freaking finally. You two were driving me nuts. But dammit!" She looks around the room and stops when she finds Paisley. "You win, Paisley. They're dating now."

"What the hell? You bet on us?"

"Of course we did." She looks at me like I'm the crazy one. "He was sending you like, a million flowers a day. You thought we weren't going to get in on that action?"

"Jerks." I shake my head and walk away before my smile breaks free again.

The rest of the day passes like my days normally do. Uneventful. Which, after the last week, I should be happy about. But I don't know. Gavin Pope's my boyfriend. It kind of feels like confetti should be thrown in the air whenever I walk into a room.

Since business was slow today, Brynn let me leave early and I took the time to do some grocery shopping. Gavin's going to be coming over more and I hate eating out all the time, especially now that I work at a restaurant, so I try to keep my kitchen stocked. Before Gregory Scumbag Thomas was arrested, my dad was driving me to and from the store, but now that the coast is clear, I grab my little grocery cart from home and hop on the train. Not having my dad nagging me about looking at every aisle, I take longer than I mean to and when I leave, the sun is long gone. I walk to the train, trying to think happy thoughts as the streetlights flicker on and off over my head.

Once at the train platform, I park my cart of groceries next to me and sit on one of the empty benches. I open my text messages, about to send one to Gavin, when a hand grabs on to my shoulder. A scream rips out of my throat, probably pushed out from my heart trying to escape with it. I jerk my shoulder out of the grasp and I'm not even all the way upright before I start to run.

"Marlee," Gavin calls my name before I make it to the edge of the platform. "It's just me."

"Holy shit!" I stop and turn around. "You almost gave me a heart attack!" I put both of my hands over my head as I make my way back toward him. My breathing is still ragged and each inhale causes the burn in my chest to go a little deeper.

This is why I avoid running and haunted houses at all costs.

"I called your name two or three times before I came over here." He reaches for the backpack I was willing to abandon. "What were you doing that you couldn't hear me?"

"I was thinking about what to text you."

"Ooh . . . you were, were you?" His voice drops, and he wiggles his eyebrows.

He looks ridiculous, but I'd still totally do him. Who could blame me? A girl's got needs.

"Not that kind of text." I pat his shoulder. "What are you doing here anyway?"

"I went to see you at HERS, but Brynn said you went to the store. I was heading there when I saw you pushing your old lady corral." He wraps his arm around me, pulling my freezing body into his warm one. "Plus it's cold. You don't want to wait out here, do you?"

"Aren't you the sweetest." I hug him a little tighter.

"I am, but don't tell anybody," he whispers even though we're alone. "You'll ruin my street cred."

When we arrive at his truck, ever the gentleman, he opens my door for me before walking to the driver's side and climbing in.

"Can I sleep at your place tonight?" he asks over the radio. "I know we both have work tomorrow, but one night in bed with you and you already have me addicted."

"Of course you can. You don't even have to ask." Thankfully, the dark sky prevents him from seeing the way my cheeks flame and the way my thighs press together, but the grin that overtakes my face is unmistakable.

"Good. It would've been embarrassing to have to explain why I have a duffel bag with my stuff in it if you said no." He points to the bag I didn't even notice under my feet.

#ShortPeopleProblems

"I'm not sure if you've noticed this yet or not, but I seem to have a really hard time telling you no."

"Since you said that, maybe now is as good a time as ever to mention . . ." He says that terrifying sentence and then stops.

"Mention what? You can't stop there, Seacrest! This isn't *American Idol*, there are no commercial breaks before the announcement." When in doubt, always use reality shows to help drive home your point.

"Did you just call me Seacrest? I'm pretty sure I have about a foot and sixty pounds on that guy."

"Oh my god. First, that was a fantastic metaphor. Second, will you just say what you were going to say already? You're freaking me out!"

"You're the only person I know who argues with pop culture references."

"Gavin!" I'm about to resort to physical violence, but he seems to sense I'm getting there and starts talking.

"I talked to Dre today. He said Naomi misses you at the games. And I want you at the games. So I was hoping you'd start going again. The next two games are away, but after that, would you want to come?" He rushes out in a single breath.

"Why wouldn't you just say that!" I slap him, feeling relieved that's all it was but still on edge from my fleeting nerves. "I'd love to go. I don't know if anybody has told you this yet, but I'm kind of the shit when it comes to showing up at the stadium on Sundays."

"No, Dre warned me. He said Naomi hasn't been able to decide if she enjoys not fearing you starting a brawl or not."

"That was one time! How was I supposed to know everyone around us would get so upset?" I try to defend myself, but when he stops at a red light and turns his wide eyes my way, I see the error of my ways. "I mean . . . if that ever actually happened it would only happen once . . ."

"I thought they were exaggerating!"

"I just get a little . . . intense when I go to games." I shrug. "I'm competitive. So kill me."

"Do me a favor, try not to start any fights when you come to the game. I think I might get a fine if I run into the stands to fight some guy." They're pretty strict about that stuff, but . . .

"No promises. Lenny's probably been bored out of his mind without me."

"Who the hell is Lenny?" he asks, probably already thinking of ways to revoke his invitation.

#NoTakeBacks

"He checks the tickets for section 112. I've been sitting in his section for years. He loves it when I give him a little extra excitement."

"God help me," he asks the roof. "No promises because she's got a fucking attendant who loves her antics."

"Not even god can help you, Pope," I say once I've stopped laughing. "Don't worry, you'll learn to love my antics."

"I have no doubt."

And the way he says it, I can't help but wonder if he's talking about more than my game-time behavior.

Twenty-four

ONCE THE TWO AWAY GAMES FINALLY PASS BY, NAOMI AND I PLAN for her to pick me up and ride to the game together. However, before that can happen, she calls and requests an emergency meeting.

I'm not shocked.

I guess some drama went down at this week's Wednesday meeting, most likely the unusual pairing of Marlee (the groupie) and Gavin (the naive).

Plus, Naomi has a flare for the dramatic and why discuss things over the phone when you can call an emergency meeting?

And in Naomi's terms . . . and mine . . . an emergency meeting can constitute a sleepover at my house, filled with all sorts of Girl Scout activities like working on our bedazzling, margarita, and gossip badges.

"I've missed these." Naomi takes a sip out of her margarita glass without lifting the glass, even though she finished painting her nails thirty minutes ago and there's no way they're still wet. "I've missed you too, but your margaritas are the best."

"Thank you . . . I think." I walk to the kitchen and grab the blender with the rest of the margarita in it.

Tequila goes well with gossip, but I have to admit, I'm a little nervous about what our shirts are going to look like. I spent a mint ordering all these crystals, so this is kind of a one-shot gig.

I pour the remainder of the drink into Naomi's glass and pick my tweezers back up, returning to my bedazzling project.

"Now that you have me drunk, are you ready to hear about the last meeting?" she asks.

"I think I'm the one who needs to be drunk for this, but sure." I'm lying on the floor, my face only inches away from my shirt as I drop the bling onto the glue. It was so much easier ordering my Alexander jersey from the jersey lady. This is stupid.

"Okay, so good news or bad news first?"

"Bad."

"Shit." She looks at me over the rim of her glass. "I thought you'd choose good news. You gotta hear that first or it won't work."

I roll onto my back, knocking over the plate holding all the crystals.

"Dammit!" I glare at her. "Why'd you even ask me then?"

I climb to my knees and crawl around the floor, collecting all the rogue bling.

"Sorry." She shrugs, not looking sorry at all. "So the good news is Ava broke up with Chris."

"Shut up!" I turn to her, eyes wide, crystals long forgotten. "Are you kidding me?"

"Nope. She dumped him for an NBA player, said a football player's life is 'too unpredictable' for her." She uses air quotes. "But we all know she means a football player's paycheck. NBA is that guaranteed money, honey." She snaps at me in Z formation.

"Does it make me a horrible person for finding this so funny?" I ask, wiping away the tears falling down my cheeks from laughing so hard.

"Not at all. Karma's a bitch. We're allowed to laugh once she's done her job." She says it like it's written in the Ten Commandments. Which, maybe it is? I wouldn't know.

"Oh good. I like that rule." I turn back to my shirt, but then I remember that was only the good news and I still have the bad to go and roll back onto my elbows. "What's the bad?"

"There are two things." She puts both hands in the air when I open my mouth to yell at her. "Hey! Don't shoot the messenger. Would you want to get sent into battle without proper intel first? No, you wouldn't."

"Ugh. Fine." I move to the couch and sit next to her. The good news was too good. I know what's coming is going to suck. "Tell me."

"Chris has a new girlfriend." She just floats it out there.

"Already?" Why this shocks me? Who knows. I already know he's got a roster.

"It's Gavin's PR chick, Madison. You know, the one you called Snobby the Snow Bitch."

The fast, Band-Aid-ripping delivery worked with the first news. This one? Not so much. This was like ripping out stitches before they were ready to come out.

"What!" I jump off of the couch into standing position. "Nay. You're messing with me. My ex is not dating Gavin's good friend who I'm pretty sure hates me, is he? This is your attempt at a joke, right?" I stare at her, waiting for her to start laughing, but she never does.

"I'm sorry. I couldn't believe it either when she showed up at the meeting on Wednesday."

"WHAT!" I don't know if I want to laugh or cry.

I dated Chris for years before those bitches let me in and Madison dates Chris for what? A week? And they let her in? No. Fuuuuuuuck no. Smells like a setup.

"And there's more." Naomi squeezes her eyes shut and bites her bottom lip.

"What the hell else could've happened? It was one meeting." I fall back onto the couch beside her, not sure if I can stand more news if it's anything like the last. "Just say it, Nay."

Her eyes stay closed as she draws in a deep breath.

"DixiewashuggingMadisonandtalkingaboutyoutoo," she says too fast for me to understand.

"Slow down. All I got was Dixie." In hindsight, I probably should've saved the margaritas for after story time.

"Dixie was hugging Madison and talking about you too," she says slower, not by much . . . but enough for me to understand and wish I didn't.

"Dixie?" All the anger has fled and now it's being filled with hurt, which really sucks, because it's so much easier to be angry. "But she just texted me the other day."

"Yeah, on Tuesday to see if you wanted to grab lunch."

I run the days back through my head and almost—but don't—cry when I realize she's right.

"She told us you said you were busy but would find a day that worked. If you would've said yes, I would've told you sooner. I promise. But since you said no, I figured it'd be better to tell you in person." She looks so nervous telling me this, and I feel terrible that she's been put in this situation. "She said she thinks you lied about the attack just so you could have a chance to sink your claws into Gavin. Don't hate me."

"I could never." I pull out Gavin's favorite move and squeeze her hand. "It's not your fault they're bitches."

"I don't want you to think I sat there while they rattled off bullshit and I didn't have your back." She sits up straight and looks me in the eyes. "I did. I went a little crazy on Dixie and that bitch Madison. I left early, and I told Dre I might not go back."

"No. Go back. The children's hospital event is coming up, and I know how much you love helping those kids. Don't you dare stop." I take a deep breath and lower my volume. "Freakin' Dixie. If they'll talk with you, they'll talk about you. My mom always tells me that. Why do I never listen to her?"

"Because—" She starts but is interrupted by a knock on the door.

I'm not expecting anybody. Brynn had to close HERS and she's opening tomorrow so she couldn't come, and . . . well . . . I don't have any other friends who would just drop by. But since the attack they haven't found James, and even though I don't think he'd ever actually hurt me, I'm still on guard more than normal.

"Who is it?" I ask, ignoring Naomi's laughter when I have to stand on a footstool to see out of the peephole.

"Me," Gavin says just as I verify his identity.

I jump off of the stool and kick it to the side, unlocking the door as fast as I can.

The players spend the night in hotels, even the night before home games. I think it's stupid, but I guess it's so the coaches can keep tabs on the grown men they're paying millions of dollars to catch a ball. They have a strict schedule and a curfew, so I'm more than a little shocked to see Gavin here.

"Hey!" I kiss him when the door opens all the way. "What are you doing here?"

"This." He puts his hands under my ass, lifts me up, and starts kissing me again.

"Holy shit," I say, out of breath and dizzy when he puts me back on my feet. "What was that for?"

"It's our first home game with you as my girl. I needed a good luck kiss before I went to bed." He leans in for a quick kiss. "I'll call you before the game tomorrow."

Before the last two away games, he's called me from the locker room right before he takes the field. The calls aren't long, but they're enough to make my heart skip a beat every time I see his name on my caller ID.

"Sounds good. I'll be waiting for it."

"Tell Dre he's in the dog house," Naomi says, alerting Gavin of her presence for the first time. "He's never snuck out to kiss me."

"Hey, Naomi." Gavin waves to her. "I'll let him know."

He glances around my messy, nail polish smelling, crystal covered apartment and when he looks back at me, his eyes are dancing with laughter.

"I like the shirt." He bends downs and whispers in my ear, "I like it on the floor too. Let's put the shirt back there as soon as we come back."

I blush scarlet, and he kisses me on the cheek and turns to leave.

"Bye, babe. Later, Naomi," he yells before the door closes behind him.

"Damn girl," Naomi tells me after I slide down the door and onto the floor. "You're in so deep."

Tell me something I don't know.

Twenty-five

I WALK INTO THE STADIUM READY FOR BATTLE.

Because Naomi felt guilty for being the bearer of shit news, we walk in together, Naomi wearing Mustangs gear for the first time ever. We're pumped about being together again for football Sunday. Unfortunately for us though, it doesn't last long.

"Naomi!" Dixie cries out across the wide, crowded concourse as soon as we walk in. "Don't you look all sparkly and festive!"

"Dixie," Naomi says without smiling.

Naomi might not like conflict, but when she's thrown into it, she's not backing down. I guess Dixie didn't know that about her. Too bad, so sad.

"Oh. Marlee! I didn't even see you." Dixie aims her bright smile at me when Naomi doesn't say more. "Are you using Naomi's extra ticket?"

I knew Naomi wasn't lying, but having Dixie standing in front of me, pretending like she doesn't know Gavin and I are together, still feels like a slap in the face.

"No, she's using mine," I lie. I was totally using Nay's, but only because Gavin's tickets weren't in section 112 and do I look like a traitor? "Gavin has better seats."

I take more than a little bit of joy watching her jaw drop at how easily I bring up Gavin.

"Oh that's right. I forgot you're seeing him now," she says. "Don't you just move on faster than a pig in heat?"

What the hell? I don't even think that's a real saying. I think she just called me a pig in heat!

"I wasn't looking." I make a mental note to tell Gavin about this later. "But have you seen the man? When Gavin Pope pursues you, it's hard to keep your defenses up. I could only let him send flowers to my house and work so many times before I gave the poor guy a break."

"Well aren't you lucky? Catching two player's eyes . . . from the same team and everything. I wonder what the odds of that are?"

All right, enough of this shit. I'm a grown-ass woman, not some scared fifteen-year-old trying to get a seat at the cool girl's table. Hell, *I'm* the freaking cool girl. She can't sit with me!

"I think if you were to ask Gavin, he'd tell you he's the lucky one. You know, Dixie, I might not have gone to Bible study with you, but I still know god doesn't like ugly. You're better than this. Petty isn't a good look." I look over to Naomi, who's biting her lip so hard, I'm surprised she's not bleeding. "Ready to go to our seats?"

"Yup," she says.

And without either of us acknowledging Dixie again, we walk away.

"Holy shit. That was *epic*!" Naomi says when we're out of earshot from Dixie.

"One down, too many to count to go." I look at her with wide eyes. "Let's hope I can keep this up."

"I got your back. I already told Dre we're staying until Gavin comes out." She pulls me to a stop at the concession stand with nachos. "No way I'm leaving you in the lion's den today."

AFTER HUGGING LENNY—who pretends not to be happy to see me, but is soooo happy to see me—we make it to her seats. Gavin's having an amazing game, the people around us are awesome, and the weather is surprisingly warm for it almost being December. We both have a great buzz going and decide the best way to keep it is to avoid the family room at halftime.

Everything is going so well, I should've known something had to go wrong.

It's the beginning of the fourth quarter.

The Cowboys have the ball. They're down by two touchdowns and getting desperate to put some points on the board.

Their quarterback—not as skilled or good looking as my QB—decides to go for a long pass. Dre's guarding their wide receiver. They jump into the air at the same time and nobody can tell who's going to catch the ball. Then, out of nowhere, a Cowboys player charges Dre, slamming him back to the ground with a crash so violent, the entire stadium lets out a unison gasp.

Except Naomi. She screams.

On the field, Dre lays motionless on the green grass. The refs blow their whistles and all the players take a knee, as the trainers and medical staff rush the field.

The fans around us, whether cheering for the Mustangs or Cowboys, stand with their crossed fingers raised in the air. It's an eerie feeling, being surrounded by so many people, not hearing anything other than the frightened tears and sniffles of your best friend.

After a couple of minutes, the crowd lowers their hands but stay on their feet. The players on the field stand and get water while they wait for Dre to stand up and walk off the field.

Five minutes after that, when Dre is still motionless, players from both teams meet in the middle of the field, hold hands, and begin to pray.

Now, I sit next to Naomi, holding her hand, listening to the prayers she repeats, telling her it will be okay—hoping I'm right.

The chatter around the stadium starts to pick up, but it feels different, like a dark cloud has settled over everyone. People come to these games to be entertained; the danger of it often gets lost until something as scary as this forces it to the forefront of our brains.

When Naomi's phone rings, she answers it right away, but it takes her a moment to get the words past the silent tears that haven't slowed.

"Okay . . . okay . . . all right. I'll be right there." She throws the phone in her purse and stands on shaky legs. "That was the trainer. An ambulance is here, and I'm going to ride with him," she tells me just as a golf cart with a stretcher attached drives onto the field.

"Do you need me to walk you down?"

"No. Thank you, but I need to be alone for a minute. I'll call you later."

"Let me know if you need anything." I stand up as she's passing me and pull her in for a hug before she goes. "He's going to be fine."

"He's going to be fine," she says to herself more than me.

Then, showing everyone around us what I already know—that she's one of the strongest women around—she wipes her tears, squares her shoulders, holds her head up high, and goes to be Dre's strength.

After Naomi is gone, the stretcher races off the field with Dre in a neck brace, and as they're headed off, the stadium roars to life when he raises his hand to the crowd.

Thank you, God.

THERE'S ONLY ONE way to describe the family room after the game: somber.

The kids who usually run around, knocking over plants and one another, are sitting with their moms, haunted looks on their faces.

The women who pair up and gossip are sitting with their loved ones, holding hands, and for once, their tongues.

Well, most of them.

But I guess the sight of me is too good for a few to pass up.

Courtney spots me across the room and walks over with her big-boobed, Botoxed soldiers following close behind.

"I would say we've missed you, but we all know I'd be lying."

What a stellar greeting.

"Are we really doing this today, Courtney?" I don't even call her Court, that's how not up for this I am. I can't get the sight or sounds of Naomi's whispered pleas out of my head. I don't have the time or energy for this shit.

"Doing what, Marlee? You always have so much to say. Do you not want to say anything now that Chris has a girlfriend with class?" She points to Madison who, once I look at her, lets her disapproving gaze travel down my body.

"I don't know if you missed the part where my best friend's husband was wheeled off the field or you're a bigger bitch than I imagined, which, to be honest, I didn't think was possible." I stop and take a deep breath. I will not get lured into this. "But I sat next to a woman as she cried, staring at the same football field your husband was on, praying to see any hint that he was alive and not paralyzed."

I know some people like to ignore things to cope, and that's fine by me. As long as you aren't using me as a punching bag to accomplish it. I'll give it to Courtney though. I might not like her, but even she seems affected by this. She drops her face to the floor, and her shoulders hunch in a way I would've thought was impossible before right now.

"I'm not fighting with you today," I say. "I'm not playing this game. Say what you want about me. I'm a groupie. I'm a liar. I have no class," I repeat the things she's said about me in the past, checking myself with every word to make sure I'm not yelling. "I don't care. If what you saw today can't make you be at least a semi-decent person who doesn't start an argument in front of a room of shaken-up children, wives, and mothers, I already know you'll beat me. No way I can sink lower than that."

When I step off my soapbox, Courtney makes no attempt at a comeback, so I find an empty chair and I put my headphones in until Gavin comes into the room to get me.

"Are you okay? How's Naomi?" he asks the second I pull the headphones out.

"I'm fine. Naomi was a mess, but you know her. She pulled herself together before she went to see him." I try to smile at him, but it comes off more as a grimace. "You had a good game though. Three touchdown passes and no turnovers."

"Thanks, but you don't have to do that." He bends down and plants a quick kiss on my lips. "It's okay to be upset and thinking about our friends. I'm not insulted. But, just so you know, Coach updated us in the locker room. There was no spinal or neck injury, they're thinking a severe concussion."

I cringe at the news. I'm thankful there's not a spinal or neck injury, obviously, but with all the recent news and discoveries about the brain damage football players have, a concussion is almost as bad.

"Fuck." I fight back the tears I want to cry for my friend. "Football is so stupid."

"It is," Gavin agrees. "But I kinda like it, and I think I'm pretty good at it too."

"You're all right," I say and feel the first signs of a smile since I heard the collision of helmets an hour ago. "Don't go letting your head get too big."

"Never." He kisses me once more, both of us in a bubble, protected from the dirty looks and hateful words being tossed our way.

He grabs my hand for us to leave and just calls out a casual, "See ya," to Madison when we pass her.

I didn't want to be bitchy today, but when Madison stutters and spits and can't even manage a simple good-bye? Well, not even the Pope could keep a straight face for that.

#NoPunIntended

Twenty-six

THERE'S A SMALL CATCH TO THE ALWAYS-SUNNY-IN-COLORADO thing.

During the winter, the sun can be out, bright and lighting up the entire, cloudless blue sky, and you think, *Hey! What a beautiful December day! Let's go do something!* Then you step outside and the dry, freezing air slaps you so hard it steals all of your breath.

You'd think after living here all of my life, I wouldn't fall for Mother Nature's cruel trick.

You would be wrong.

And now I'm working on dragging Gavin down with me.

"Marlee, it's too cold to go ice skating." He's not going down without a struggle.

"Please." I stick out my bottom lip, and although it might seem ridiculous to most, we cannot say no to each other's pouty faces. "You need a break from studying film, and I need a break from watching you study film."

"There are only two more games this season and if we don't

win, we're out of the playoffs. I have to be on my game, the defense is struggling without Dre. I need to study."

"And you are studying, but you need a break. Remember how when I was stuck on my paper, you pulled me out of my apartment and took me to the arcade and then the next day I was able to finish?" I can see his resolve starting to slip. "Let me do that for you. Give your football brilliance a rest for the day. Go ice skating, come back and drink some hot cocoa . . . I even bought jumbo marshmallows."

"I don't know. I really need to get all this down."

"Then after skating we can spend the rest of the night warming up . . . naked . . . in bed." I approach him and straddle his lap.

"Let me get my jacket."

I touch my mouth to his before I slowly slide off his lap. Watching his eyes darken as I peel myself off of him, the thought of skipping straight to naked and bed does go through my head.

But we don't.

Yay willpower!

WINTER IS MY favorite time of the year.

Actually, I think I say that about every season.

But it's true for winter.

Besides the icy roads and the cold air that holds my lungs hostage, there's nothing I don't love. Oversized puffy jackets? Love. Boots with the fur? Love. The feeling of being nice and warm under your blanket when the rest of your house is cold? Love times two. Ice skating beneath the twinkling Christmas lights above the rink they put up every year? Best. Feeling. Ever.

As soon as Brynn realized how serious Gavin and I were, she made it so my schedule matched his the best it could. Which means instead of working on my marketing plans for HERS or perfecting my bartending skills, I'm spending my Tuesday night appreciating all life has thrown my way. Especially Gavin Pope.

"I can't believe skating was your idea and you don't even know how to do it."

Of course Mr. Perfect slipped his skates on and jumped onto the ice with no problem. Whereas I slipped my skates on, jumped on the ice, and fell so hard I thought I broke my ass.

"The last time I went ice skating, I was like eleven, and I was awesome. It's just, sometimes, I forget I'm not a kid anymore and I might not be able to do everything I used to." Admitting it to Gavin physically pains me. For some reason I cannot at all remember—because I wasn't even a very good ice skater when I was a kid—I thought I would come out here Nancy Kerrigan–style and kill it.

"So what are you going to do, Blanche? You gonna come out here with me or spend the entire time attached to the wall?" He skates over and stops in front of me.

"Is it weird that I'm turned on by a *Golden Girls* reference? Because I totally am."

"Come on, you dragged me out here so you're going to skate. Hold my hands."

Gosh. So bossy.

But I can never resist an opportunity to touch any part of Gavin.

"Fine, but disclaimer, if you fall, it's not my fault."

"Got it, not your fault." He grabs both of my hands and pulls me across the ice.

And it is so much fun.

Gliding across the ice, the cold air hits my face as my hands are wrapped tightly in Gavin's. My smile is so big my cheeks hurt, and I can't stop laughing at the way Gavin's forehead creases from concentration. We stay that way, Gavin skating backward, me holding on for dear life, while the people around us stare. Staring because either they recognize Gavin or they recognize themselves in the young couple with hearts in their eyes.

"Okay! Let me go now," I tell Gavin. I think I've finally found my balance.

"Are you sure?" He's watching me like a dad letting go of the bike as their kid learns to ride without training wheels.

"Not at all." My butt still hurts from my first fall. "But let go before I change my mind."

So he does.

And I skate.

Well . . . I give it a valiant effort.

I make it about ten feet before my ankles start to wobble, and my body sways. My arms spin around like propellers trying to keep my body upright. But as I flail and my shrieks mix with laughter, I know I'm going down.

Right as I start to fall, Gavin's strong arms wrap around my waist and for one shiny, hopeful moment, my butt has been saved. But then, Gavin's legs start moving at supersonic speed and I'm still going down, just not alone.

We hit the ice with a crash so hard, I'm surprised the ice doesn't crack. We're both moaning and groaning until I hear Gavin from behind me.

"Fuck."

And that doesn't sound like my favorite four-letter word anymore. No, now it sounds like the scariest thing I've ever heard.

"Are you okay?" I turn to him faster than I thought possible on ice.

"My ankle twisted when I fell. It's probably no big deal, but I think we should head out." He nods his chin and when he does, I notice the crowd, armed with camera phones, circled around us.

Fan-fucking-tastic.

I stand up, feeling secure on the ice for the first time all day, and help Gavin up. To the people watching, I'm sure he looks fine. But I know him and when he stands, he slightly pinches his eyebrows and his jaw tightens. As much as I want to ignore it, I know this is more than a tweaked ankle.

We walk to his truck in silence and as he's opening my door like always, I snatch the keys out of hands.

"What are you doing?" He tries to take a step toward me, but his face scrunches up in pain, and he stops.

"I'm driving."

"What? Why?"

"Because I saw the way you looked when you stood up on the ice and just now when you tried to get your keys," I tell him in my most mom-inspired voice. "So you're going to sit in the passenger seat while I drive and you're going to call Jason."

Jason is the team's trainer, and he has his phone on him 24/7 in case of incidents like these.

I wait for Gavin to argue, but instead he aims a weak smile my way, climbs into the truck, and pulls out his phone. Gavin always fights back, even about stuff he doesn't care about, so him just getting in? It causes the worry in the pit of my stomach to grow.

The drive back to his condo is relatively short. As I navigate the tight, one-way roads, it reaffirms what I already knew: driving anything larger than a Prius isn't a good idea for me. I feel like a kid at Chuck E. Cheese riding in one of the cars that is way too big for them. Thankfully, we make it home without any added injuries, and Jason doesn't sound too worried about Gavin's ankle.

Once inside, I make Gavin hobble his tight ass up the stairs and get him hot chocolate and an ice pack. When the cocoa is distributed evenly between his oversized mugs and as many jumbo marshmallows that can fit are in them, I bring them upstairs.

When I'm climbing up the stairs, ice pack freezing under my arm and cocoa splashing dangerously close to the edge, I hear

Gavin talking on the phone. At first I can't decipher what he's saying, but as I make my way to the room, it all becomes clear.

"I'm fine, Madison." He sounds tired and annoyed, which seems like the appropriate response to the shrill, whiny voice I'm sure is coming from the other end. "Marlee and I went ice skating. We fell. I'm fine."

When I walk into the room he tries to smile, but it's easy to see he's in pain.

"What do you want me to do about it now? I can't help that everyone carries phones and all phones have cameras. It's not my fault all of America is always connected to social media." In the time I have known Gavin, I've seen him lose his temper approximately three times. When I left Chris, at the fashion show, and now. I can hear the volume of Madison, but I can't make out the words. "What do you suggest I do, Madison? Should I stay at home all the time? Should I not go out with my girlfriend? Should I only do football ever?"

She says something else and I swear, Gavin's phone almost snaps in half.

"You really want to go there, Madison? Maybe if your lowlife boyfriend could catch the passes I throw him, we wouldn't be on the bubble for the playoffs. I'm having the best season of my career, I think it's safe to say she isn't a distraction."

Of course she went there.

I know they're friends, and I'm sure she can be sweet. But she's a horrid bitch, and I hate her.

#BadBlood

"I wasn't out smoking crack. I took my girlfriend ice skating. I don't know why you're trying to get me so worked up about this. It's your job to handle it, Madison, not mine. Marlee's here and I'm not spending my night talking to you about this. Figure it out and call me in the morning."

I still hear her Chihuahua voice barking through the earpiece when Gavin hangs up on her and throws his phone across the bed.

"You know I hate to admit this more than I did about you being a better skater, but Madison is kind of right."

"What are you talking about?" He takes the mugs out of my hands, places them on the side table, then pulls me onto his lap. "I'm having the best season of my career. Donny called me yesterday telling me the Mustangs are already talking numbers to bring me back next year. He thinks you're my good luck charm and told me if I do anything to mess up our relationship, he'll fly here to kick my ass. And that's saying something because Donny hates everyone."

"Maybe before this, but I can tell you're hurting and it's my fault for dragging you out there."

"No. I signed the disclaimer relieving you from all responsibility of injury." He tilts my chin up and touches his lips to mine. "I'm fine. I wanted to go with you, and I had a great time. Now we're going to stop thinking about it. You're going to strip out of all of those clothes and lay next to me while we drink our hot chocolate. Then we're going to take turns warming each other up until we fall asleep, as promised."

I mean . . .

"Okay."

It was a fantastic plan, except after we stripped out of our clothes, the hot chocolate was cold chocolate before we got to it.

Twenty-seven

THERE'S SERIOUS TRUTH BEHIND THE SAYING "IGNORANCE IS bliss." I know this firsthand now.

You'd think, after all of these years dating an athlete and the surprise of Gavin coming to the Mustangs, I'd give in and just download the free ESPN app for my phone. But . . . I don't.

Even though Gavin and I try to spend as much time together as we can, it's still not much. So when we're together, we try not to talk about work. It's lovely. I spend all my free time with a man who, if you ask Mustangs fans, is listed right under Jesus. He could be with anyone and he chose me. I've gotten to know him so well over the last few months and every little tidbit makes me feel like I'm unwrapping a gift.

After #IceSkateGate we don't talk much about the fall. I know his ankle is bothering him a bit. I get him ice and he uses my lap to elevate it, but other than that, he seems fine. He mentions very briefly he's on the questionable list for the next game, but I've been around for a while and most of the time, questionable gets a thumbs-up. Especially when it's the starting quarterback.

When Naomi calls to come over and watch the game with me,

I notice the tightness in her voice right away. I figure it's because Dre is still on the inactive list, and even though he can't play, they're still making him stand on the sidelines and travel with the team. But no matter how many times I ask what's wrong, she won't give me a straight answer. Until she gets fed up with me asking and says, "Maybe you should call Gavin."

Ominous.

We hang up and I go to call him, but before I do, I notice an unread text cluttering my clean phone screen. As soon as I open it, I wish I hadn't. I know what Naomi was worried about, and I know Madison has just received the ammunition to hate me for eternity.

> Hey babe. I didn't get cleared for the game. I'll call you
> when it's over.

Oh. No.

Then I do the thing you should never, ever do.

I Google him.

Don't get me wrong, I love the internet. It's the only reason I ever have recipes to make, I don't get lost, and how I can kick Gavin's ass in *Jeopardy!* all the time. But the internet is also where faceless assholes cloaked in anonymity get the confidence to say the vile things they would never say in person. They're everywhere—Facebook, Twitter, Instagram—but the truly terrible ones always seem to gather in one place: the comments section.

You know how girls have a bad rep for being catty and gossipy and mean? Well, I'd be willing to bet money men are a thousand times worse on any given Sunday.

I know this because ta-da! Meet their new target.

Me.

Now, to be fair to these giant asshole men picking on a woman they don't know and saying things that, in my opinion, should get them arrested, Madison's the one who threw me under the bus. Apparently when Gavin said handle it, she heard, "Here's your chance to slander and passively attack my girlfriend. Have fun!"

And boy, did she run with it.

Not only is my name listed in every single article, so is the fact that I'm the ex-girlfriend of Chris Alexander. Reading article after article, even I think I might be a gold-digging groupie who did nothing short of drugging, kidnapping, and then depositing Gavin's unwilling body on the ice. Plus, thanks to all my friends at the rink that day, there is a crystal clear image to go with the multiple accounts of our trip.

One article not so cleverly titled "Pope's Costly Sin" is basically an entire article simultaneously telling men they're the rulers of the universe and they're too weak to stand up to the wicked, tempting women in the world. The sexism shows no limits.

By the time Naomi shows up at my place, I'm on the brink of hysteria. Laughing, maybe crying, no . . . definitely laughing at the absurdity of the situation. My boyfriend took me ice skating and fell. That's it. But to some of these people, you'd think I committed murder.

The hell with politics. Screw religion. I had united men and women, white and black, all on the common ground of hating me. I don't know if it's an accomplishment or a reason to seek out witness protection.

"Are you okay?" Naomi asks as soon as I open the door.

"Why wouldn't I be? I, Mrs. Harris, am public enemy *numero uno*." I wave my index finger in front of her face.

"I know. The chatter started on Wednesday when he sat out of practice, but they kind of hinted Kevin would be starting today instead of Gavin, and people lost their damn minds. I know Gavin ignores this stuff as much as you, but with Dre being out, he's treating ESPN like a soap opera and reporting every last detail to me. I'm blaming it on the brain injury, but he's driving me nuts."

And being the best friend I could ever ask for, she punctuates this very unfortunate news with two bottles of wine pulled from her giant purse. "These are for both of us, don't try and hog it."

See—that *is* the only reason to carry a duffel disguised as a purse around.

"I'm trying to ignore it."

"Marlee."

She says my name like she's said everything. And truth be told, along with her pursed lips and the serious side-eye she's throwing at me? I crack.

"Okay. Fine! That's a lie. I've read every article I could find and then every single comment left on them. I even snooped through some sports forums. People have Photoshopped my head into a GIF of Kanye's 'Gold Digger' song!"

And the bitch laughs. Come on!

"If you want me to seem sympathetic, which I am, I'm going to need you to not tell me things like that."

I narrow my eyes and go to find the bottle opener. These wines aren't surviving the night.

"Oh stop it. You can't tell me your head bobbing around on a video girl's body with Kanye dancing next to you wasn't hella funny!"

"You just said hella, which voids everything you said previous to it."

"Hella, hella, hella!"

"I can't with you right now." I hand her a glass of wine and cheers her before we both chug the contents of our glasses.

Because you know . . .

#HellaKlassy

"Anyway. The GIFS were funny. The words were not. It's one thing for Courtney and Madison to hate me, it's another thing entirely when it's the whole city."

"I bet Courtney was giddy hearing about Gavin's injury. She

might even like you now if she thinks you'll be able to get Kevin his spot back."

"She's delusional. Kevin was losing his spot with or without Gavin. He had an average season last year and a terrible preseason. Kevin's on his way out, I hope she's enjoying her final season in charge of the Mustangs."

"True. And for someone who 'hates football'"—she uses air quotes. I freaking hate air quotes—"you sure are mighty informed."

"Not about other teams though," I defend myself. "You've gone to games with me. You know how hard I go for them. But that's only when I'm sharing a bed with one of the players. If I don't know somebody on the team, then I don't care about them."

"Whatever the case, you need to download the ESPN app on your phone before I leave. I'm over having to blindside you because you're too busy to type in your Apple ID password."

"Fair point. Having an advanced warning would be nice." I grab my wineglass and plop down next to her on my comfy couch.

"I don't know if I'm glad to hear you're giving in or worried that you're not denying something like this will happen again."

"I mean, there is one more home game left, and I'm thinking with the recent headlines declaring me enemy of the state, I might cause quite the reaction when I show my bedazzled ass at the game."

"Remind me not to sit by you next week."

"Please. Deny it all you want, but you love it."

I just know the Mustangs better win today. I think it's bad now? I don't even want to imagine what it'll be like if they lose and are out of the playoffs.

Twenty-eight

THEY LOSE.

Of course they do because Kevin Matthews is their backup quarterback and he's terrible. He threw three interceptions in the first half alone, and the rage toward the slut who drugged Pope and threw him down on the ice grew as the game went on.

By the end of the game, I was afraid if I opened my curtains, a mob complete with pitchforks would be filling the street.

They weren't, of course.

But it doesn't ease the fears running through my mind. Football is religion to these people, and wars have been started over less. And even though there's still a game left, the chances of the Mustangs making the playoffs are practically nothing.

So when my phone rings in the middle of the night, waking me from a dreamless sleep, every horror movie I've ever watched flashes through my head before I see Gavin's name lighting up the screen.

"Hey," I try to answer, my voice scratchy from sleep.

"I'm outside your door. You wanna let me in?"

Duh.

I was already halfway across my apartment when he asked.

"Eh. I think I'll pass."

"Liar. I heard your sheets, and I can hear your footsteps through your apartment," he says, laughing. "You know, for being so petite, you walk harder than a rhinoceros."

Busted.

"Do not." I open the door, my phone still at my ear.

"You do, but a super sexy rhino."

"You really need to work on your sweet talk, Pope." Not true. Only Gavin can make me feel butterflies when he compares me to a rhino. "But I'm glad you came to visit the evil seductress who injured you."

"Evil seductress? What are you talking about?" His head slightly flinches, and his eyebrows scrunch together—no idea what I'm referring to.

"I'm glad I'm not the only one who doesn't stalk the internet and stare at the ESPN app all day." I close the door and follow him to my room. He strips out of his suit (gray this time, still perfectly tailored—pants nice and tight, cropped at the ankle, jacket equally snug) and falls into my bed naked as the day he was born.

Death threats and all . . . I'm the luckiest woman ever.

Once we're both in our cuddle positions under my comforter—the new one Gavin bought me for Christmas after I raved about his every time I spent the night in his bed—I hand him my phone. While he was changing, I pulled up one of the articles pointing all fingers toward me being the reason Gavin was injured and therefore, the reason the Mustangs lost. This article was my particular favorite as it not only told the world where I grew up and went to high school, but that I'm also the head of marketing for HERS.

"What the fuck is this?" Gavin semi yells, scissoring out of the bed.

And I was comfortable, I should've waited until the morning.

Ooh! But maybe he'll want to work off his aggression in bed?

"Apparently when you told Madison to handle it, she did so by throwing me under the bus. My name, my job, my dating history? All there." I plaster on my most fake smile. "Did I ever tell you how much I love Madison?"

"I can't believe she'd do this." His tone has changed, and the outrage he had only seconds prior is gone. Now he just sounds broken . . . betrayed.

God. I hate Madison.

"I get what she was doing to take the heat off of you. She did her job very effectively by making you the victim. She protected her client and her friend."

"But she did it in a way I clearly told her not to. She knows how I feel about you, I can't believe she would throw you into this mess."

"How do you feel about me, Gavin?" I crawl across the bed toward where he's pacing.

At my question, he stops moving, brings his hand to my cheek, and looks me straight in my eyes.

"Well, I was thinking since the chances of going to the playoffs are slim to none now, I could take you on a trip when the season ends."

"A trip?" Intrigued with where he's taking this, I sit up on my knees. "To where?"

"Surprise." He smirks. "You tell me the days you can get off, and I'll plan the trip. Sound good?"

"Sounds amazing!" I'm not huge on surprises, but I think I can get over it if the outcome is alone time with Gavin.

"Oh, and also, I love you." The words come out quietly, but I don't need him to yell it. The power, the sincerity, is enough to knock me over. "I know this is fast, and I don't expect you to say it back. But I know, without a doubt, what I'm feeling for you is love. I've had girlfriends before and I've never felt an ounce of what I feel for you."

My stupid mouth, that never closes, chooses this moment to forget how to work.

I stare at him, mouth open, eyes wide for who knows how long. If it was any other man, I'm sure their ego would've been demolished by now. But it's not any other man, it's Gavin. And instead of insecurity or anger at my reaction, he's staring at me almost laughing.

"It couldn't have been that big of a shock. I'm with you every chance I get, and if I'm not next to you, I'm on the phone. I'm smitten, Marlee. Those articles may have been right in calling you a seductress." He winks at me, effectively getting my mouth to function again.

"I'm not a seductress," I tell him without any fight in my voice. "I'm just in love with an amazing man."

When I'm finished speaking, the only noise in the room is our elevated breathing. Neither of us make a move to say something else or to touch each other. Instead, we stare at each other, taking in this moment. Both of us knowing after tonight, our relationship will never be the same. Knowing this isn't a casual fling for either of us, emotions . . . hearts . . . are on the line.

"I'm going to kiss you now." Gavin breaks the silence. "I'm going to kiss you, and then I'm going to make love to the woman I love. The woman who loves me back."

"That was so much better than calling me a sexy rhino," I say and watch his dimple appear.

"Lay back, Marlee. I told you I love you, now I'm going to show you."

He's standing in front of me, every perfect, chiseled inch of him on display. His erection standing large and proud, as if it too is declaring it's love for me. He's giving himself to me in a way I've never experienced. Unselfishly. Without wanting anything in return except to let him love me.

So angry mob and pitchforks be damned. The outside world is

no longer so much as a memory in my head. Because Gavin Pope loves me and I love him right back.

I do as he says.

The second my head hits the pillow, Gavin's body is covering me. His mouth hits mine and lacks the usual gentle touch. These kisses are frenzied, demanding. The power of his need is being poured out through his lips.

The angry mob and the dancing GIFs all fade to black, and I'm left alone with their football god, who spends the rest of the night worshipping me.

Twenty-nine

HERS IS PACKED WHEN I WALK IN THE NEXT AFTERNOON.

We usually have a decent lunchtime crowd, but nothing like this.

New Year's just passed, maybe it's women spending time together at the end of the holiday season? Either way, I don't care. I'm in love, and I've already had two orgasms this morning. Nothing is messing up my good vibes.

I'm making my way toward the employee room when I spot Brynn across the dining room. She's smiling and talking with a customer, her hands flying all over the place, the expressions on her face changing with every word. I stop outside of the door, waiting for her to head my way when she's finished taking the order. She sticks her notepad in the pocket of her apron and turns toward me. Except when she does, she doesn't smile and yell a greeting across the room like she normally does. Instead, she stops in her tracks and her eyes grow to the size of quarters before she sprints toward me, just missing other waiters and diners as she does.

When she reaches me, she opens the closed door and pushes me inside so hard, I almost fall on my ass.

"What the hell?" I ask once I catch my balance.

"I had to warn you!" she shouts into my face as if I'm not only a foot in front of her.

"Warn me about what? That you're really a Powerpuff Girl?"

"Did you see the crowd? I think they're here because of you."

"Really? You think the new promotions we put out brought them in?" I ask, despite Brynn's mild freak-out.

"No! I mean, you know I love your promotions, but the majority of the people out there asked if you worked here the second they walked in. I think they're all here because of the stuff with Gavin."

Okay.

So something can mess with my good vibes.

#PleaseDontKillMyVibe

"Please tell me you're messing with me to get back at me for the time I poured you vodka instead of water." I fold my fingers together and bring them to my chin.

"I wish I was." She reaches for my hands and wraps hers around them. "I'm so sorry. I'm sure most of them are just lookie-loos and want to get a gander at Gavin Pope's girlfriend, but I'd understand if you wanted to head home."

"You're sweet, but no," I tell her with steel in my voice. "They can say whatever they want on the internet, but here? In my job? They have another thing coming if they think I'm going to run and hide."

"You're a rock star. Let me know if anyone gives you a hard time though. I told my dad what was going on, and he offered to come in and sit at the bar like your own personal bodyguard." Mr. Sterling, as nice as he is, would be a terrible bodyguard. He's all of five foot seven and one hundred and sixty pounds. My smile must hint at where my mind was heading because before I can respond, Brynn starts talking again. "Oh. And he said he'd bring your dad too."

Oh.

Shit.

My dad has a heart of gold and is as sweet as sugar . . . until you mess with his little girl. Then? #DaddyDontPlay

Like one time, this boy in third grade, Derek Fuller, decided I was going to be his next target. It started with the occasional tug on my pigtail and then grew to pinching. Then he started with the words. And I know they say words don't hurt. But you know what? Screw them. Words hurt the worst. He would tell me how my hair was ugly and that I was fat. What a little asshole, right? Who calls someone fat in third grade? He would chase me around the playground yelling how stupid I was and how nobody liked me. Then, one day, he called me a half-breed and told me my dad shouldn't be allowed to marry my mom. I went home that night in absolute tears. I mean, I won't say I was color-blind—I loathe that term—but when I saw the different colors in my family, I felt nothing but lucky. And Derek tarnished that.

When I told my dad what happened? Shit. Hit. The. Fan.

Not only was he in school with me the next day, setting up a meeting with teachers and the principal and Derek's parents, he called out of work for a week and sat at the back of my class, watching and making sure Derek didn't so much as look my way. Some kids might've been embarrassed to have their dad at school, but not me. I loved every single second he was there. I loved the way Derek's smug grin turned to pure fear when he walked into class the next day about to shout more poison at me.

And even though I'm a grown woman, I have no doubt in my mind that my Dad will call out of work and sit at the bar waiting to unleash on the first person who looks at me wrong.

"Oh no! Did Mr. Sterling call him?" I pull the door open, looking around for the giant black man completely out of place at a restaurant cluttered with *Housewives* pictures.

"Not yet. He said he'd call him if you're getting a lot of grief and needed backup."

"Oh thank god. Because unless you want my name in the news again because my Dad beat up some guy at HERS for accidentally coughing my way, it'd be for the best if we left him out of this mission."

"I'm not going to stand here and sit by while some skank runs her mouth or some psycho football fan comes at you. If I have to call in our dads to make sure it doesn't happen, you aren't stopping me." Her mouth is set and her arms folded across her chest. Dammit. She's assuming her power pose.

"Fine. But let's hold off on our biologically mandated protection until we know how things are going to go, okay?"

"Okay, but the first sign it's getting bad, I'm calling."

"Thank you," I say. I head to my desk to get some marketing work finished before I join them on the floor. Maybe if I work back here for a couple of hours, the crowd will die down enough for me to do my job in peace.

#AGirlCanDream

I was right.

People have a lot of courage when they're hidden behind their computers or phones. When they have the chance to say things to your face though, they don't have the nerve.

Not that I'm complaining. I talk a big game when it comes to dealing with the trolls attacking me at every chance on every article they can find—I lost an entire day of my life arguing with them. But I'm pretty sure if somebody said the crude, awful things being said about me to my face, I'd crumble to the floor and start sobbing.

I WALK INTO HERS before we open on Wednesday morning for a quick meeting. I don't know what it is about Wednesdays and meetings, but they seem to follow me everywhere I go. We talk about the sales, the marketing and promotions I'm working on, and any new ideas we may have thought about over the previous week. However, unlike the meetings with the Lady Mustangs, we get shit done. They're productive and I actually look forward to them.

"We have a reservation for twenty this evening," Brynn says. "I asked where they heard about us and they said a friend recommended us. How exciting is that? Our first big party!"

"So exciting!" I give her a high five. "I'll be in the back, but let me know if you need any extra help."

The afternoon passes in the blink of an eye, and once I'm caught up on emails and the new project I'm working on, I join Brynn out front. The sun has already set and I see a few snowflakes falling in front of the streetlights. I'm counting our bottles at the bar when I hear the front door open and a familiar voice calling my name.

"Marlee!" Naomi says.

"Hey! What are you doing here?" I'm excited to see her, until she gets closer and I see the look of terror on her face. "What's wrong? Is Dre okay? Is Gavin okay?"

"Where's your phone? I've been calling you for hours!" She ignores my question about our guys and causes my worry to increase. My heart races, and my palms sweat as I prepare for her to tell me Gavin was injured at practice or Dre's recovery went south.

"It's in the back. I don't check my phone when I'm at work." I rush the words out, only thinking about one thing. "Nay. Are the guys all right?"

"Oh, honey, this is so much worse than a football injury," she tells me before the front door opens and giggling fills the room. I look over her shoulder just in time to see Courtney walking in with Madison.

"You've got to be kidding me," I whisper, my teeth clenched. "Why didn't you tell me?"

"I tried! Up until this afternoon, I thought we were going to the sushi place by my house. I'm guessing they held up telling me so I couldn't warn you. Are you going to be okay?"

"Dammit. I should've known it wouldn't be long until they showed their faces here." I close my eyes and take a deep breath, trying to regain my composure. I refuse to give the reaction they're hoping for. "Okay. I'm fine. Here, I'll show you to your table."

Naomi watches me with pursed lips and narrowed eyes, but even under her disbelieving stare, my plastic smile never wavers. She sits in her seat at the same time Brynn arrives at the table.

"Hey, Nay! What are you doing . . . ?" Her eyes widen as she figures out the answer to her question before she even finishes asking it. "Oh shit. The Lady Bitches are our big party?"

"Yup. Batten down the hatches, cause I have a feeling shit is about to get ugly."

And right on cue, Madison and Courtney appear at the opposite end of the table.

"Marlee? Oh my goodness. I totally forgot you worked here." Courtney should really ask Naomi for some acting tips because this fake surprise thing she's trying to pull off is about as inspiring as Mariah in *Glitter*.

Madison, on the other hand, doesn't even try. Her annoyingly perfect face doesn't even acknowledge my presence. Fine with me. This is the first time I've seen her since she info-dumped my life to all of the crazies on the internet, and I'm pretty sure if she said something snotty to me right now, I'd ninja leap over the table and kick her in the face.

Disclaimer: I don't know how to ninja leap, but I feel like it'd just come to me.

"Hey, Court!" I call across the table and watch with joy as her smile fades a tiny bit. "I hope you enjoy your dinner. I'm at the bar tonight, but I'm sure you'll love it."

Before she can respond, I turn on my heel and hustle my way to the bar, which is where I stay as Amber, Dixie, and the rest of the wicked wives bring themselves in from the cold.

Brynn and Paisley both work their table. They're always great about good service, but once they realize who these women are, they take it up a level. After they take their orders, I make sure to have them put in an order of our street tacos for Nay. No way is she only eating a salad with me nearby.

Once their meeting comes to an end, I bring them over a few bottles of Skinny Girl on the house to sip on while they gossip. Even when I know most of said gossip is going to be about me. #BiggerPerson

"So . . . you're a bartender?" Courtney asks, disdain evident, before I can make my escape.

"I'm the head of marketing, but I help with the bar when I get a chance."

"How nice for you. You look much more at home behind a bar than you do at the games."

I know she was making a jab at me. It's just too bad it makes no sense. I know this is my opportunity to get away, but instead of taking it, I climb into the mud with her. #NotTheBiggerPerson

"How are you feeling today? I know Sunday must have been pretty hard for you." I pull my eyebrows together and try to look as concerned as possible. When I notice the smile on Naomi's face out of the corner of my eye, I know I'm successful.

She isn't expecting me to come back at her. Only a minute in and I already have her color rising. I know I'm supposed to be all customer service and kindhearted, but they bring out the ugly in me. After the game Kevin had, I can't believe she has the audacity to try and stir shit up with me.

"I was going to ask you the same question. I've been reading the articles they've been posting. People are pretty upset with you." She tries to mirror my expression, but all the Botox makes it impossible.

"You read?" I ask at the same time Naomi takes a sip of her water, causing her to spit it across the table and onto Dixie's empty glass.

"Shit," she croaks out in between coughs. "I'm so sorry."

"Really, Naomi. Get a grip," Madison—MADISON!—says.

Oh. Hell. No.

It's one thing to come after me, I can handle it. But go after my friends?

No, bitch.

"I'm sorry, Madison. Do you have something to say?"

"Not to you." She crosses her arms and looks at Naomi instead of me.

"No. I think you do. First, you give my personal information to anyone who will print it, then you show up at my job, and now you're being a straight-up bitch to my best friend. What's your deal?"

Now, I may talk a lot (like tons) of shit in my head, but it's rare for me to say it out loud. Confrontation isn't my thing, but sometimes it has to happen. And this is one of those times.

"You're not worth my time, Marlee. You're nothing but a pathetic cleat chaser, and I have no room in my life for someone like you." Her arrogant tone carries across the room and causes all the chatter at surrounding tables to stop.

"Madison." Naomi tries to wrangle her in. "You need to stop."

"Was I talking to you, Naomi?"

Here you go, ladies and gents. Dinner and a show. There's a two drink minimum and please, don't forget to tip your waiter.

"Really? Someone like me? You're dating my ex. You've chosen a profession centered around athletes, and I'm the cleat chaser? Do you hear yourself?" I can't decide if I want to laugh, scream, or cry, so I settle on a mix of all three. It might not be the best option, but at least it gets her to look at me.

"Loud and clear. You date Chris, you slept with god only knows how many of his teammates, then, the second you see an opportunity to get in with a player who makes more money, you leap at it. Playing victim, acting like Chris was the cheater, faking a mugging. All some pathetic attempt at getting your greedy hands on Gavin." She stops and points one manicured finger at me. "You. Are. Trash."

I'm pretty sure my jaw is on the floor when she's finished with her rant, and the ninja skills I was hoping for never kick in.

"What in the actual *fuck* are you talking about?" I'm dumbfounded. How she can say all of those things as if they're absolute facts is either disturbingly impressive or just plain disturbing. "Did someone tell you those things, or is your pretty head so screwed up all you do in your free time is fabricate these outrageous stories about me?"

"You hate me because I see you for what you really are, don't you? That I don't buy the innocent, naive victim story you're selling." Her face is all scrunched up, and for the first time, her outside starts to match her inside. "You should count your blessings I love Gavin and didn't want him to hear the truth about you in the paper."

"And you should count your blessings nobody's caught on to your brand of crazy and locked your ass up."

"Screw you, Marlee. Just you wait," she carries on, oblivious to the camera phones around her. "Gavin's going to wake up one morning and realize you're the biggest mistake of his life. And I'll be there waiting."

"And you're going to be Grandma Barbie waiting that long because . . ." Pause for drama. "It's. Never. Gonna. Happen." I roll my neck with each word.

"You're a toy for Gavin—a fetish." She cuts me with her

tongue. "His sister's my best friend. She doesn't trust you. His parents are best friends with my parents. Our mothers have planned our weddings since we were in diapers. Do you think his family is going to welcome you with open arms? And does Gavin seem like the kind of guy to choose a girl like you over his family?"

I roll up my sleeves, and I swear I'm only seconds away from taking my earrings out. #SheMustNotKnowAboutMe

"Why don't you just spell it out for everyone around us, Madison? What do you really mean when you say a girl like me?" I know damn well what she means, the same thing Derek Fuller thought in third grade.

"A girl like you." She unfolds her long legs from her chair and stands. "A cleat-chasing, rap-video-starring, ghetto bitch."

On one hand? I have to kind of give the girl props for owning up to the shit she was thinking.

On the other hand? Oh no she didn't.

I'm can't decide whether I should prove her right or wrong when Brynn steps in and takes away the choice.

"Enough!" Brynn yells. "Madison, get out. And, Marlee, you know I love you, but you have to leave. I can't have this shit going on in my restaurant."

Fuck.

At her restaurant. The same one I've been working so hard to help build its good name and reputation.

In one night and—guessing by the number of phones aimed my way—multiple videos, I could've ruined it all.

"I'm so sorry," I whisper through the tears I won't let her see fall and the guilt that feels like it's wrapping hands around my neck. "I'm so sorry."

I don't look at her, or anybody for that matter, as I walk out of the dining room to collect my things. I write her a note and leave it on her desk. I take the back exit out, my pride and shame both preventing me from showing my face again.

Thirty

ON MY WAY HOME FROM HERS, I TAKE A LAST-MINUTE DETOUR TO Gavin's place. I don't want to tell him about the fight, but the more I think on it, the more I think it'll be better if he hears it from me instead of Madison, or even worse, Chris.

I walk up his snow-covered walkway, my boot prints ruining the perfect blanket of sparkling snow. Once I reach the front door, I pull out the key Gavin gave me and let myself in. Layer by layer, I unwrap myself from my hat, jackets, and scarf and hang them in his entryway closet.

I don't know if it's because my ears are burning from the cold or if part of me is still at the restaurant, but either way, I don't notice the man sitting in the living room watching me make myself at home until he makes himself known.

"Marlee fuckin' Harper!" Gavin's agent, Donovan "Donny" Ratiglia, says across the condo.

I scream and jump at least a foot off the ground. But when I land, my knees are so shaky, I fall to the ground, dropping the hanger I just strategically loaded with all my winter protection.

"Shit!" He runs across the room to help me up. "Sorry, got a little excited to meet the fuckin' girl who's got our boy playin' the shit outta this fuckin' game!'"

I've overheard a few conversations between him and Gavin over the months, but I thought Donny's cussing was the exception, not the rule. Looks like I was wrong.

But I've liked him from the moment I saw him the first game of the season. He may be a little crude, but a few f-bombs can't cover the goodness shining out of him.

"It's nice to know at least one person in the world doesn't hate me with Gavin," I say. "Speaking of, where is he?" I ask once I realize he's not in his usual spot on the couch.

"He went to grab dinner." He takes a seat on a stool in the kitchen. "And ignore the fans. Some of them can be fuckin' ruthless and that's saying a lot coming from me."

"I wish it was only the fans I had to worry about." I open the fridge and pull out the bottle of wine I put in there a couple of weeks ago. "But they aren't my biggest problem anymore."

"Oh shit. You wanna tell Donny about it?"

I don't answer right away. I focus on uncorking and pouring my liquid courage. I climb onto the stool next to Donny and sip my wine in silence while I figure out if I should tell him or not. I've already created problems with one person in Gavin's life, I don't want to make the same mistake twice. But Donny will do what's best for Gavin, and I could use him in my corner.

I open my mouth and spill. "Madison hates me."

"Fuck Madison," he says, like I'm crazy for caring what she thinks. "She's fuckin' miserable and hates everybody."

I knew I liked him.

"But Gavin cares about her, and she made it very clear that his family does too." I fold my hands in my lap and keep my head down. "We had it out at my job tonight. It got really ugly, and I'm willing to bet there will be video online before I go to bed. It's why I came over. I don't want Gavin to be blindsided by it."

"She did this at your job? I can't stand her. Always fuckin' drama with that one."

Damn. Look at Donny spittin' truths.

"Yup. I got sent home early." I finish my wine and take my glass to the sink. "Hopefully I'll still be employed tomorrow."

"If it happened the way I'm sure it did—because I've seen the way Madison summons the drama her way—your boss will forgive you. But listen." He stands and walks toward me. "Let's keep this to ourselves. I went to the facility with him today and had it out with a few of the higher-ups. He was cleared to play this weekend, but he's having a rough fuckin' go. Keep it under wraps until the after this game for me?"

I know I shouldn't agree. I should be honest and tell Gavin right away.

But I don't.

How could this ever go wrong?

"WHY THE FUCK do you like this icebox, Mars?" Donny mutters from beneath his down jacket, two scarves, and a hat he's pulled so low, it might as well be a face mask.

"Donny. You live in New York. Geography wasn't my strongest subject, but I'm pretty sure they don't have the warmest of winters."

"It's different. The cold isn't so cold."

"You're right. It's worse because Manhattan is on the water, so it's straight-to-your-bones cold. Colorado is a dry cold."

"Oh my god." Naomi cuts in between us. "Will you two stop it already? Cold is cold is cold."

"Who pissed in your Cheerios?" Donny is nothing if not a man of beautiful, poignant words.

Since our secret powwow in Gavin's kitchen, Donny has been

at Gavin's house every single day, despite the fact that he has a suite at the Four Seasons. We've spent a lot of time together.

He's killing me.

Only about five feet six inches tall, what he lacks in height, he makes up for in volume. He's loud and crass and obnoxious and a whole host of other issues.

But, and I will deny this if he ever finds out, I'm kind of obsessed with him.

I was right when I thought I saw a man who deeply cares for Gavin. In a business all about show me the money, it's not an easy trait to find, but Donny has it in spades. Even if he does tell everyone I got Gavin with my "black girl magic or whatever they're calling it these days."

See? #YoureKillinMeSmalls

"Can't you call one of your friends with a fucking box and have them come get us?"

"I don't know if the cold has placed a temporary freeze on your brain or if you just never listen to me. I didn't have many friends before Gavin and since him, I have exactly one. And you're sitting next to her."

"Oh for fucking fuck's sake. Why the fuck didn't Gavin get a goddamn box?"

Donny also curses so much he's caused my cheeks to heat a few times. And I love a good f-bomb, so that's saying something.

"Because he got here as the season was starting, and he only has a one-year contract. You're his freaking agent, you're supposed to know this stuff better than me." The second quarter is about to start and there's no way I can listen to his bitching for the rest of the game. "If you're cold, go downstairs and watch the game on TV."

"Why the hell would I fly all the fuckin' way out here to watch this shit on TV?"

"It's your only option to warm up. Either shut up and sit down or go to the family room."

"Thank you," Naomi says at the same time Donny says, "Harsh."

Eh. Can't win 'em all.

BUT GAVIN CAN win.

His game is flawless.

It's hard to believe he was out last week with a twisted ankle. You'd never guess there was anything wrong with him the way he's playing. There's no hesitation on his part, nothing is slowed down. If anything, he looks sharper and quicker out there.

In the third quarter, a lineman breaks free and my entire body tightens, preparing to watch Gavin take a hard hit. But he never does. He spins out of the Hulk's grip and throws the ball almost fifty yards to Marcus, the rookie Chris took under his wing who has now surpassed him on the depth chart. Marcus jumps into the air like Superman, his body parallel to the grass beneath him, and comes down with the ball in the end zone.

And Donny finally forgets about the weather for a second.

"That's what the fuck I'm talkin' about, Pope!" He pulls off one his scarves and swings it over his head, hitting the guys behind and in front of us.

"Watch what you're doing, little man," the guy behind us says to Donny.

"Little man." He looks at me and laughs. "What this goofy fucker doesn't understand is if I stood on my wallet, I'd be six feet taller than his broke fuckin' ass."

"Asshole," the guy behind us mutters.

Donny might be aggressive, but at least he keeps all eyes off me.

Well . . . until we go to the family room after the game is over, that is.

We walk into the room a little later than most. After Wednesday, I'd be lying if I said I wasn't at all nervous about facing some of the women again. And while I don't necessarily regret the things I said, I should've walked away.

As soon as we enter the room, all eyes come to us. Some with looks of sympathy, some with indifference, but the majority with disdain. But I was prepared for this. Because of Dre's concussion, he's out of the locker room so fast, Naomi doesn't even go downstairs after the game. But I have Donny and a new book downloaded on my Kindle app in case he gets pulled away. I'm covered.

But what I'm not prepared for, and I should've been, is the way Donny can't sit quietly through it all.

"What the fuck?" His voice, which is always loud, seems much louder in the small, quiet space. "Why's it so quiet in here? We won—or was everyone else watching the Colts play today?"

I'm pretty sure it's a rhetorical question and everyone else seems to think so as well. Until, of course, Madison makes her way from the rear of the room.

"Because, Donovan." She walks up to him in her five-inch pumps . . . that she wore to a football game . . . and stops an inch too close to his face. "Your friend Marlee there? She's the reason we aren't going to the playoffs."

Boring.

Are we really doing this again?

"Cut the shit, Madison." Donny brushes her off. "The Mustangs are out of the playoffs because your fuckin' boyfriend dropped eighty percent of the passes Gavin threw to him and couldn't find his way to the end zone if someone gave him a map. It's because the backup quarterback played worse than my fuckin' four-year-old niece and blew the last fuckin' game."

While Donny is talking to her, the room falls to complete silence. No tapping on phones, no chewing of food, definitely no chatter. Donny has gained everyone's full attention, and Madison doesn't look like a Snow Bitch. She's bright red and the snarl on her lips is so pronounced, she resembles a rabid dog.

"Fuck you!" Her high-pitched voice echoes off the walls around us. "You don't know what you're talking about!"

"I know you've had a thing for Gavin for years and him picking Marlee over you has you spitting nails." While everyone else watching this conversation seems extremely uncomfortable, Donny's at ease. As if he's been planning this moment for years and I just gave him the opportunity to let loose.

"Shut up!" She's completely lost it now. She doesn't seem to realize her reaction has confirmed everything Donny is saying.

"You know," I say to Donny, "I think I'm just going to head home. Tell Gavin I'll call him later."

"And she finally takes the hint." Courtney's voice carries across the room.

It'd be easy to hit back, but the fight in me is gone. They're vampires and they've sucked me dry. Even if they didn't hate me, why would I ever want to be friends with women as terrible as them? I worked my ass off trying to get them to like me and instead of them focusing on all of the charity work I've done, the times I showed up early to events to set up, they couldn't see past my empty ring finger.

I feel bad for Gavin that his season is over, but not having to see these women for a while is not something I'm mad at.

Bitches.

The whole bloody lot of 'em.

Thirty-one

SINCE I STILL DON'T HAVE A CAR, NAOMI ALWAYS SWINGS BY TO take me to the games, and I ride home with Gavin. But thankfully for me, on game days, I have no problem catching the train.

I stand on the platform, surrounded by a sea of orange and blue. The fans, most of whom seem to have indulged in a few beverages during the game, are a mixture of thrilled at the win and pissed about the season being over. I watch, kind of in awe at the way a game these people really have no stakes in can bring out such strong emotions. How it can create such bonds, as if they're all united in orange and blue and all of those in the opposition's colors are automatically the enemy.

We climb on the train when it arrives and by some small miracle, I'm able to find a seat. I sit down, open my new book, and try to lose myself in anything other than football.

We are at the second or third stop when two men in Alexander jerseys (warning number one) approach me.

"Hey. Why are you so quiet over here?" asks the one in the ridiculous bright orange hat shaped with a Mustang head.

"Just reading a book." I keep my answer as short as I can, trying to be polite, yet dismiss them at the same time.

"Reading? On a Sunday after the best fucking game of the season?" asks the other shorter and chubbier guy.

"Yup. Reading on a Sunday." I don't look up at them and hope it's enough for them to catch a hint.

Shocker.

It's not.

"I'm pissed that was the last game of the season," chubby guys says. "I thought we'd go all the way with Pope here."

"If only that stupid bitch didn't get him hurt we would've."

Ooookay.

This isn't sounding promising for me.

"I don't get it. These guys could have anybody they want and they're just passing around the same piece? What could be so great about her?"

"I don't know, but if I ever found her, I'd be sure to try a taste."

Now I feel sick.

Obviously they don't recognize me, but that doesn't mean somebody else won't. I close my Kindle app on my phone, pull up my text messages, and start typing one out to Gavin.

> Hey. On the train surrounded by Super Creepers. Can
> you meet me at my stop?

"You're finished reading?" The guy I have appointed as Creeper Number One asks from above me.

"Yup." *Short and sweet, Marlee. You do not owe them conversation.*

"Who were you texting?" Does alcohol make all people lose sight of social norms and personal boundaries?

"My boyfriend, not that it's any of your business."

"No need to be rude, sweetheart," Horsehead, aka Creeper

Number Two, says, and I want to barf at the sexist, condescending name.

The train slows to another stop, and I almost drop to my knees, praying they'll get off. But instead, the people filling the seats next to me get up. Both of them shoot a sympathetic glance my way as they exit the train.

Gee. Thanks for the show of support.

Before the Super Creepers can sit in both of the seats next to me, I slide down until I'm rubbing thighs with a new stranger and toss my purse in the opposite seat. But, again, neither of my pursuers gets a clue.

And unfortunately for me, when I moved my purse to the other seat, I wasn't thinking about my bedazzled Pope jersey being put on display.

"Damn. That's a sparkly-ass jersey. You must really like Pope."

I cross my arms is a pathetic attempt to shield the jersey they've already seen and ignore them.

"Oh. You can't speak now?" Creeper One accuses. Because, of course, I'm the bitch. It couldn't be their crude words and aggressive behavior.

I still don't say anything.

The instructors in the self-defense classes I took warned women not to speak because they feel obligated, that trying to be kind is what gets women hurt.

And after the last week, being a bitch isn't difficult to pull off. I've learned from the best.

We're at the stop before mine, and the doors slide open. Nobody gets off, but quite a few more people get on. One girl in particular looks really familiar, but I'm having a hard time placing her. She sits across the aisle from me, her eyes down to the dirt-stained carpet. I'm watching her, trying to figure out where I know her from, when she looks up and her gaze collides with mine.

"Hey." A small smile crosses her face. "Don't I know you?

"I was going to ask you the same thing."

"Oh. You do know how to talk," one of the Super Creepers says, but I don't look their way to see which one.

The sun catches the crystals at just the right angle to hit the girl across from me in the face. She stares at my bedazzled shirt.

"Oh my god!" Her eyes widen. "You're the girl that works at HERS! The one who's dating Gavin Pope!"

Oh crap.

"No. That's not me," I say, but the words come out too fast to sound anything but defensive and full of shit.

"It is! I was there the other night when you got into the argument with a really pretty, bitchy lady. I posted a video of it on YouTube. It's already up to almost five thousand views!"

"Congratulations?" Does she want a cookie?

I haven't watched the video, but like I guessed, it was uploaded before my head hit the pillow that night. I take a deep breath and close my eyes. Freaking Madison. Still causing me problems even when she's not around.

"No fuckin' way. You're the girl?" Horsehead says, coming way too close.

"Damn," Creeper One says, sounding a thousand times creepier than he did before. His heavy, drunk eyes linger across my chest. "You are pretty hot."

"Not that hot," Horsehead says, his eyes narrowed on me, cheeks red with anger. "You're the reason we're out of the fucking playoffs! All because you can't keep your fuckin' legs closed."

The girl across from me stares with wide eyes, listening to the two dirtbags hovering over me. She mouths a silent *I'm sorry* my way, but it doesn't make me feel any better . . . or safer for that matter.

Before they can say too much more, the train begins to slow for my stop. I zip my jacket back up, grab my purse, and stand. As soon as the doors open, I'm booking it. But as I'm waiting, sour, hot breath is at my ear and a very unwelcome hand is trailing its way down the back of my jacket.

"What do you say? Wanna slum it for a bit? I'm guessing since you had to catch a ride on the train with the rest of us, you and Pope are finished."

I gather all of the strength I'm not feeling at the moment and turn toward the drunk guy currently invading my space. "Get your hands off of me right now." I spit out the words, but instead of him backing off, he seems entertained. My attempt at calling him off has accomplished the opposite.

"Don't worry," he whispers in my ear, even closer than before. "I like when they get a little feisty. Doug likes it too."

I have to fight back the wave of nausea that rolls over me. Doug (I guess is his name) is on my left, so close his hat is hitting me in the head with every bump we go over. His angry glare feels like it's burning a hole in my head. On my right, whoever this guy is, is getting closer with every second that passes. His nose is touching my ear, and his hand is approaching the bottom of my jacket.

But just as his hand is about to make contact with the thin leggings covering my butt, the train doors start to open. Before they open all the way, I jump out and break into a full-blown sprint, dodging the other people exiting at the same time. I look over my shoulder and see both Doug and whatever-his-name are running after me. Thankfully, unlike the dark night months ago, the sun is still out and I feel confident in my ability to outrun these guys. I turn the corner off of the platform and run smack-dab into a brick wall. Except this wall has hands and they grab my waist, steadying me on my feet.

I look up to see who I ran into, fully prepared to scream bloody murder, when I look into the concerned, blue eyes of Gavin Pope.

The moment his arms wrap around me, the adrenaline I was running on flees, and I have to choke back the urge to vomit.

"Are you okay?" he asks. "Where are they?"

I turn in his arms, searching the crowd until I see both men turn the corner, still running as fast as they can. Sardonic smiles twist across their creepy faces when they see me, until a second later, they notice the large figure behind me.

"What the fuck?" Gavin growls.

"Shit, man. I'm sorry. We didn't realize she was still yours," the chubby guy says between heavy breaths.

"She's not mine, you sick fuck. She's not some piece of fucking property you only respect because she belongs to another man. You respect her because she's a fucking woman who deserves to take a train home without being harassed by assholes like you."

"Calm down, man," Horsehead says with his hands in front of his chest. "We didn't mean anything by it. We were just having a little fun. Weren't we, sweetheart?" He directs the end of his statement to me.

"Don't call me sweetheart, asshole." I pull out of Gavin's arm, feeling way too pissed to be scared anymore, and I'm sure having Gavin at my back doesn't hurt. "No. We were not having a little fun when that asshole wouldn't take his hand off me and you both chased me down."

"Don't be like . . ." he starts to say but stops when he sees Donny approach us with two uniformed officers. I watch with glee as the drunk haze they're in starts to clear and the color drains from their faces.

"Gentlemen. It's seems we have a problem here," says the very handsome African American officer.

"Yes," Gavin says from behind me, his angry voice sending shivers down my spine. "We most definitely do."

"We're already starting to draw a crowd, Mr. Pope." The officer motions toward the crowd forming a circle around us with their cell phones up. "Would you mind if my partner took them in and we went someplace more private to get the details?"

"I'd appreciate that, Officer . . ."

"Officer Graham." He reaches his hand out toward Gavin.

"Officer Graham. Thank you." Gavin returns his handshake. "My car is around the corner if you'd like to follow us to my place."

"Sounds good, Mr. Pope."

Without exchanging any more words, Gavin, Donny, and I walk to Gavin's truck. Donny climbs into the back seat and we sit quietly listening to sports talk. Well . . . I don't listen. I stare out the window thinking of every worst-case-scenario ending to what just happened. I also start budgeting in my head because I'm pretty sure this marks the end of my time on public transportation.

"This is stupid. Those guys were assholes, but they didn't get crazy until the lady mentioned the video and outed me as your girlfriend." I break the silence, still pissed about how everything went down.

"What video?" Gavin asks.

Oopsies.

"Some video from work." That's only a half lie and I've never watched the video, it'd be irresponsible of me to say any more.

"It's a video of Madison losing her fuckin' shit the way she always does while Marlee's at work." Donny fills in the blanks for Gavin. "They named it 'Gavin Pope's Girl's No Nun.' Fuckin' brilliant."

"What?" Gavin looks to me for an answer even though I'm not the one who told him.

"Thanks a lot, friend." I turn and glare at Donny, but he doesn't care.

"Again," Gavin says. "What?"

"I don't even know. I've never watched it." I tell Gavin the truth and hope he'll drop it.

"I have." Donny pipes in . . . again. "I was going to show it to you later, but what better time than the present?" He passes his phone to Gavin, and I can hear my voice before he even looks at it.

"You know what, Donny?" I put my knees on the seats and turn around to look at him.

"What?" he asks, but he knows what I'm going to say.

"I really don't like you."

"Stop lying." He takes a sip of the beer he snuck out of the stadium. "I love you, you love me, it's like fuckin' *Barney* in this car."

"Whatever." I roll my eyes and plop back on the seat.

"I can't believe neither of you told me about this video," Gavin says, but never takes his eyes off of the screen.

The next ten minutes are the slowest, most awkward ten minutes of my life, and I learn how god-awful my voice is. At least, how bad it is when I sound like a hysterical freaking maniac. All I was missing was the smeared red lipstick and the purple hair and I was the freaking Joker. Not a good look.

When it ends, Gavin passes Donny back his phone without muttering a word.

I don't take it as a good sign.

He reaches for his phone in the cup holder and starts dialing.

I still don't have the best feeling.

Then he starts speaking.

"Madison? I've been better. You know what? No. You're fired." Oh shit. Now I know I'm screwed.

"No, Madison. Marlee didn't tell me anything. You did. I watched the video from HERS. The shit you said? The vile shit that left your mouth after you brought up my fucking family? Yeah, I have no room for that in my life. You want to run around, disrespecting the woman I love, then you should've been prepared for this."

"Gavin!" I yell after he pushes the end button. "What did you just do?"

My eyes are in danger of popping out my head, and I'm having a hard time hearing over the sound of my heartbeat racing in my ears.

"I fired Madison. What the fuck did you think I'd do after I heard the shit she said to you? Fuck!" He punches the steering wheel so hard, the horn goes off. "Why'd you hide that from me?"

"Because I knew you'd react like this!" I throw my hands in the air. "I told you before we started dating I don't want you fighting my battles for me. I don't want you to fire Madison because of me! I can take care of it on my own."

"Not everything's about you, Marlee! Did you ever think about that? That I wouldn't want a person like that working for me? That I wouldn't want someone who treats the person I love like fucking garbage around me?" His nostrils are flaring, and the vein in his neck is throbbing. "I know you can fight for yourself, and I've been pretty damn good about letting you. Now it's time for you to let me fight my battles."

A knock on the window pulls my attention from a heavily breathing Gavin to Officer Graham, who's standing at the driver's window.

Gavin takes a second to collect himself and then rolls down the window. As if his freak-out never happened, he smiles at the officer and gives him his address before putting the truck in gear and driving the last few blocks to his place in silence.

But right before he pulls into his garage, he reaches over the center console and laces our fingers together.

And with the one sweet, simple gesture, I know we're going to be fine.

Thirty-two

"RISE AND SHINE, BABE."

I hate perky morning Gavin. It's hasn't even been a week since the season, but I thought he'd take this time to sleep until noon like normal adult humans with no daily commitments. Wrong. If it wasn't for his lips trailing down my neck and his beard tickling my chest, I'd be way pissed.

But they are. So, instead, I'm just super turned on.

Hot guy superpowers . . . turning anger into lust with a brush of the lips.

"The season's over. You have no reason to wake up early. Sleep, you freak." Some of the words are accidentally more moan than not. Moaning does not help your case if you're wondering.

"Come on. It's vacation day." He nips at my earlobe.

Dammit.

Ear biting and vacations? Those are my biggest weaknesses.

I pop out of bed faster than I think I ever have at the reminder of what we're doing today. I'm in nothing but undies, my hair is a disaster, and my lips are still swollen from the night before, but the way Gavin's gaze travels slowly down my body, you'd think I was red carpet ready.

"You're so fucking beautiful it hurts." His voice is much deeper than it was only moments prior.

"Love you." It's all I can say when he tells me these things, when he looks at me like I'm the only woman in the entire world worth living for, when he reminds me with one small gesture what I missed out on for so long and how lucky I am to have found it. Even if for only a little while.

Sorry.

The skeptic in me is still alive and well.

"Take a shower, get dressed, then meet me downstairs. Our driver will be here soon, and I have everything scheduled down to the minute."

"Then I hope you scheduled an extra hour for incidentals."

"Why do you think you're already awake? I didn't deploy the ear biting for no reason." He swats at my butt as I turn toward the bathroom.

"So . . . does this mean you won't be joining me in the shower?" I call over my shoulder, exaggerating the sway of my hips. "I hope I don't get lonely."

"Dammit, you evil seductress." His footsteps quicken behind me. Before I get the chance to run, he has me tossed over his shoulder and is biting my ass.

"And don't you forget it," I tell his butt, which I'm eye level with.

LUCKY FOR ME, Gavin implements a very generous buffer time.

After we finish breakfast, I grab my jacket, boots, and purse. Gavin grabs our luggage, and then we head out the door. I'd packed winter things—which was Gavin's only hint.

Waiting in front of his place is a black town car. #Classy-WithaC

The second we step outside into the deceivingly sunny, cold air, the driver, an older man in a suit, hops out of the car to retrieve our luggage. I let him take mine, but Gavin puts his away himself. I hope wherever we're going is slightly warmer than here.

When we arrive at the small airport, instead of the long lines and the mindless waiting at the gate like I'm used to, we're checked right in, ushered through security, and guided straight to our plane.

Read that again.

Our. Plane.

WHAT?!

I mean, I've flown first class a few times, but never, ever have I flown private. I've always said I didn't want to fly on a small plane, but that's before I stepped foot on this one. Because let me tell you, quality over quantity, my friends.

When we walk on board the charter plane, the pilot, Asher; copilot, Cory; and flight attendant, Giana are all waiting to introduce themselves. It's all very formal and intimidating. #First-WorldProblems

Once we're in the air, Giana brings us our lunch menus.

Yeah, lunch menus. As in more than a bag of stale pretzels.

"Can I have the chicken Caesar salad, light on the dressing, heavy on the champagne refills, please?" Just because the plane is fancy doesn't mean I've forgotten the fact that we're floating in the air, testing the limits of gravity, teetering on the edge of a death dive to the earth beneath us.

Not that I'm dramatic or anything.

"Of course, ma'am." Ma'am? How old does she think I am? "And for you, Mr. Pope?"

"I'll have the stuffed chicken, please."

"Perfect. I'll get that right to you," she says and I swear, when she does, her voice drops three octaves and her blouse unbuttons itself.

Gavin drops his hand to my knee and gets my attention. "Are you excited to find out where we're going?"

"Was that a rhetorical question? Because duh. I'm dying here!" And I'm a little bit tipsy.

"I can't wait until you see." He pulls my legs into his lap and slips my boots off one at a time. Then his million-dollar hands massage my feet.

My head falls back and an exaggerated, champagne-emboldened moan slips out. "Holy moly. No wonder you have those things insured. It's like magic flows from your fingertips."

"I'm glad you like them, because they love touching you."

"Stop right now. I cannot handle getting caught in the middle of dirty talk by a stranger." I'm gonna need a lot more champagne before I can handle that much humiliation.

"When you pay for a private plane, the main thing you're paying for is privacy. Just say the word and I can have Giana sitting in the cockpit with Asher and Cory."

"The word." No time like the present to join the mile-high club, right?

Apparently Gavin agrees because instead of just pushing the call button for Giana to come to us, he sprints to the front of the plane where she's sitting. I watch them talk for about half a second before I realize that even though she will respect our wish for privacy, she's still going to know what we're doing. And with that knowledge, the ability to look her in the eyes ever again opens the emergency exit and jumps out of the plane.

My libido, however, stays firmly in place. An hour of awkwardness is well worth the price for any amount of time with Gavin's hands on me . . . and anybody who disagrees is a dirty liar.

I don't allow my gaze to return to the front of the plane until

I hear Gavin thank Giana and the cockpit door closes. Gavin saunters—yes, saunters—toward me with an open bottle of champagne in one hand, an eye mask in the other, and a look of mischief on his face that makes my insides quiver.

"You want to get drunk and get some beauty sleep? That's a way better idea than what I thought you were talking about," I say, and a growl slips from the back of his throat. I have to bite the inside of my cheek to keep the smile that's threatening to take over my face from breaking free.

I love giving him a hard time because when I do, he feels the need to defend his manhood. And let me tell you, the only thing better than imagining what Gavin has planned for me is hearing him lay it all out, word for dirty word.

"Sleep is the last thing you're about to get." He places the champagne and mask on the table and turns to face me.

I don't even have time to formulate a smart-ass response before his large hand is on the back of my neck, gently pulling my face toward his as he drops to his knees in front of me. His free hand falls to my thigh and starts to follow the upward path of the seam on my leggings. My heart rate increases and my breathing becomes louder with every inch they travel, doing nothing to mask the anticipation coursing through my body. His fingers are so close to being where I want them most when I become vaguely aware of his breath against my neck.

"And, babe, just so you know, you won't be getting much sleep until we get back to Colorado," he whispers in my ear.

The breathing I couldn't slow down suddenly disappears and my eyes I didn't even realize were closed fly open. But he doesn't stop there.

"I have you to myself. No jobs, no responsibilities, no pain-in-the-ass press running bullshit stories. Just you and me and a bed. And if you think I'm going to let these next days go by without me getting my hands on you every possible second, you're out of your mind. I've been waiting all season long to have unrestricted access to you and I'm not missing a single opportunity to do so . . ." He moves his hands to the top of my leggings and starts to roll them down and over my hips. "You are out of your mind."

By the time he's finished with his little speech, my leggings are somewhere behind me, my bare ass is on the leather seat, and I'm staring at him openmouthed like he's some kind of sex magician . . . which is pretty much what he is.

"I . . . you . . . please." I barely mange to stutter out. His words are like foreplay to foreplay. All he has to do is whisper in my ear and I'm primed and ready to go. And considering Gavin is sitting between my spread legs, almost eye level with the proof of what his words do to me, he will soon find out. But he never responds. He just sits back on his heels, both hands wrapped around my ankles, and watches me.

"Gavin." I try to make his name come out sounding strong, but it's more of a whine . . . or a moan . . . a whoan? "Why are you staring at me? Please, touch me."

"I will." He finally breaks the silence. "Just give me a second to look at you."

He drops my gaze and lets his eyes roam my half-naked body. But he's not just ogling. Yes, the look in his eyes is appreciative— even as it follows the unfortunate curve of my even-more-pronounced-while-sitting-down tummy—but there is something more. Something deeper is at work behind his eyes. I don't know what it is. All I know is it's so powerful it's almost physical. Goose bumps break out over my skin wherever he looks. I try to close my legs when he gets there, but his hands at my ankles keep them open.

"You are a fucking goddess, Marlee." He looks back to my face. "Every inch of you is fucking perfection and I cannot believe I got lucky enough to have you. That I'm the person who gets to experience the beauty that only you can bring me."

Ummm. . . .

Wow.

"I think most people would say I'm the lucky one," I whisper back. My inability to accept a compliment is still fully intact.

"Then most people would be wrong. Because my life was nothing more than an empty condo and work before you. And now it's overflowing with beauty."

Holy shit.

"Holy shit." I make my thoughts known. "Are you trying to ruin me?"

"I wasn't, but if that's the result of telling you, then I guess so." He lets go of my ankles and his hands start moving up my legs. "I know our relationship hasn't been an easy road so far, but know I plan on telling you how much you mean to me almost as often as I show you."

He finishes talking at the same time his hands reach the top of my legs and he dips one of his fingers inside of me. Between this and everything he just said to me, I almost come immediately. My back arches off of the seat, my eyes snap shut, and there's not a chance in hell I could tame the moan coming out of my mouth.

"Look at me, baby."

I barely hear him over the roaring of blood in my ears and opening my eyes has never taken so much effort. But when I look at him, I know it was worth it. Because as soon as our eyes meet, he adds another finger and drops his mouth to my sex.

Now feeling it is one thing—one amazing, wonderful thing. But seeing it?

Oh.

My.

God.

Gavin doesn't drop our eye contact either. With his fingers inside me and his tongue on my most sensitive part, he watches me with hooded eyes. It's the most intimate moment of my life and I almost cry when I feel the tightening at my core beginning to build. I try to hold it off, wanting to stay in this moment for as long as possible, but I can't control it. I freeze for a second before my entire body starts shaking uncontrollably. Colors explode behind my eyelids and my head flies back. I scream so loudly, I know without a doubt the entire crew—and maybe even people on the ground—can hear me. But I don't care, I'm not holding back *anything*.

"See?" Gavin says between kisses up my chest. "Fucking beauty."

Feeling wrecked in the best possible way, the only words I can manage are, "Inside. Now."

"Bossy," he says, but I can feel his body shaking with laughter on mine. "But if you insist."

I pull off my shirt and bra, throwing them over my head to join my leggings, and push my breasts against his bare chest. "I insist."

His breath hitches and I watch as his blue eyes turn navy. Then, without a word, he picks me up and flips us around so he's in my seat. He positions me just so and when I drop my hips down, he's inside of me, filling me completely.

"Oh my god," I breathe into his throat.

Even though we've done this multiple times now, it still takes me a minute to adjust to his size. Gavin never rushes me. He lets me take my time while his hands draw circles on my back.

Once the small bite of pain fades, an urgent, throbbing need replaces it.

Up and down.

Slowly at first, I begin to move.

Up.

Down.

Gavin's hands drop beneath my ass, lifting me to the very tip of his erection, then letting me drop.

I start moving faster, harder. Taking as much of him as I can.

"Fuck yes." Gavin encourages me with a strained voice. The need in his voice only makes my need for him grow.

He drops his free hand between my legs and starts rubbing delicious circles while I rock my hips, keeping him deep inside of me.

It sneaks up on me this time.

I clench around him and a soundless scream rips from the back of my throat. Gavin tenses underneath me. His fingernails dig into my back and even though I can't see it, I know tomorrow there will still be scratches as a reminder of this moment.

My body, still trembling and glistening with sweat (being on top is a legitimate workout), collapses down onto Gavin. I rest my forehead on his, willing my breathing to calm, but when his lips move to touch mine, I know it's a lost cause.

"That." Deep breath. "Was." Deeper breath. "Amazing." Exhale.

"It always is." Gavin's mouth curves into a cocky smile. "Champagne and then ready to go again?"

Is he insane? Again?!

"Absolutely."

#MileHighClubInitiation

SINCE WE DIDN'T fly over the mountains, all I know is we flew east.

We step off the plane and the first thing I notice is the cold. Not the dry, easy-to-deal-with cold I'm used to, but the wet, sink-to-your-bones, never-feel-warm-again cold you can only get when you're near a large body of water.

Now, maybe if I hadn't indulged in the rest of the champagne or my mind wasn't still focused on the new mouth and finger combination Gavin came up with on the plane, I would've put two and two together. I would've come to the fairly obvious conclusion that we were in New York before we walked out of the front door of the small airport and straight into the smiling faces of Thompson and Elizabeth Pope.

But I don't.

I put my best plastic smile on my face, push everything Madison told me about them to the back of my mind, and try to pull myself together to meet his parents.

"Mom . . . Dad . . . what are you guys doing here? What happened to the driver I hired?" Gavin sounds as surprised as I feel.

Oh thank goodness. I'm not gonna lie, if his idea of a good surprise was meeting his parents after a long flight, I was going to be a little concerned about our future.

"You can't expect we'd let some driver see you before us." Her eyebrows go up as her attention shifts toward me. "We weren't aware you'd be bringing a guest though."

"Mom. I told you about Marlee."

"Oh yes. Marlee. The one who got you injured."

No. Nope. Never. Get me back on the plane, I'm going home.

"Mom!" Gavin yells at the same time his dad bursts into laughter.

"I'm kidding, Gavin. Always so serious." Mrs. Pope pats him on the arm and turns her somewhat appraising gaze toward me. "We've heard so much about you, Marlee. When his sister called to tell us Gavin was bringing you, we knew we had to rush to meet you before he hid you away for the rest of your visit."

"Nice to meet you too, Mrs. Pope," I force out. Never in my life have I been more aware of my less-than-desirable appearance. "I've heard so much about you and your family."

"Sorry, Gavin. I tried to talk her out of it, but you know how your mom gets when she wants something." Thompson Pope, if I may say, is so freaking handsome. If he's any indication of how well Gavin is going to age, sticking around is now mandatory.

Gavin doesn't say anything in return. He just nods and runs a hand through his hair.

"Honey. I don't understand this hair. Can't you get a haircut? Remember the one you had in high school? You looked so handsome."

"I've been bugging him to get a haircut for the last month and he won't give in," I tattle. "I guess he likes the Jesus do he's got going."

Gavin groans, I stifle a laugh, and if I'm not mistaken, Mrs. Pope's smile becomes a little more genuine.

"Well, get in the car, you two." She claps her hands. "Let's get this show on the road."

Gavin grabs our luggage to put in the trunk and when he does, his mom slides into the back seat, motioning for me to sit next to her. I hesitate for a moment, worried about the proximity in relation to me having sex hair and possibly smelling like alcohol, but I get in anyway. Better to be thought of as a nice floozy than a bitchy one.

"Don't you dare turn on rap, Pope." I poke his shoulder when I see him reach for the radio. "You know this is my favorite song."

"This is my favorite song too!" Mrs. Pope says about the country music filling the car. "What other songs of his do you like?"

After we've successfully matched our top five favorite songs, I think I've won Mrs. Pope over. #SaintLukeBryan

AFTER GAVIN GETS into the front seat, following a string of hushed words about big-mouthed sisters and pushy moms, we slowly make our way across Long Island to a little city named Oyster Bay.

Gavin had told me before he was from here, but I could never picture it.

Now I know why. I wasn't able to imagine how a town so close to one of the largest cities in the world could still be so charming and peaceful.

I love it and the only thing better than the scenery is the company.

I was nervous to meet Gavin's parents, and after everything Madison had spit at me, I was straight-up petrified.

But now, meeting them at last, I couldn't love them more. Mrs. Pope—or Beth as she keeps telling me to call her—is my favorite. If I didn't love my parents so much and it didn't make the guy I'm sleeping with my brother, I would ask her to adopt me.

To pass time as we're stuck in traffic, Beth chats my ear off, filling me in on stories of Gavin's past. Like when he was four and refused to go to the bathroom in the house and would run to the backyard every time he had to go. And the time he got suspended from school because a boy was picking on his sister, Emerson, so he went to her class and refused to leave until the boy apologized. It's creepy to swoon over middle school Gavin, isn't it?

"Is this your home?" I ask Mrs. Pope when we reach the end of the long, tree-lined driveway.

"No, this is Gavin's. Isn't it adorable? And wait until you walk around the property. It has access to the water. It's cold now, but during summer, it's really very lovely."

"I bet it is." I have to use all of my self-restraint not to press my forehead against the window to get a better view before I open the door to take it in in all of its classic glory.

The house is the polar opposite of his condo back in Denver. Where his condo is everything modern and clean lines, his house in New York is a classic colonial on a lot of land. It's stunning, it's just not what I expected.

"Well, my dear." Mr. Pope draws my attention as he sets luggage on the brick-lined walkway ahead of me. "This is where we leave you or that wife of mine won't let you out of her sight. Don't let Gavin sneak you away without seeing us again."

"I won't Mr.—I mean Thom." I catch myself. "Thank you for the ride. It was so nice meeting you."

"The pleasure was all mine," he whispers before giving me a quick hug.

"Marlee!" Mrs. Pope calls from where she's standing with Gavin. "Now don't you dare let him keep you away from us. We love you already and want to see more of you before you go home. And Emerson will kill Gavin if she's the only one who misses you."

Well, of course, it would be a shame for anybody to miss out on my marvelous presence. #Sarcasm

"I won't. Now that I know where we are, he won't be able to get me back on a plane without meeting her and letting me squeeze on that scrumptious grandson of yours."

"Isn't he yummy?" Hearts appeared in her eyes the instant I mentioned Finn, Gavin's eighteen-month-old nephew. It's understandable. I'm not even related to him and I'm obsessed with the blue-eyed, head-full-of-red-hair little guy.

"He really is."

"Okay then." She claps her hands and rounds the car to the passenger door. "Now that I'm convinced you two won't disappear, we will leave you. Let's go, Thompson."

"Coming, dear," he says from beside me, the words so sugary sweet they sound anything but.

They get in the car, Mrs. Pope waving to us and her lips moving a million miles a minute while Mr. Pope nods along and drives away.

"So." Gavin pulls my attention from beside me. "Those are my parents."

I turn to him and for the first time, he appears shy and nervous. I don't know if it's because of his parents or if he's nervous to show me this part of him, but after all of the not-so-shiny parts of my life he's witnessed? He has no reason to ever worry.

"They're amazing. I love them." I give him a quick peck on the lips and squeeze his bum. "Now show me around this place! It's beautiful."

"I want to show you my bedroom, but if I take you there first, you won't be seeing the rest of this place until tomorrow."

I have no idea how he manages to be so nonchalant when he says those things.

#Perv

"Oh." I feel the now familiar heat spreading across my cheeks. "Well if we must . . ."

"Oh thank god," his whispers to the sky before looking back to me. "I thought you'd never ask."

He was right. Once we got into bed, I didn't get the house tour until the next morning.

Thirty-three

I NEVER THOUGHT OF MYSELF AS AN EAST COAST GIRL. I LOVE COL-orado, and there wasn't one place I ever went to that was able to shake that belief.

Until Oyster Bay.

In our three days here, we've explored downtown, visiting some of his favorite places from his childhood, and he even took me to the cemetery after I admitted my strange fascination with them. But most of our time is spent in his amazing house, which is filled with contradicting styles. The modern clean furniture Gavin likes contrasts with the original 1888 moldings. Marble counters and stainless-steel appliances on turn-of-the-century tiles. A giant flat-screen TV tops his hand-carved fireplace. This is probably the most wonderful home I've ever stepped foot in.

"I don't even like to cook, but I think I would learn just to have an excuse to be in your kitchen." It's late in the afternoon on the third day of our trip and we still haven't seen his family again.

"Too bad I don't have much food to cook because watching you walk around my kitchen wearing what you're wearing is definitely on my bucket list." He sticks his head around the freezer door to look at me in nothing but my lace panties and matching cami. "But for now, we can either have frozen lasagna or order in. Which do you want?"

"Hmmm . . . give me a second. This feels like a really big decision," I joke, about to pick the lasagna when the doorbell rings.

"Fuck. Who the hell is that?"

"How should I know?" But I do have a feeling. It doesn't take a genius to figure out that it's probably a family member. Because of that, I take off up the stairs when he goes to open the door. Last thing I want is for his mom to see me sitting in her son's kitchen half naked.

Right before I'm about to slam the bedroom door shut, an unfamiliar voice drifts upstairs, and I'm able to keep the door from closing at the very last second. "Were you planning on seeing your nephew before you left or do you think you're too good for us now?"

Oh shit.

I hope I'm wrong, but I'm thinking his sister may not be as big of a Marlee fan as his mom.

"We're going to call mom tomorrow. Marlee's been asking when she gets to meet you and Finn," Gavin tells her, and I want to cheer. I was always Chris's excuse to get out of things. I love how Gavin always takes the fall, even when he doesn't have to.

"Why do I doubt that?" Emerson says, each word dripping with disdain.

Good news? I was right!

Bad news? I was right. She's definitely not my fan.

"Listen, Em. I love you, and I can't wait to see Finn, but if this is how you're going to act around Marlee, you can leave."

"God. Madison was right." I can't see her face from a level up and behind walls, but I'd be willing to bet there's a nasty snarl on her face. "This girl makes you blind."

Our trip was going way too well. I should've known something big was about to happen.

"Do not mention Madison, Emerson." Oh. He called her by her full name, a page ripped out of the dad book. "You have no clue the things she's done. I already talked to mom about her a week ago. I'm not hiring her again. I don't know if I'll ever talk to her again."

"This is absurd, Gavin," his sister yells, startling me so much, I hit my head on the door frame I'm leaning against. "Madison has been one of your best friends since you guys were in what? First grade? And you're going to throw it all away over some girl who already doesn't have the best reputation?"

"Emerson." His tone is so cold, I get goose bumps.

"Gavin." Oh. Looks like the name response runs in the family.

"If you're going to act like this and take Madison's word over mine without even asking my side of the story, then we're done here, and we can try when we're back next time."

"We? You're going to come back with *her* again?"

All right, now I'm not sure I care if she likes me because I'm not too crazy about her either.

"Yes. I am. Marlee's my girlfriend. I love her. When I come back, she'll be coming along." Poor guy sounds exhausted. Logically, I know this isn't my fault, but I can't help but feel guilty hearing them fight because of me.

"You just feel like you have to keep watch on her so she doesn't cheat on you with your teammates like she did to her ex."

Oh hell no.

"Are you fucking kidding me right now?" At least he doesn't sound tired anymore. Now he sounds flat-out pissed. "Don't come here with that bullshit. I was in the locker room with him while they were still together, and he was always bragging about how many girls he fucked over the weekend. Never once was there any whisper of Marlee cheating on him. You know why? Because it never happened."

"Why would Madison make up something like that? I get that you like this girl, but you aren't using your head."

"Take a search around YouTube and get back to me. Look up 'Gavin Pope's Girl's No Nun,'" he tells her, his tone softening. "Madison isn't who you think she is. She's vindictive and for some reason, has made it her mission to bring Marlee down. I understand she's your friend and you want to believe her, but she's lying to you."

"Don't patronize me, Gavin. I'm not six years old anymore, I don't need you to try and protect my feelings, just like I don't need to believe everything you say. You want this girl in your life? Fine with me. But don't expect me to sit around and let you bring her around *my* family. When you get yourself together, come see me. But don't you dare bring her with you. I will not allow my son to be around somebody like her." Then the door slams and tires screech as she speeds away.

Ouch.

I may not be Emerson Pope's biggest fan, but there is no denying the effectiveness of her closing. The girlfriend or the sister/nephew? Quite the ultimatum.

What am I supposed to do with it? I can't ruin the life of the guy I love. It's like all I do is bring problems into his life and the situations keep escalating. Causing problems with his family is a burden I can't carry and I know, because he's Gavin, he's going to try and protect me from it.

When I hear his footsteps up the stairs, I walk to the door and meet him. It took him a while to join me after Emerson left and now the purple and pink sky is being chased away by the black night.

"I'm assuming you heard what went down?" he asks when he sees me.

"Yeah." I shift on my feet, my eyes focusing on the old wood floors. "I'm so sorry. I didn't ever mean to put you in a situation like this."

"Hey." His hand moves under my chin, forcing my eyes to meet his. "You didn't. Madison did. That had nothing to do with you."

"You're sweet for saying that, but it does have to do with me. I knew Madison liked you the moment I saw you two in the elevator with me and Chris."

"I'd thought of her as a sister. It wasn't like that between us."

"For you, maybe. But for her? She loved you. And not in the he's-my-best-friend-I've-known-him-forever way either. No, she was biding her time until you realized she was the love of your life, put a ring on it, and then put all the babies in her."

I wish I still had the ability to have some sort of sympathy for her, but she has sucked it out of me with her evil, emotion-sucking, vampire ways.

He ruffles his already messy hair as he walks across the room and stares out the window. "But how does she think fucking with you would make me like her?"

"Gavin. I don't know." I cross the room and stand beside him, looking at the dark night sky. "I know she's your friend—" He starts to cut me off, but I talk over him. "Yeah, yeah. You're pissed at her now, but she's still been your friend for what? Twenty years? Even if you want to, it's not so easy to shut off a friendship. But I think in her messed-up mind she thought she was helping you. Warning you away from the big bad slut. And no matter what I told her, I was never going to be as good as her."

"Well, fuck." He drops his head and takes a step away from me. "I don't even know what to do with that. Do you care if I go for a run?"

"Of course not." My response is immediate, but not entirely truthful. "Go, clear your mind."

But even though he doesn't say it directly, I know what he means. He needs space to think . . . space away from me. I just hope once his mind is clear, I'll still be in there.

Gavin changes into some of the workout clothes he left behind and when he leaves for his run, he just shouts a quick good-bye.

I have no idea when he comes back.

I fall asleep alone.

Thirty-four

WE'RE LEAVING TOMORROW—WHICH SUCKS—SO WE'RE SPEND-
ing today with Gavin's family. Well, probably just his parents.
Last night and this morning are the first time in months I've woken up alone. But instead of discussing it, I just focus on baking
a red velvet cake to bring to his parents' house tonight.

My red velvet cake is always a hit, but there is one tiny little
detail: I suck at shopping. At the store this morning and I forgot
to buy cream cheese. And you cannot have a red velvet cake without homemade cream cheese frosting. It's a law.

I am near a full-blown panic because I can't show up at his
parents' house with a red velvet cake with plain old vanilla frosting now can I? No! But lucky for me, I'm dating Gavin Pope who,
at the first sign of my meltdown, offers to run to the store to grab
cream cheese, becoming a real-life superhero.

The timer on the cake goes off at the same time there's a knock
on the door. He always buys too much at the store, and his hands
are probably too full to open it.

"One sec!" I call to him, balancing the two cake pans on my
oven-mitt-covered hands.

There's another loud knock as I'm setting the cakes on the cooling racks on top of the flour-coated countertops.

Hey. I said I was a good baker, not a neat one.

"Here I come! You were quick." I run to the door, twist open the locks, and when I swing the door open, I'm met with familiar eyes on an unfamiliar face.

Emerson.

Of course it's her. Murphy's an asshole.

"Oh hi, Emerson, hey." I'm so taken aback by her presence I stumble over my words. "Gavin ran to the store really fast, but do you want come in and wait?"

"Sure. Thank you."

Her tone is much different than it was yesterday, thank you Lord. She doesn't seem annoyed or disgusted to see me, and I'm taking that as a good sign.

She walks into the family room, then stops and swings around to face me.

"I'm not sure if you heard what I said yesterday, but I want to apologize to you." She sounds sincere, but I was in a relationship with Chris for years while he lied straight to my face, so I might not be the best judge. "It was rude of me to make the assumptions I made."

Okay. Now that? I'm pretty sure if I looked at her palm, those exact words in Mrs. Pope's handwriting would be there.

But who am I to kick a gift horse in the mouth?

"Thanks." I walk into kitchen to avoid eye contact.

"It smells awesome in here."

She tells no lies though, my red velvet cake never fails. I'm a little thrown by the compliment, but I guess she's trying.

"Hope your family likes red velvet." I point to the cake pans on the cooling racks. "I asked Gavin for suggestions, but he was no help, so I guessed."

"So Gavin. If you need him, he will be there in a heartbeat, but little details? He has no clue."

Do we know the same Gavin? Because my Gavin doesn't forget a single detail. I mean, he kept my necklace for years!

"Really? That seems unlike him." I'm trying to take the high road, but this better-woman crap is hard. I really want to say he only forgets things that don't matter.

"He still has no idea what my favorite color is and it's been the same since I was nine." She comes into the kitchen and sits on a stool at the island.

"What's your favorite color?" I feel like we're on a first date asking that question.

"Yellow." She points to her yellow diamond wedding ring and yellow pea coat.

"That's my favorite color too!"

Look at us. Bonding and shit.

I put the few dishes I've gotten messy in the dishwasher. When I finish, she has her head tilted, watching me inquisitively and my need to not be in silence kicks back in.

"Are you guys coming tonight?"

"What really happened with you and Madison?" she asks instead of answering my question and yet again, I'm wishing I would enjoy the silence for once.

"I'm not sure anything happened, to be honest." I put the dish towel on the counter and move to the seat next to her. "I think she hates any woman Gavin shows attention to because she's in love with him. But with me dating Chris, it gave her all the extra ammunition she needed to *really* hate me."

"You have to understand. Madison has been my best friend since before I could walk. Our parents are close and we grew up together."

"Emerson." I take her hand into mine when I see her eyes beginning to gloss over. "I don't want to get between you and Madison. I already feel guilty about what's gone down between her and your brother. But I can't give you a specific moment where I said or did anything other than falling for your brother. Which, by the way, was not something I wanted."

Her eyes widen with surprise at my last tidbit and I don't blame her. She's his sister, she knows what a catch he is. I doubt there are many women on the planet who would even think twice about falling head over heels for him.

"You didn't? Madison has been telling me you've been chasing him since the moment he got there."

"Well, Madison has quite the imagination," I say with a little too much attitude and have to take a deep breath to get it under control. "Listen, besides your brother, Chris is the only other guy I've ever dated. And when it ended, it was nuclear-level bad. Honestly? It's embarrassing and not something I like to talk about, but I can tell you I had no intention of dating an athlete ever again. But no matter how hard I tried to deny my feelings for Gavin, he wouldn't go away." The smile I always have to fight when I'm talking about Gavin breaks free. "Your brother's kind of like a knight in sweatpants. After so many times, I had to accept what we have."

"Shit." She purses her lips. "Does Gavin have wine?"

"Already on it." I walk to the fridge and pull out an unopened bottle.

I pour two extra-large wineglasses to the rim and bring them to the island. We sit on the hard stools in silence until the creaking of the front door opening snaps us out of our heads.

"Um. What the hell did I miss?" Gavin eyes shift between me and Emerson until they settle on the almost empty wineglasses.

"Just a little girl talk," I tell him as Emerson takes her final sip of wine.

"Yeah, bro." She stands, scratching her stool against the hard-wood floors. "Walk me to my car?"

"Um. Sure?" he answers.

Gavin's still standing in the same spot, staring at me. "Go!" I motion after his sister.

"What did I miss?" he mumbles under his breath as he heads to the door.

Hell.

I'm asking myself the same damn thing.

Thirty-five

GAVIN HAS HINTED AT IT IN THE PAST, BUT HERE AT HIS PARENTS' house, there's no denying the fact. The Popes have some serious money.

Their house is the non-poser version of what Chris wanted his to be. There's a chandelier in every single room. Even the bathrooms. There are old paintings his mom points out that have been passed down for generations. Even the silverware she set the table with is from her great-grandma.

Gavin's been trying to play it cool since we walked into the quiet house, but he chose football over drama for a reason. It's clear to see that Emerson not being here upsets him. I wish he hadn't come home while we were sitting together. His hopes got too high.

"Come." Mrs. Pope directs us into the kitchen. "I have a few appetizers and wine for us while dinner finishes."

We follow her in and sit down at the kitchen table covered in finger foods. Her definition of a few is clearly different than mine.

"This is amazing, Beth," I say as I formulate a game plan for how I can eat as much of the cheese as possible.

"Oh, it's nothing." She waves off the compliment, but by the way Gavin laughs and shakes his head, I know this isn't nothing.

I'm busy launching a full-on attack on the prosciutto-wrapped mozzarella when we hear the front door open.

"Nonna!" the sweetest little voice I've ever heard calls out. Finn bursts into the kitchen, followed closely by Emerson and her husband.

I glance at them for a second before all my attention turns to Gavin, who looks like someone breathed life back into him. His eyes shine with love, and the dimple I've missed finally makes an appearance. It takes every bit of my strength not to jump up and fist pump like I'm on *Arsenio*.

"Hey, Gavin," Emerson says before looking to me. "Good to see you, Marlee."

"You too." I ignore the way her smile changes from natural to forced when she talks to me. At least she's talking to me.

"Well then." Mrs. Pope, forever the hostess with the mostess, gets our attention. "Now that Emerson has brought me my favorite grandson, dinner is ready."

AFTER DINNER, WE'RE all sitting around the table, some of us with the top button of our jeans undone, when something I've never seen before happens. The guys each give their lady a kiss, gather the plates, and go do the dishes.

Now my dad is pretty fantastic, but never once in my entire life have I seen him wash so much as a spoon. He'll go to the store and buy plastic dinnerware before sticking something in the dishwasher.

"Oh yes, dear," Mrs. Pope says, no doubt noticing my look of awe watching the guys standing by the sink. "If we do the cooking, they do the cleaning. I'm a wife and mother, not a servant."

While the guys finish up in the kitchen, Mrs. Pope excuses

herself for a second and comes back holding four giant photo albums.

"You have no idea how long I've waited for this moment," she says as she sits down next to me and spreads the albums on the table.

"Get ready, babe," Gavin whispers in my ear when he walks into the room. "I was the cutest kid ever, and my mom is about to spend the next two hours proving it to you."

"He doesn't let me take pictures anymore so I have to search the internet for good ones the team posts and reminisce about the days he would just say cheese."

"Finn's way cuter than I ever was, Mom. Start taking more pictures of him."

"That's true," Emerson speaks up. "Finn makes you look like a troll."

"Haters gonna hate," Gavin sings—yes, sings—to her.

Emerson sticks her tongue out at him and blows a raspberry, while his mom swoops Finn into her arms and silently shakes her head at her grown children arguing like toddlers. Once she's out of the room, we all dissolve into a fit of laughter. It feels nice, getting along. Emerson might not be on my team yet, but I have faith she'll get there eventually.

Thirty-six

LIFE GETS A LITTLE CRAZY FOR ME WHEN WE GET BACK FROM OYS-
ter Bay. HERS missed me while I was gone. With football over,
two new seasons of *Real Housewives* starting, and our idea for
Bravo trivia to win free drinks, it's getting busy. But poor Gavin
has nothing. He misses football, and even though we might have
just left them, he misses his family too. I think our trip out east
made him realize how much he misses being home.

But luckily (and I use the term very lightly) for Gavin, Donny
flies in to talk about the upcoming free agency and see where
Gavin's head is.

"Gavin. You aren't really telling me you want to spend another
season in this fuckin' icebox, are you?"

I try to hide my smile behind my huge wineglass when Donny
shouts across the table of one of Denver's nicest restaurants.

"More importantly, you aren't telling me that *I'm* gonna have
to visit this fuckin' place for the next four fuckin' years, are you?"

"Donny, come on, watch the language, could you? We're in
public." Gavin still notices it, apparently. "And yes, that's exactly

what I'm telling you. Talk to Jacobs, get them to their best offer, and give it to me to sign."

"Other teams have been making moves. The Giants quarterback announced his retirement, and I've heard through the grapevine they're interested."

"I'm not," Gavin says. "Talk to Jacobs. Talk to me. Let's get this finished so I can move on with my off season."

"What?" Donny asks. Poor guy sounds desperate. "Are you sure? You've always wanted to be a Giant! This is The Dream, man."

Maybe Gavin did, but that was before he came here. Everybody loves Colorado.

Well, except Donny, but there's clearly something wrong with him and he doesn't count.

"Positive. Football isn't going to last forever, but Marlee will. I want to stay with her. Plus, I love it here and the organization is great. Talk to them."

We've exchanged "I love you's," I've met his family, and we practically live together. But still, hearing him tell Donny how much I mean to him without so much as batting an eyelash sends my heart to moon. Never underestimate the power of a public declaration of love.

Even more than that though, the relief I feel hearing Gavin giving Donny the order to stay in Denver is unmeasurable. He has been downplaying his upcoming free agent status, but this isn't my first rodeo. Nothing in the NFL is easy.

Colorado is my home. My work, my family, my friends—they're all here. We're still a new couple, and I've spent most of my adult years following around a man and doing as he says. I'm not interested in doing it again. I love Gavin even more knowing he's not going to put me in a situation where I have to choose between me and him.

"You and that fuckin' black girl magic, Marlee. Got him spell-bound."

I laugh when I hear a person at one of the surrounding tables take an audible gasp. Donny shouldn't be allowed in public.

"You can't say stuff like that out loud." But then I lean across the table and whisper, "I don't know if I'd call it magic, but I have been putting something on him."

"Fuckin' Christ! I wish I had somebody puttin' somethin' on me." His voice gradually raises from his normal loud to really loud, screaming. "Lucky fuckin' bastard over there. Makes the money. Gets the girl. I guess it's only right he has to live like a fuckin' icicle."

"Donny! We were just in New York. It's even colder there than it is here. You need a new argument."

"I don't care if it's cold there." He huffs. "If I'm gonna put my ass on a plane out of New York, it better be to some place warm. San Francisco 49'ers, fuckin' Arizona. You got my ass coming to Chicago first and then fuckin' Denver. Why are you doing this to me?"

"I don't even know why I keep you around." Gavin shakes his head. "Now I'm going to have to pay for all the tables next to us so I don't end up having to hear from the Mustangs GM about the complaints they got for my behavior tonight."

"They should mind their own fuckin' business!" He looks directly at the elderly man ahead of him when he yells it.

"Fucking hell." Gavin groans.

"This wouldn't be a problem in New York. People keep to themselves."

"Denver, Donny." Gavin's hand tightens around his fork, and I can tell he's struggling to keep it together. He always ends up like this after talking to Donny. But they love each other. And they're both very good at getting the other one money.

"Yeah, yeah. I hear you," Donny mumbles. "I'll call Jacobs in the morning."

Squeee!

I want to jump up and run a victory lap around the restaurant yelling, "My man's staying," but since Donny's already embarrassed us enough for the evening, I keep it buried deep down and raise my glass like a classy broad.

Once the bill—correction, bills—are paid, we take Donny to Gavin's place and then head to mine. I told Gavin since he's at my place so often, he should put his on AirBnb for some off-season compensation. He laughed. I was serious. If he would have listened, he could have made back some of what he had to pay for dinner.

"I'll be so glad when your contract is signed and free agency is behind us."

"Not too much longer." He looks over at me while we wait at a red light. "I'm thinking we'll need another vacation after that. Back to New York or an island somewhere."

"Back to New York." The words fly out of my mouth. "Your house is like paradise, and I already miss your family. I can totally picture living there. Walking on the beach, watching Finn for your sister, and one day opening my own little storefront in town. I can see it all."

Even in the dark, I can tell he likes my answer.

Family matters to the Popes and having sat at his mom's extraordinary dining room table listening to her stories about the rambunctious toddler who would turn into the man I love, it's become important to me as well.

I'm an only child and I don't have a big extended family. The idea of having a huge family where everyone loves and supports one another is all I've ever dreamt of. Okay, Gavin too.

"New York it is," he whispers before the light turns green.

"But just to put it out there, summer is pretty long. Maybe two vacations wouldn't be a terrible hardship."

"Mars." He grabs my hands and gives it a soft squeeze.

"Gavin."

"You in a bikini on a beach? What's the opposite of a hardship?"

"Wine, Gavin. You know I can't answer a question like that after wine." Hell. I can barely answer sober.

#NotAnEnglishMajor

"Well, whatever the opposite is, that's what being on vacations with you is like."

Wine and compliments? He's so getting laid tonight.

Thirty-seven

THE BEST FEELING IN THE WORLD AFTER A LONG SHIFT ON YOUR feet is the moment when your ass finally takes over for you.

Business at HERS never slowed after football season ended. And since it's March, Brynn and I are both optimistic it's only going to keep getting better.

After my showdown with Madison, I've made a big effort to be my most professional self at all times when I'm at HERS. Whenever I'm here, I turn my phone off so I'm only checking it while I'm on break.

Tonight, when I turn my phone back on, I have ten unread text messages and four new voice mails from Nay.

"Where the hell have you been?" Naomi's voice blares out of my phone.

"At work. Is everything okay?"

"You mean to tell me you still don't have the freaking ESPN app on your phone?" she scolds me.

Oops. I hate cluttering up my home screen with apps, especially ones I don't care about.

"Is it Gavin?" I start to panic a little because that stupid app has only brought me bad news in the past.

"No, it's Chris! They released him!"

Oh shit.

I should feel bad for him. Maybe send him a text or a postcard letting him know I hope he'll be okay. But, karma is in my ear, whispering about what a bitch she is, and I laugh.

"Shut up!" I say when I can breathe again. "I wonder who is more pissed right now, Chris or Madison."

"Probably a draw. Chris lost his job, Madison lost the key player in her quest for revenge . . . You know. Typical relationship stuff."

"If only I could be a fly on the wall right now." I put on my coat and walk out into the restaurant, where Brynn is taking a customer's order. Paisley is behind the bar. I wave a silent good-bye to them both and push through the door into the cold Colorado night.

Snowflakes fall from the sky, dusting the sidewalks so they look like they're covered in glitter. Couples cuddled together pass by me, groups of friends bounce on their toes, pulling their jackets tight around them, waiting for the train to arrive. I keep my pace nice and slow while I gossip with Naomi on my walk to Gavin's condo.

"I know. I bet she broke up with him the minute he told her. It was obvious to everyone around them she didn't really like him. If he didn't treat you like dirt, I'd feel bad for him. But as it is, I'm laughing my ass off at his dumb self."

See why we're best friends?

"That's what I said!" I yell and startle the guy with huge ear gauges and no coat smoking outside a tattoo shop. "Sorry!" I say right away when he narrows his eyes at me. I've had enough incidents while I'm walking alone to last a lifetime.

"I wonder if Madison is still going to try to stay."

"Who knows? Ideally the Snow Bitch would return to her ice castle."

"One can hope," Naomi says as I round the corner onto Gavin's street. I spot his building easily not only because it's his house, but because he keeps it lit like a Christmas tree when he knows I'm coming. Tonight though, there's a car I don't recognize parked in the driveway, and after my conversation with Nay, I have a sinking feeling I know exactly who it belongs to.

"Ummm . . . Nay? Madison wouldn't happen to drive a new white Range Rover, would she?"

"Yeah, I think she does. Why?"

"Because it's parked in Gavin's driveway right now."

"Oh shit," she breathes out. "I guess that answers our question about her relationship with Chris."

"Yep, and I think she's throwing her Hail Mary right now. I'll call you tomorrow and fill you in." I end the call and pick up my pace before Nay is even able to reply. Not because I'm worried Gavin will fall for it; no, not at all. I'm worried I'll miss Madison's face when she gets shot down . . . again.

I test the door when I get there to see if I need to get my key, but it opens. I walk in and close the door behind me as quietly as possible so I don't interrupt the voices coming from the living room. I slowly make my way toward them, but I stop just outside the wall and peek my head around.

I wished to be a fly on the wall and I have a feeling this is the closest I will ever come.

"Gavin, you have to understand that I'm trying to protect you," Madison whines through her crocodile tears. "You aren't seeing the real Marlee Harper. She's fooling you."

Really? She's back to this? All of the time she spent with Chris and she couldn't come up with anything better than the "Marlee is a cheater" act? Not to mention, I don't know why people keep insulting Gavin. Do they think basically calling him stupid is going to sway him to see their (completely fabricated, covered in horse crap) way?

"Madison," Gavin says. For once I'm able to decipher the one-name response.

"I'm not lying to you. Why do you think Courtney hated her so much? If you would open your eyes, you would see everything so clearly."

"Courtney didn't like Marlee because Courtney's a bitch, which, with my open eyes, I'm figuring might be the same reason you two became instant friends."

Burn.

Madison's back is toward me, but Gavin's windows are like perfect mirrors, and I can see the way her jaw drops open perfectly. I'm so glad I ran that last block. My blistered feet protested, but look at the payoff.

"Listen, Madison. I agreed to listen to you out of respect for your family and the fact that I've known you for so long. I wasn't going to mention how you tried to bring my sister into your bitch-fight. I wasn't going to say how low it was of you to try and get to Marlee by sleeping with one of my teammates. I was prepared to be the bigger person and let us go amicably our separate ways." His face is like stone as he delivers his words, and even though I want to love watching Madison getting shut down, I find no joy in how badly Gavin hurts telling her this. "But then you come in my house and attack my girlfriend . . . again. You lie straight to my face because I know you, Madison, and you're anything but stupid. You know what you're telling me is bullshit but you keep on going, throwing every bit of friendship we've ever had in my face. Spitting on our history. For what? What's Marlee ever done to you that's so bad you're willing to throw our friendship away?"

"Because she isn't supposed to have you!" She stomps her feet and screams so loud, the glass vase Gavin fills with flowers for me every Saturday rattles on the counter. "I am! I've been with you every step of the way, and then she weasels her way right into the spot I was born for! You love me, you just won't let yourself feel it!"

Gavin stands there stunned.

"Feel it!" she repeats. I watch in horror as she grabs the back of his head and pulls him in for a kiss. But before her mouth reaches his, he pushes her away and moves to the other side of the room.

#UnrequitedLoveFor400Alex #HowAboutThingsISawComingFromAMileAwayFor1000

God. I love being right.

The only sound coming out of the living room is her harsh breathing. Gavin watches her and all of the heat he had has disappeared. His eyes have gone soft and his previously ramrod straight back hunches over.

"I don't love you, Madison. I love Marlee." His voice is so gentle, it's like he's talking to a scared, injured animal.

In a way, he is.

A wounded snake in the grass.

#ZeroCompassionZeroGuilt

"But . . . Gavin, please." Her voice breaks, and even though I can't see them in the window now, her thick voice does nothing to mask the tears I'm sure are falling.

"No, Madison. You were one of my best friends, but you ruined that." He walks to her and pulls her into a hug. "Maybe one day I'll forgive you, but that's not today. Hopefully this will be the wake-up call you need for you to get your act together. You can't treat people the way you've treated Marlee the last few months. You're better than that."

She might say something in response, but it's muffled into Gavin's shirt and the sound of her sniffles—which, side note, is such an unpleasant sound. Just sucking your snot back in. Gross. Gavin doesn't seem to mind though, but Gavin's also a saint, so he doesn't count.

I can't look away from the scene playing out in front of me. I know this is the last time Madison is going to come in between us, and even though I'm being a total creeper, hiding in the shadows, this is closure for me too. Relief courses through my system and a realization comes over me. I had been carrying around stress waiting for the next dirty trick Madison was going to pull. Having her gone, I feel like I'm floating.

When I peek around the corner again, Madison is still crying, and I know what's coming next. Even though I've been invading their privacy for the last ten minutes or so, I quietly retreat to Gavin's bedroom and let them have these last moments together without me.

I'm lying in Gavin's bed, trying to focus on my book instead of sneaking back downstairs to listen again, when Gavin walks in.

"Hey." I sit up and put my glasses and book on the nightstand. "You okay?"

"I'm fine." He collapses on the bed and rolls over until his head is in my lap. "Glad it's over."

"I bet. It looked rough." He's grown his hair since the end of the season, and I pull it out of the man-bun on the top of his head so I can sift my fingers through it while we talk.

"How much did you see?"

"Enough to know she was still trying to make me look bad and to know you still aren't having any of it . . . also that she loves you." I cringe. Listening in the moment felt fine, admitting to it now does not.

"Yeah, that sucked." His eyes close, and he nestles his head deeper into my lap. "When she called asking to come over, I really hoped she was going to make things right."

"It sucks when people we care about disappoint us, but maybe in a few years she'll come around and we can all be friends."

"Doubt it, but it's nice of you to say it."

Dammit. At least I tried?

"You know what else is nice of me?" I nudge his head off of my lap and climb on top of him. "What I'm about to do to you now."

I set forth unbuttoning his pants, removing his boxers, making sure the night ends on a high and it does . . . just not until well into the next morning.

Thirty-eight

FREE AGENCY HAS ARRIVED.

Now to put it in terms for people not in the sports business, it's the time that could either bring a career to new heights or end it. It's when a contract ends and other teams are allowed to court a player (#DuggarTerminology) or no teams call and a career is over. #MakeItOrBreakIt

In years past, it's been stressful. This is the first year I've actually kind of enjoyed it. Chris, obviously, always got an offer, but it was never like it's been with Gavin. Chris was never satisfied with the offer, but he knew he wasn't going to get better. With Gavin, it's been like a bidding war on speed. Donny has officially demolished any doubts I had about him. The contract offers he's been coming to us with have, quite literally, made me light-headed. Let's just say Gavin is firmly located in the two-comma club—eight, nearly nine digits.

He isn't, however, located next to me like I've grown accustomed to. Three days ago his mom called him complaining about how much she missed him. Usually during the off season, Gavin spends it entirely in Oyster Bay, but this year, I stole him. And being the amazing man/son/person he is, he flew out yesterday afternoon to surprise her for a couple of days. He wanted me to come, but considering we just returned from the last trip, I had to say no.

We FaceTimed last night before bed and again this morning. It doesn't come close to having him in bed with me, but you know . . . beggars can't be choosers and all that jazz. I've texted him a few times throughout the afternoon and still haven't heard back from him. I'm sure he's busy with his family, and I'm trying my hardest to avoid being clingy. It's just . . . I'm freaking clingy, all right! Not having him next to me when he could potentially receive a record-breaking contract offer has me batty.

"The waiter hasn't even taken our order and I'm already seconds away from throwing your phone away," Naomi says when I look at my notification-less screen . . . again. "Turn off your ringer, put it in your purse, and do not look at it again."

"You're right. No more phone." I toss it in my bag like she said and turn back to her. "Thanks for inviting me to lunch. I haven't been to your neck of the woods in a long time."

Naomi called this morning, not long after Gavin and I finished FaceTiming, and invited me to lunch at my favorite little café by my old house. They have the best sandwiches and a killer wine list, and Nay knows those are the only things I need in life. The sketchiest van could pull up next to me, the driver could be wearing a ski mask and have a voice disguiser, but if he said there was bread and wine in the back of the van? You better believe my ass would be climbing in. #WillRiskLifeForBooze&Carbs

"I'm glad you came. Gavin told Dre he was going out of town. I think he wanted us to keep an eye on you. Shut up," she says faster than I can even open my mouth. "I wanted to go to lunch with you anyway."

"You missed your football wifey? I'm not mad the season's over, but I miss you too."

"That's part of it," she says mysteriously, but the waiter comes to take our order before I can have her explain.

"Naomi! Marlee!" Josh, our favorite waiter, calls our names. "It's been way too long. I've missed your faces around here."

I'm sure he missed us getting tipsy and leaving outrageously large tips even more.

"You know I'm a waiter/bartender at HERS in Five Points. You get to come visit me next."

"I think everyone who follows Mustangs football knows you work at HERS."

Touché.

"How could I forget about my Denver's Most Hated status?" I'm still pissed at Madison for that shit.

"We all still love you here." Brown nose. "Do you ladies want your usual? Two bacon, caramelized onion, and brie grilled cheeses and a bottle of the shiraz?"

"Yes, please," I tell him at the same time Naomi says, "Not today."

"Then I'll give you two a moment to look over the menu." He smiles at us then heads to another table.

"You're getting adventurous on me?"

"You could say that . . ."

"So are you switching the wine, food, or both?"

"Both."

"Then I'll order the shiraz, but you do know I'm going to steal a sip of whichever one you decide to try." I grab the wine list off of the table and try to find another one I want to have.

"I'm not having wine." Those foreign words snap my attention back to her in an instant. "And I can't have brie either."

Oh.

My.

God.

"If you aren't about to tell me you're pregnant, there's a ninety-nine percent chance I might never speak to you again."

I have been hounding her about having a baby since I met her. Not only are she and Dre the most beautiful couple and it would be a crime against humanity not to bless us with a baby sharing their genes, but they're the best people who would make the best parents. But like so many stories, when they began trying to get pregnant about two years ago, they couldn't. She puts on a strong face, but I know how hard this has been on her.

"It's a good thing I'm telling you I'm pregnant then."

And I scream. In the middle of a cute little café filled with snooty women who take tennis lessons and lunch, I leap out of my seat, and I scream.

"Naomi! You're going to be a mom!" I pull her into a hug. "I call dibs on godmother, and I'm throwing the shower!"

Some people may say it's in bad taste to call dibs on these things. But screw them. That's why I'm not their friend. If there's one thing I love more than carbs and wine, it's parties and babies. My best friend's baby? You better believe I'm calling that shit early.

"I knew you would call it." When I can barely hear her, I realize I'm hugging her so tight, I'm accidentally smothering her in my bosoms. "Thank you," she says on a deep breath when I release her. "I knew you would call it, which is why Dre and I have already appointed you godmother."

"Oh my god!" I hug her again, still screaming. Screw the other patrons. #WhoGonnaCheckMeBoo "This is the best day ever! Hurry up and order. We have a mall to hit and maternity clothes and gender neutral baby clothes to buy."

IT TOOK SOME convincing, but after Naomi slipped on her first pair of maternity jeans, she was all in.

"I'm so buying some of those leggings," I tell her from my seat outside of the dressing room. "I'm going to put them on and drag Gavin up to Black Hawk with me. We will gamble, drink the free drinks they bring you, and eat at buffets all day and I'll be comfortable as fuck. Where do you think I can find a sequined visor and matching fanny pack?"

"You do know we are in public and other people can hear you, right?" She walks out and does a little spin in the cutest emerald shift dress I've ever seen. Unbeknownst to me, probably because I've never shopped for maternity clothes before, they have a fake little belly you can strap on for women who aren't showing yet but want to buy clothes. If it's any indication of what Nay will look like pregnant, it's going to be unfair to the rest of the women (aka me) who are destined to spread *everywhere* while pregnant. "What do you think?"

"It's amazing. You're going to be the most chic pregnant woman ever. But since when did maternity clothes get this cute? I thought you were supposed to be in muumuus and jeans that made your ass look terrible."

"Smart people probably still wear those because they don't want to spend two hundred dollars on a dress they will only wear for nine months." She looks in the mirror and smooths the dress over her cotton-filled bump. "But I'm not smart. I'm totally buying this."

"As you should. Dre isn't a baller for nothing. You're having his baby! This gives you unlimited access to the credit cards." #MarleeLogic

"Agreed." #NaomiLogicToo. "Take a pic. I want to send it to Dre."

She hands me her phone and I snap about a thousand pictures of her in various poses before she goes back to her maternity wardrobe search.

I sink back into the chair while I'm waiting for her to show off her next outfit and look at my phone for the first time since I put it away at the restaurant. When I see the little notifications showing three missed calls and a new text from Gavin, a giddy thrill shoots through my body.

> I've got news. Call me when you can.

"Nay, do you mind if I go call Gavin back real fast?"

"Of course not." She walks out in the black, long-sleeved version of the dress before, holding her phone toward me. "One more first . . ." She stops talking when her phone chimes in her hand at the same time mine vibrates in mine.

Strange.

Her eyes go wide, and her face loses some of its color.

"Are you okay?" I toss my phone onto the seat and grab her bottle of water from the dressing room. "Here, have some water."

"Um. Mars?" Her voice is quiet, and she shifts from one foot to the other, something she always does when she's nervous. "Did your phone go off too?"

"Yeah . . ." I do not like where this is heading. "Why?"

"Look at it." She's watching me so closely, I'm not sure she's even blinked.

I do as she says. There's an ESPN notification on my screen. My sweaty, shaking hands make it so I have to try more than a few times before I'm able to enter my password correctly. And when I do, I wish I hadn't. I read and reread the headline until I know I'm not reading it wrong. No. In my hand, there's a picture of my boyfriend, the smile I've grown to love. The eyes I've told my secrets to are staring right back at me under a headline announcing his new contract.

GAVIN POPE SIGNS RECORD-SETTING, SIX-YEAR CONTRACT
WITH NEW YORK GIANTS

He lied.

He didn't go to New York to see his mom. He went to sign a contract for a team on the other side of the country after telling me for weeks he was staying here.

New York.

Not Denver.

Not me.

#PersonalFoul

Thirty-nine

I WAS SO BUSY RUNNING THE LAST THREE OR FOUR WEEKS OF MY relationship through my head, I'm not a hundred percent clear on how I got home. I think Naomi drove me back to my place after we left the maternity store so I wouldn't have to deal with my world crashing down and an overly chatty Uber driver during rush hour.

Now, numb on my Ikea couch, staring at my ceiling and ignoring the sports commentators on my TV, I'm trying to think of any point where he might have mentioned playing for New York. I can't think of a single time. I remember Donny telling us they might be interested, but Gavin shut it down so quickly, I never thought twice.

Stupid.

He has a home in New York. Family, friends, history.

Why wouldn't he want to go back if he had the opportunity?

The broken, crushed, and betrayed part of me is screaming, *Because of me! He wouldn't want to go back because of me!* The cynical, jaded part I've become so accustomed to after years with Chris, however, is feeling resolved. *He's a quarterback in the*

NFL. What did you really expect? You know athletes. What's the definition of insanity, Marlee? You're slipping.

I am.

It was stupid of me to expect something different.

Why would I think my measly marketing job at HERS would hold the same weight as a person who is offered 130 million dollars? I know I shouldn't be mad at him. I mean, what person in their right mind would say no to that kind of money?

My problem is he hid it from me. He left for New York knowing what the outcome was going to be and he didn't tell me. Lies by omission are still lies.

And he knows.

He. Knows.

After the way things ended with Chris, sneaking and lying are absolute deal breakers. So either he didn't think I deserved to know, he didn't want me to know, or he didn't think of me at all.

I thought we were partners. Yes, it's a new relationship, but I thought we were headed someplace. I *ass*umed we were on the same page.

Wrong yet again.

I turned off my phone after I read the ESPN alert and promptly called Brynn to let her know I need an evening to wallow in self-pity before I can go to work. I thought it was a good call. I haven't cried, but I know if my dad calls asking questions or Gavin sends me a text, I will lose it. And I hate losing it.

When I feel like I have no control over anything around me, it's very important for me to keep my emotions in check. Like each tear will water and sprout drama. Not showing emotion lets me keep the power. I refuse to give people the satisfaction of knowing they upset me.

I never thought I would have to shield myself from Gavin. But hey. What do I really know anyway? Apparently nothing.

I'M LYING ON my couch, half drunk, half sugar high, and possibly infected with salmonella from the amount of raw cookie dough I've consumed, when Gavin uses the key to my apartment that I gave him.

Shit.

"Are you kidding me right now, Marlee? What's wrong with you? Why is your phone off? I've been trying to call you for hours."

I was planning on the silent treatment, but after he barges into my home acting like he's the one who's been wronged, I think, *Eh. What the hell. Let's set this shit on fire.*

"Wow! Look who it is, ladies and gentlemen." I stand up and start clapping. "The man of the hour. The king of *New York*, Gavin Pope. Setting records and getting paid, baby!"

I'll fully admit to being on the excessive side of dramatic, but what can I say? When I commit, I fucking commit.

"What the hell, Marlee?" He flinches slightly, and his eyebrows furrow. "What's your problem? I thought you'd be happy for me."

Oh this mother-effer.

"I'm thrilled for you, Gavin. Why wouldn't I be? My boyfriend got the contract of the century. He's going to be moving across the country. He's been lying to my face for the last month." The pounding in my head and my chest have synchronized and I'm shaking so badly, I have to sit down before my legs give in and I fall to the ground. "I'm fuckin' peachy."

"That's why you're acting like this?" he asks incredulously. "You think I lied to you?"

"There's no think to it, Gavin. You've been telling me since the end of the season you were coming back to the Mustangs. Today you signed a contract with New York. Lies."

"I didn't lie. I was trying to surprise you!" He's raking his hands through his hair and he's redder than I've ever seen him.

"Surprise me with what, exactly?"

"With New York! You were just telling me you wanted to move there and open your own business! Saying how you loved my house . . . my family. I thought you'd be happy to get away from Chris and all the bullshit that's tainted our lives since I got here."

"You can't be serious." I stare at him wide-eyed, and if I wasn't so pissed off, I'd laugh. "Gavin! We were talking about a vacation when I said that, not a freaking relocation! What about my family? My job! You want me to up and leave all of that without you even talking to me about it?"

"We'll figure it out. New York will be great for your career. I even called my real estate agent out there, she's already trying to find you a spot for your storefront." He starts pacing, his long legs making quick work of crossing my tiny space. "Come on, Marlee. Not only is this going to be good for you, this is the biggest deal of my entire life. Is it too much to expect my girlfriend to answer her phone or return a text?"

"IS IT TOO MUCH TO EXPECT MY FUCKING BOY-FRIEND TO TELL ME HE'S MOVING ACROSS THE COUN-TRY!" Dammit. He made me lose it. "Too much for you to tell me everything we've planned for the last month is total bullshit? Not to assume that I'll follow you across the country like some puppy? That I don't find out about the biggest deal of your life from the stupid ESPN app in a maternity store dressing room? Is that too hard for you?"

All of the color in his face drains and I think I've finally hit my mark when he starts to stutter a response. "Wh-what? Y-y-you? Maternity? You're pregnant?"

"For fuck's sake." I roll my eyes to the heavens. "No, I'm not pregnant. Naomi is."

"Oh thank god." He exhales and pulls out one of the stools from my kitchen table.

"Nice, Gavin. Really freaking nice." For some reason I can't explain, his relief at learning I'm not pregnant stings almost as much as the lies.

Almost.

"What? You want to be pregnant?"

"No, but we aren't talking about that now." I'm not going there. He will not see the hurt. Anger? Fine. Sadness and hurt? #AllTheNope

"Then what are we talking about? This is ridiculous. I got the contract I've been waiting my entire life to get and I get to celebrate that with you. I'm sorry you found out the way you did, but this is a good thing."

"Get out!" I rise to my feet again, my legs now feeling sturdy while it's my mind that's shaky. "I'm not doing this with you right now. You lied to me! You know how I feel about that."

The telltale sting of tears is building behind my eyes, but I'll be damned if I let them fall.

"You're always comparing me to Chris," he says quietly. "Always waiting for me to mess up."

"I didn't have to wait too long, did I?"

As soon as the words slip out of my mouth, I regret them. When I'm angry, I tend to go for the jugular with no regard as to what may come. And by the giant step back Gavin takes, I think this is one of those times.

"I guess you didn't." He rubs the back of his neck and turns toward my door. "I'm gonna get out of here for now and let the dust settle for a bit. But this isn't over, not by a long shot. I'll call you later."

"Yup." I fold my arms across my chest. Whether I'm trying to comfort myself or prevent them from reaching out toward Gavin, I'm not sure. "Bye."

"Bye, Marlee," he says to the door, not even giving me the common courtesy to look at me before he walks away.

Fine by me.

Except . . . when the door slams shut behind him, the tears I've been fighting so hard to keep away finally fall. I lean against the door, listening as his heavy footsteps fade away, praying he will stop and come back to me.

Instead, I hear the stairwell door slam shut.

I fall to the ground, letting the soul-wrenching sobs take over my body, allowing the noises that don't even sound human escape.

And when I'm all cried out, I know what I need to do to protect myself.

Forty

WE DON'T TALK AGAIN FOR THE REST OF THE DAY.

Or the next day.

Or the day after that.

I guess the stubborn qualities we both possess aren't always a good thing.

I know he feels like I'm in the wrong, Mrs. Pope tells me so when she calls me begging me to go over to his place and work things out. Being the mature woman I am, I refuse and tell her to tell him he's the one who should be apologizing.

He doesn't apologize, and I don't hear from his mom again.

We play this game with each other for a week before he reaches out, asking to meet at Fresh before I go to work. I agree. I might be mad, but I miss him too. My stupid heart makes things so much more difficult than my brain prefers. Shamelessly, I wake up an hour early, primping and curling, adding an extra swipe of mascara, like he'd notice and drop to his knees in an apology.

I arrive at Fresh a few minutes early so I can order my own coffee. Don't ask why it feels so important to not let him spend the four dollars on my vanilla latte. It just is. Maybe even more important now knowing he's the highest paid athlete in the NFL.

I've fallen into the trap already. I know how easy it is to get complacent. Coffee turns into dinner, dinner turns into a new pair of shoes, shoes stay in his huge closet and before I know what's happened, I'm shacked up with some football player, dependent and back to square one.

When they hand me my latte, Gavin still isn't there, so I find an open table tucked against the exposed brick wall in the back. I pull out one of the clear acrylic chairs that I always lie and say are comfortable because I think they're cute, but in reality it's like sitting on the floor.

I wait for twenty minutes before I start to think I might have been stood up. Gavin is so punctual, it's annoying. So being late isn't alarming, it's a slap in the face.

I'm gathering my empty coffee cup and pushing away from the table when the energy in the place changes. The patrons who were sitting quiet moments ago are now doing a pretty crappy job at whispering loudly. Movements become more hurried. I look at the couple across from me and follow their eyes toward to door. And there, looking his normal, gorgeous self, is Gavin.

His eyes meet mine moments after I notice him. A big, goofy grin appears on his face. When he starts to walk toward me, his chin dimple that's normally concealed with his beard is just noticeable under his scruff. I can't stop the way my thighs squeeze together. I guess my heart's not the only part of me that's a traitor.

And dammit if being in his presence doesn't put a chip in my already weakened armor.

"Hey," he calls out and draws the attention of everyone my way. So much for my nice, quiet, semi-private table in the back. "Sorry I'm running late."

"Not a problem," I lie.

"I'm going to grab a coffee for myself. Do you want anything?"

"No, thank you." I wave my empty cup at him. "I'm good."

"Be right back then." He leans in the way I grew so used to during our time together and hesitantly touches his lips to mine. "I've missed doing that. You look gorgeous."

"Extra mascara." A peck on the lips. All it took for me to revert into my say-anything-turn-to-mush self was one little peck on the lips.

And when his eyes crinkle at the corners and his blue eyes turn liquid, I'm tempted to say screw coffee . . . screw me. It's on the tip on my tongue, but my brain kicks back in and I manage to grab the last bit of self-restraint as it slips through my fingers and hold on for dear life.

You will not have sex with him. You will not have sex with him. You will NOT have sex with him.

I chant the mantra in my head the entire time he's getting coffee. My mom always made me write my spelling words a billion times so I wouldn't forget them. She always said, "Repetition is the key to mastery." Hopefully it works in this case as well.

He sits in the chair across from me and takes a deep sip of his large coffee, which is very unlike him. Usually he orders a medium coffee, sometimes small. Never large. It makes me take notice of other things about him. Like the way his hair is long, even for him. Or the dark circles surrounding his bloodshot eyes. Even his outfit, which is really freaking hot, is wrinkled and worn. It's a look I remember well from the long, frequent nights Chris spent partying.

"Did you just get here?"

"Um . . . yeah?"

"No." I shake my head, trying to find the right words. "I mean, did you just get here from being out all night?"

"Oh. Yeah." He shrugs like it's no big deal. "I went out with TK and a few of the rookies. The young ones know how to party."

What an asshole. We see each other for the first time in a week. I come in early after a morning spent finding the perfect outfit and making sure I looked my best and he comes in late, wearing the clothes from last night, and possibly still drunk.

Is he insane?

Or is he just like every other football player with an overinflated ego and no regard for others?

"Seriously, Gavin?" I try to tamp down the irritation currently threatening to blow all over my favorite coffee shop. "We haven't talked in how long? Then the first time we do, which, in case you forgot, was your idea, you can't even go home and shower first?"

"I'm not here to fight with you." His bullshit attempt to calm me only pisses me off more—I'm not the drunk, late one! I don't get the lecture here, he does!

"Neither am I. I thought maybe showing up on time, dressed and showered would have tipped you off to that point." I close my eyes, draw in a deep breath, and try to relax. "Why did you call then?"

"Our first mini-camp is this week. I'm going. I want my teammates to know me before training camp. I want them to understand I'm as dedicated as they are." He takes a sip of coffee and when he looks at me again, I don't see the tiredness anymore. I see hope and happiness.

I feel like an asshole. He's the new starting quarterback for his favorite childhood team. His family will be able to go to his games. He'll get to see his nephew as he grows. And all I've thought about is me.

"So I've been thinking about things." He leans forward, reaching a hand across the table, lacing our fingers together, and dammit if that minimal contact doesn't weaken my resolve. "I messed up."

"Yeah," I agree, tightening my grip on his hand. "You kinda did."

"I know how hard you've worked to get HERS going and how much you love your apartment. I want to take your stress away, not add to it, and you finding out about New York the way you did was fucked up."

Wow.

I was hopeful, but I was not expecting an apology.

"I really appreciate that, thank you."

"I've been trying to figure out how to make this move work best for both of us," he says. "This last week I talked to Brynn and your parents to try and figure things out."

Wait.

Quarterback say what?

"Work shouldn't be too hard. Brynn said she'll give you a recommendation letter and whatever you need for work. I even had her make a list of good potential matches in Jersey and New York. Your parents said they'll help you pack and can store whatever you don't want to take in their basement. And get this." His smile grows and I can tell that this terrible plan is about to get even worse. "I called your landlord to see about subletting and he said he didn't have a problem with it as long you give him an extra deposit, which I dropped off to him last night. So you can still keep your apartment."

Gavin looks so happy and proud of himself across from me, I almost feel guilty for the rage rushing through my veins. I mean, he called my landlord? I would trade in all of my wine for the opportunity to see what is going on inside that brain of his. And also, in what world is it okay for my landlord to talk to someone not on my lease about my living situation? There are so many things wrong here, I don't even know where to begin.

"What are you talking about, Gavin?" The words come out so syrupy sweet, I don't even know who I am.

"We can stay in the Oyster Bay house for the summer, but I'm thinking we should find a place in Hoboken for the season so we don't have to deal with tunnel traffic." He puts his hands up in surrender, white teeth still on display. "Don't worry, I haven't even glanced at places. I want you to be there to pick the house out with me."

"Oh my god. Gavin." I cut him off before he can talk any further. "Let's go back to my place to finish this conversation."

I've been in the paper enough in the past few months to know I don't want to be again. And if I say what I want to right now, I have a feeling I'll be on YouTube and maybe ESPN as well.

No thank you.

"That's a good idea. We can hammer out the rest of the details and then go grab some boxes. Brynn said she could come over later to help too."

"Wow." I smile at him but I know it doesn't reach my eyes. "You just thought of everything. Called all my friends, my family, just not me. Nice."

My back is so straight, it feels like somebody shoved a metal rod up my spine, and despite the coffee I drank and my thick, fuzzy sweater I put on, I'm shivering.

Or maybe I'm shaking indoors. I can't really differentiate between the two at the moment.

"I figured if I could tie up loose ends, it would help. I know how stressed you get, but you're gonna love living on the East Coast. Promise." He looks so young and innocent without his beard, so sweet and earnest, I almost say thank you.

But then I remember what he's done. How he's crossed about every single line I've drawn. How disrespectful he is for going behind my back.

How manipulative.

So I don't thank him. Instead, gathering what's left of my little patience, I slowly stand, throw my cup away, and make my way to the front door. I don't look behind me or ask if Gavin's coming along. I know he is.

"Thanks, Yaya!" I call to my favorite barista before I hit the street.

"Welcome, Marlee. See you tomorrow?"

"You know it," I say at the same time Gavin's loud, powerful voice rings out behind me declaring, "Nope. She'll be in New York tomorrow."

Oh yeah.

We have a lot to discuss, and I have a very bad feeling it won't end well at all.

Forty-one

SINCE LOSING HONEY-BLOSSOM, I'VE REALLY GROWN TO APPRECI-
ate the quiet walks to and from work. But not right now.

Walking to my apartment with Gavin is anything but comfortable. It may be March, but spring is still nowhere to be seen.
Neither of us makes an effort to break the silence between us, only
the sounds of cars as they pass keep me grounded to reality.

We walk up the stairs, Gavin trailing close behind me, and I
unlock my apartment door like I've done with him so many times
before. I have been in a Gavin-induced slump that resulted in lots
of takeout and minimal cleaning. Thankfully, after we decided on
coffee, I straightened up my place just in case he decided to come
over. And by cleaning, I mean I shoved everything in the closet.

"It smells good in here. Did you get some new candles?"

"Yeah, I picked up a few the other day." Last night. I figured
they were my best chance at disguising the lingering scent of
heartbreak and betrayal.

"You'll definitely have to bring those with us."

Ughhhhh. I guess we're doing this now. I was hoping for a

little mindless chatter, maybe even some more awkward silence. Anything but this.

"You keep saying this stuff like we've made the decision to leave, but we haven't. I haven't even talked to you in a week. Why are you all of a sudden acting like nothing happened?" Despite the giant knots in my stomach and the pounding in my head, my voice is calm and even.

"Because this is stupid, Marlee. I love you, you love me. I get I should've told you about New York, but I thought you'd be happy to start our life together. I wanted to surprise you. Can we stop being stubborn now and move on?"

Oh sweet baby Jesus. I'm not sure if I'm more pissed he's brushing off my feelings about this or if I'm more stunned that he could really be this oblivious.

"I'm not being stubborn, Gavin. And I'm for damn sure and not just acting mad for the sake of being mad. Do you hear yourself?"

"Then why are you mad? Please, enlighten me, because I don't get it. There are more opportunities than you can imagine in New York. Marketing jobs? Everywhere. My family you said you loved will be right down the street. And me, your boyfriend, got the contract of the century! How is there anything wrong with any of that? You're being kind of irrational right now."

Oh no the fuck he did not.

It's not what he's saying that causes me to snap, it's the way he's saying it. Like I couldn't possibly have any merit behind my argument, like I'm overreacting. Like I'm crazy.

"I don't want to leave my job! I don't want to leave my family! Did you ever think of that? Did you ever think, 'Hey, Gavin, maybe Marlee has a life outside of you and you should ask her opinion before expecting her to jump like a freaking dog'? Did you? Even once think my opinion mattered at all?" I take a deep breath and close my eyes. "I can't believe you have such little respect for me. That you think so little of what I do that you'd just expect me to walk away from it all without a blink of an eye. What did you think was going to happen? I'd move, get pregnant, and give up my career like your sister and mom to raise babies? That's not what I want!"

I sit down on my couch, cradling my forehead in my hands and dragging them through my hair. I focus on the pattern of my rug, willing myself to hold it together for just a little bit longer. I'm worried if I look at him I'll either break down or give in and neither of those are acceptable.

"It's great that you have the career you want and the contract everyone around you envies. But could you just step outside of your self-absorbed bubble for one second and think about me? Think that I've spent my entire adult life being dragged around by Chris, pushed into the shadows, my dreams put on hold because he had the 'real' career?" I stand on shaky legs and cross the room to where he's standing. I wrap my arms around his waist, praying he will feel how desperate I am for him to understand. My throat starts to clog up and the sting behind my eyes kicks in. *Oh no, Marlee. You hold your shit together. You will not start to cry right now.* "Do you understand how worthless you've made me feel this past week? Today?"

He closes his arms around me and kisses the top of my head.

"That's not what I meant to do. You know how much I care about you. How much I respect how hard you work," he whispers above me.

"How do I know that?" The volume falls from my voice. I pull back just enough to look him in the eyes, to let him see my eyes glossed over with tears. "You went behind my back to talk to my employer, to my family. You told them I'd be leaving without so much as a text message to me to see if I wanted to."

"I know you're mad, but I—" He trails a finger down my cheek.

"I'm not mad." I put my hand over his, stopping him from going any farther. "I'm hurt, and I'm disappointed that the man I love and respect has shown such disregard for me and my feelings."

"Mars . . ." He stops and for the first time ever, I see his eyes shimmer with tears. No tears fall, but it's enough to make me feel like I've taken a punch to the gut, to make me want to apologize.

But I don't.

I don't say anything. I let the silence fill the room. It's funny, you know, when saying nothing says everything.

As much as I want to fix things and make him feel better, I won't do it. I refuse. If we are going to get over this, I need him to fully grasp and understand how badly he screwed up. And if I give in, not only will I never forgive myself, I won't forgive him either.

"So what are we going to do?" He steps away from me, and I mourn the loss of his touch right away.

"We aren't going to do anything." I let my tears fall. If this is the end, I want him to know how much this meant to me. I'm not the same Marlee I was when I left Chris. The only person I have to be strong for is me and sometimes, being strong is letting it all out. "I'm going to get ready for work and you're leaving for New York."

"I don't want to leave without you." He walks to me, but this time, I'm the one who pulls away. "Marlee, come with me. See how things could be. Spend a few more days with me."

"I can't," I say, still backing away. "I know how things will be. It will be amazing, and we'll fall deeper in love with each other, and I might even stay." I hold up my hands to prevent him from coming any closer. "And then who knows? Maybe I'll get to stay in a big, lovely house while my big, strong boyfriend goes off to work and brings home the big paychecks so I can go to lunch and buy handbags and things will be different than they were with Chris. But we both know that won't happen."

"I'm not telling you to stay home or quit work." He's louder than he's been all day. His face turns red, and he drops his head. "I just want you to try." He looks back to me and the tears he's been holding back are falling down his face. "Please."

It's like I've been stabbed in the chest. I stumble back until I feel my couch behind my legs. I collapse onto the couch, trying to catch my breath, grabbing my chest, willing the pain to fade. The last thing I want to do is hurt Gavin.

"I can't come," I choke out between sobs. "Please don't ask me again, Gavin. Every time I tell you no, I can feel a piece of me breaking off, and I know if you keep asking, I will come." My body is shaking, and I can't make out Gavin's face through the tears clouding my vision. "Please, Gavin. Don't."

"I won't." His voice, calmer than mine, still holds the same broken edge, and I see his body slump. "I love you, Marlee. I'll be back."

I hear him walk out of the door and it slowly creaks as it closes behind him.

I don't even get up to lock the door. I just slump over on my couch, letting the tears fall until they run out and I fall asleep on my mascara-stained pillows.

Forty-two

THE ONLY THING MORE INFURIATING THAN A MAN IGNORING your wishes is a man doing exactly as you say when you come to find out, you're not quite sure you meant it.

#IMeantThatIMeantThatIDidntMeanIt #GotIt?

Gavin did as I asked.

He left.

He went to New York. Well, technically, he went to New Jersey. Not that I've been Googling him like a stalker or anything, but I've learned through random ventures on the internet that the Giants don't play or practice in New York, so the name is really misleading.

#FootballFunFacts

Back on subject. Not only did Gavin leave, he had a training camp so phenomenal, all the reporters were asking about the changes he's made. If it was his diet, if it was being back home, if it was the pressure of living up to his contract? What they didn't ask, but it was all I could think of, was how he got rid of his needy, whiny, pain-in-the-ass girlfriend.

Blah.

Why couldn't he have played like shit to make me feel better?

Even though I technically had the week off since Gavin stuck his nose where it didn't belong and talked to Brynn, I couldn't mope around in my apartment. The only thing worse than reading about him was sitting on top of the mascara stain on my couch and watching *Jeopardy!* by myself. The day of our fight, I showed up at work later than normal—looking like shit if the look of horror on Brynn's face was anything to go by. She didn't question my showing up or my swollen, red eyes. I think she expected it. Unlike Gavin, Brynn knows me. She had to know this was coming. She treated me with kid gloves and gently suggested I work on marketing in the back. Aka—don't scare away the customers.

It's sweet.

It only lasts for a few days though. Because real friends only let you mope for a maximum of seventy-two hours before they're contractually obligated to snap you out of it.

Luckily for me, my friend owns a bar and after closing one night, we take tequila shots and I lay it all out there.

Brynn throws back shots with me as I spill all of the details of the night, but she doesn't say anything. She doesn't need to, nothing she says will change the results. #AcceptanceIsTheFirstStep

My parents, on the other hand, were a completely different story. Because my mom had been secretly fretting about my emotional state since I broke up with Chris, she was calling me ten times a day since Gavin left. It was sweet at first, but after the hundredth time she told me she just knew I was jumping into things with Gavin too quickly and that I "needed to learn to love myself and be alone," I started ignoring her calls. Which meant I was also not going over for dinner, which meant I ate ice cream for dinner and have gained seven pounds on top of the fifteen I still want to lose. #CantStopLosing #ExceptWhenImGaining

But other than my avoidance of family and their misguided,

though well-meaning, advice and my toddler eating habits, I'm doing fine. I can walk down the street without crying and I can handle my responsibilities. And even though I write Gavin a thousand text messages, I never hit send.

Camp's during the weekdays, and he has weekends off, so by the time Friday rolls around, I'm checking all flights from New York to Denver and staring at the door to my apartment and HERS whenever I think he could be arriving. He said he was coming back. He would have to come back home.

Each week, I get my hopes up that this is the weekend he'll come home, but it never happens. One night I give in to reading up on the Giants.

I open their website and the first thing I'm met with is a freshly showered Gavin, smiling for cameras and reporters.

I watch the interview all night long.

I watch as he shoots his dimple-baring grin to reporters. I listen over and over again to him telling them he's never been happier, that he's home and never wants to leave. I rewind and replay and rewind and replay the part where he winks at the beautiful blonde asking him where he'll be staying during the short break in camp.

"I have a place in Oyster Bay." Wink.

Wink.

Wink.

I see the wink when I close my eyes, when I look to his empty side of the couch, when I walk past his condo too many times to be considered sane.

And after I stop thinking of the wink, I realize he told me and the rest of the world that he was going home. He just reminded me home for him isn't Denver, it's Oyster Bay.

While he's gone he sends a few texts, but they become shorter and more infrequent as time goes on. And my heart becomes hardened in a way I'm not sure I can ever recover from. The only good thing to come out of it is that the quality of my work at HERS goes way up. And I was already the shit, so I'm killing the game. To hell with modesty.

It isn't until I'm walking to the train a month after he left that Gavin texts me he's coming back to Denver and will see me later that night.

I wish I could say the giddy feeling I felt came flooding back, but it doesn't. Instead, it's the opposite. It pisses me off. It feels like a repeat of the last time he left. How does he know I'm not busy? Why, after everything we went through, is he still assuming I'll drop everything and run to him?

I send him back a quick text telling him I'm busy and ask to meet the next evening after I get off at HERS. I don't actually have plans, but that's beside the point. It's the principle, people!

"So, what are you going to say?" A barely showing, pregnant Naomi asks from the other end of the couch.

"I really have no idea. I have no idea where we are or where I want us to go." I take a sip of the virgin strawberry daiquiris I made us. "Part of me wants to forgive him and to go back to where we were, but I don't know if that's possible. I'm still pissed. Maybe even more so since he flew to the other side of the country and is only now coming back over a month later."

"I get that. It's hard to forgive somebody when you know they're sorry, it's damn near impossible to do it when they show no signs of remorse."

"Can I tell you something I haven't said out loud yet?" I ask her.

"Of course." She sets her glass and bag of tortilla chips down and gives me her full attention.

"I don't even think I'm mad at him anymore. I think I'm mad at myself. Chris screwed me up in a way that takes longer than a month to heal from. When Gavin said I always compared him to Chris, he wasn't wrong. I was offended at first because I was always thinking of how much better Gavin was, but looking back on it, I think I did it because I was waiting for Gavin to show me he was the same as Chris." I look at the floor, unable to hold eye contact any longer. "I lied when I said I was ready for a relationship. Yes, it was messed up how Gavin went about things, but if I was a normal, not severely damaged person, we could've worked through it. I'm not ready to see him because I've finally accepted that I can't be with anyone. Not until I'm content with myself."

"Damn. That's some deep shit," Naomi whispers. "How many episodes of *Oprah* have you watched since he left?"

"All I watch is OWN, and I'm catching up on her book club list. She's been my therapist," I admit.

"I can tell." She reaches for my hand and laces her fingers between mine. "As much as I want to tell you to just go back to him, I think you're right. You need time to be you. I think Gavin is a great guy, but there's a lot that comes with being with the NFL's golden boy. If you don't figure out who you are on your own, you're going to fade to black again."

"I see you watched that *Iyanla* too?"

"Girl, who are you kidding? Without her I'd be on *Snapped*. I love Dre, but there are days he drives me batshit crazy."

"Preachin' to the choir, sister." I grab the fancy remote Gavin programmed to go with the TV and turn on OWN.

What better way to spend my Friday than not drinking and crying on the couch?

#WhoHaveIBecome

I GO INTO HERS early the next morning.

I'm obsessing over the new promo we're working on, when there's a knock at the door. It's still early, almost ten o'clock, and HERS doesn't open for another hour, so I'm taken aback when I hear the tapping on the glass.

I figure Brynn forgot her key again, because she always forgets, but when the front door comes into view, a man I've never seen before is standing there with a few boxes stacked up behind him.

"May I help you?" I ask the guy who looks like every other hipster strolling through the neighborhood.

"I'm looking for a Marlee Harper," he says with zero enthusiasm whatsoever. "I have a delivery for her."

"I'm Marlee Harper." Without any further questions or proof of identification, he picks up one of the boxes behind him and asks to come in. I point him to my office in the back and make myself busy in the bar while he makes quick work of bringing the boxes in.

He walks out the front door and the only reason I know he's done is because I watch him pull out his phone and make a call while heading down the street.

So much for customer service I guess.

I walk back into my office to finish my work and become temporarily paralyzed.

Every inch of my desk—and Brynn's too—is covered in flowers. I don't even need a card to know who they're from. The flowers that have overwhelmed the office are the same flowers Gavin used to buy for me every Saturday—roses and peonies. My favorite.

I don't realize I didn't lock the door after hipster delivery guy left until I hear it open.

I don't look behind me as I call to Brynn. "Wait until you see the office."

"Do you like them? I figured I had a lot of Saturdays and apologies to make up for." But when she answers, it's not Brynn at all, it's Gavin.

I guess I know who the guy called now.

I turn to him so fast, I almost lose my balance. Then, taking him in in all of his beautiful Gavin glory for the first time in over a month, I almost fall over again.

"What are you doing here?" I ask instead of thanking him for the flowers like a person with manners would do.

"I missed you. You said you were working today, so I figured I would start begging for forgiveness early." His hands are in his pockets, and he looks nervous. I'm relieved to know I'm not alone in that feeling, but I feel guilty too. Because I know that he went through all of this trouble to get me flowers for nothing.

"Gavin, no. You don't need to beg for forgiveness."

"I do." He starts walking toward me. "I messed up. I was so excited about my contract that I didn't even think about what I expected you to walk away from without warning or time to think. Then I ran and didn't come back. I fucked up."

"Really, you don't." I look up to him as he comes into my space and struggle not to touch him. "We both messed up. You were right when I said I compared you to Chris. I overreacted, and I stole your happiness in one of the biggest moments of your life."

"You didn't. I missed you so much. This last month has been hell." He takes one more step toward me in an effort to wrap his arms around me, but before he can, I step back.

The way the smile falls from his face and his eyebrows scrunch together is like a punch to the gut. I know what I'm going to say is the right thing, but at the moment, it doesn't make me feel any better.

"Gavin, no." I meant for the words to come out strong and powerful, but instead they're a whisper. "I can't."

"What? You just said you aren't mad at me anymore."

"I'm not." I look around the room, trying to find the words to explain how I feel. "I'm not mad at you. I know you didn't mean to hurt me. I'm over that, truly. But I can't be with you."

There. I said it.

"What? Why?" He grabs my hand and that small touch makes me question myself.

"Listen." I take a deep breath and pull my hand out of his. He watches the movement and is staring at my hand as I start to talk. "If you would've come back the week you left, you would've found me on your front porch with my suitcase packed. But over this last month, I've realized I'm not ready to be in a relationship." My eyes start to water. "I'm a mess, Gavin. And as much as I love you, I can't give you what you deserve when part of me is still damaged from my last relationship."

"But I can help you."

"No. You can't fix me." I wipe the tears from my cheeks. "I've never been alone, Gavin. And as much as I wish I could figure it out with you by my side, I know I can't. Because you are amazing and you love me and you don't want to see me struggle, but I need it. I need to figure things out on my own. I need to fix myself without running to you or Chris or my parents. I have to do this by myself. If I don't, I'm going to end up being a person I hate, and I will resent you."

God.

I've never hated my mom being right more than I do at this very moment.

"I know how strong you are." He pulls me toward him despite my effort to pull away. "You don't have to prove it to me."

"I'm not proving it to you. I'm proving it to me."

I've been preparing for this since he told me he was coming, but nothing could've gotten me ready for the feel of his tears as they fall onto my face, or the way he lets his mouth kiss the path his tears travel.

I reach into his hair, feeling the silky locks against my fingertips. It's one of the things I've missed most, besides the feel of his rough beard on my face as we kiss, so I take that too.

I crush my lips to his, tasting both our tears as we try to tell each other through the kiss the things we can't manage to speak. He tells me to try. I tell him I can't. He apologizes for his mistakes. I apologize for it ending. And in the end, I thank him for loving me, even though I wasn't ready to be loved.

We stop kissing but don't pull away. Watching each other as we let our tears fall openly and freely, mourning together what could have been great, but just wasn't right.

When our tears have stopped and our breathing has calmed, I rest my arms around him, giving in to the feeling of his arms wrapping me tight one final time.

"I'm so sorry, Gavin," I whisper.

"Me too," he whispers into my hair. "You do this and when you're ready, come find me."

Then he slowly backs away and opens the door, never letting our eye contact drop, until my door closing in front of him leaves us no choice.

And he's gone.

Again.

For the last time.

Forty-three

Four Months Later

EATS & BEATS IS ONE OF THE MOST INFLUENTIAL AND REPUTABLE marketing firms in the country. They're responsible for all the major promotions for some of the most famous restaurants and nightclubs around the world.

And thanks to the kick-ass work Brynn and I did over the last six months, HERS is their newest client. Even better for me, they loved my work so much, they helped Brynn find a replacement for me and I am the newest member of the Eats & Beats team at their headquarters in New York.

"Hello, Miss Harper," my boss, Paul, calls to me as I make my way to my desk. "Figuring out the subway, I see."

"I sure am. Ten minutes early today." I do a little dance, thrilled to have finally conquered my commute from Jersey to Manhattan.

"I'm very impressed. Leslie was late every day for the first month when she started here."

"Hey!" Leslie shouts from the coffee machine. "I thought we

agreed never to speak of that again. Marlee is at least from a decent-sized city. I came from a town in Iowa with a thousand people and only four stoplights. It was a little overwhelming."

"Always excuses with that one," Paul whispers loud enough for her to hear.

It's only the end of my first week, but I could not love my new job any more. It makes every tear, every second of self-doubt, every second of loneliness worth it. This week has only reaffirmed what I knew was right four months ago when I let Gavin walk away.

I'm a better person now, and I'm crossing my fingers Gavin will be open to seeing it.

"You don't even need to bother starting your computer. I got an email this morning and we have a meeting with a new restaurant in Soho. Come on, Leslie, you're coming too." He throws his briefcase strap over his shoulder. "But we're taking a cab."

THE RESTAURANT WE go to is a new sushi place with an urban edge. It's not decorated in the calming colors I've come to expect with sushi places, not at all. This place has graffiti painted on the wall, neon lights shining around the room, and the craziest menu I've ever seen . . . and thanks to my job, tried.

After we got all our business out of the way, the owners insisted we stay for lunch. Something none of us objected to. I love sushi, but I'm also broke as fuck and will never reject a free lunch.

We're waiting for the chicken and maple rolls we ordered to arrive when my phone vibrates in my bag. Naomi had a doctor's appointment today and promised to call me after, so I excuse myself from the table to take the call.

When I step outside and look at the screen, I see a Colorado number I don't know. My mind shoots right to the worst-case scenario. Something went wrong at the appointment and Naomi is calling me from the hospital.

"Hello?" I answer.

"Marlee?" A deep voice I haven't heard in months comes from the other end. "It's Chris. How are you?"

Of all the people in the world? Chris?

"I'm well. How are you?" I step back against the building, avoiding all of the foot traffic around me.

"I'm all right." He sounds good. Like the Chris I used to know, not the stranger he became. "Listen, Marlee, I know this is going to seem random, but I've been thinking a lot about you lately."

"Chris." I try to stop him.

"No. Please, just let me say this."

Wow. Please? Big step.

"All right, but I'm at work, so this can't take long." I glance at my watch and set a mental timer.

"Thank you." I can hear him exhale a deep breath into the phone. "I've been thinking about the way I treated you. About the way things ended. I want to apologize. You deserved a lot more. You're the best, most true person I've ever had in my life."

#KnockMeOverWithAFeather

"I always knew it, but after being released from the Mustangs and not being picked up by any other teams, so many people have shown me their true colors. And I know if I hadn't treated you the way I did, you'd still be standing next to me."

"I would have. I didn't love you for football, Chris. I loved you for you," I say.

"I love you too, Marlee. I always have. It's why I'm calling. I want another chance."

I suck in a deep breath. "It's amazing to hear you say those words to me. It really is. But, Chris, I *loved* you. I will always have love for you and cherish some of our time together, but I've moved on. I'm not in love with you anymore."

It's weird having such a personal conversation in front of so many strangers. People walking past me, oblivious to what's going on in my life.

"It's still Gavin, isn't it?" He's not accusing me. It's like he's stating the obvious.

"No, Chris. It's me. I've changed. With or without Gavin, this is a decision for me." I open the door to peek back inside and see our food has arrived. "It was great to hear from you, and I wish you the best, but this is where we should end things."

"Yeah, okay," he says. "Bye, Marlee."

"Bye, Chris."

I end the call and walk back toward my new boss and coworker, feeling a lightness I never knew existed.

"BYE, MARLEE!" LESLIE calls to me as I head out at five o'clock.

"Bye, Leslie." I wave to her. "See you Monday."

I hop on the elevator and take it from the fifteenth floor of our Manhattan office building to the ground level. I push out of the revolving door and am immediately swept up in the crowds constantly filling the New York City sidewalks.

I still haven't adjusted to the humidity as it hits me like a wet slap in the face and my hair that I worked so hard on straightening early this morning instantly curls up. I don't wear my headphones while I walk to the train here. There's too much going on. The people talking on all sides of me, the street vendors yelling out the deals they have, the constant sounds of sirens and horns blaring, it's music in its own right. Maybe I'll tire of it one day, but not today.

The day after I arrived in New Jersey, I did nothing but ride the subway. I wanted to master it before my first day of work. And the last thing I wanted was to be late because I couldn't find my way. Now, only a week later, it's already feeling second nature. I mindlessly walk down the steps and into the terminal. I stand side by side with strangers who don't even look up before filing onto the train.

But today, instead of getting off at my normal exit, I take it for three more stops. I get off with the other passengers clothed in their red and blue gear and follow them until we approach the fields where the Giants are stretching on the field before their evening practice for training camp.

"Who cares about the rest of the team?" the woman behind me says loud enough for anyone to hear. "I just want to see Gavin Pope's ass in those pants. Yum-my."

She's not wrong about that. Nobody does a uniform justice like Gavin. I'm convinced if they did contracts based on asses alone, he'd still be the highest paid in the league.

Walking through the gates and fighting the crowd for a spot on the bleachers is another first for me. I've never had to do this. I've always been led to nice shaded seats with the rest of the family members. I've never had to put my game face on at training camp, but as I make my way to the one empty seat behind four guys without shirts and their stomachs painted, I think that might change too.

"I can't believe we spent that much money on that pretty fuck-boy. We could've gotten a quarterback who's just as good for half the price. He better not blow our season over some bitch like he did for the Mustangs."

Breathe, Marlee, breathe. There are four of them and one of you. Naomi and Lenny are back in Colorado. Do not start a fight.

"I know. Pope fucking sucks!" yells the guy next to him.

The people next to me roll their eyes and the people below them turn and glare, but nobody says anything.

Except me.

"Says the guys sitting in the bleachers covered in paint."

Dammit.

"What'd you just say?" the first loudmouth says. Incidentally, he's also the one with the biggest gut. Correlation? I'm not sure.

"I said you sure are doing a lot of talking from your spot on the bleachers. Last I heard, the people who really know the game are on the field."

If my intention was to fly under the radar, I'm failing miserably. Faces that were focused on the field are now turning toward me. People who wanted to say something to these jerks but didn't start clapping for me. The support would be lovely, but it just further angers the men I already pissed off.

"And you know so much? You're sitting on the bleachers too."

"Yes, I am. I'm sitting here trying to enjoy watching men who actually know the game play it, and instead I'm stuck next to Al Bundy and foot soldiers who think because they played football in high school they know everything there is to know."

I've used the Al Bundy reference before, but nothing is a more effective insult. As soon as the name comes out of my mouth, I win. I used Uncle Rico once, but I had to explain, which took away from the actual joke.

Like right now, Loudmouth is stuttering, trying to come up with a decent comeback, but looks like a fish out of water instead.

Mission accomplished.

"Well, well, well," a loud, frighteningly familiar voice calls from behind me. "Look at you, causing scenes across the country. I bet after that little show, nobody would know you aren't from here."

I turn around slowly, eyes closed the entire time, whispering useless prayers that I'm not going to see the face I know belongs to that voice. When I can't prolong it anymore, I count to three in my head and open my eyes.

"Donny." I try to sound excited, but instead it sounds like my stomach hurts. "How are you?"

For real, God? I know two people in this state and you sit one

behind me? I get that I don't go to church often, but this punish-
ment is excessive, harsh, and kind of cruel.

"I'm good. I got our boy . . . wait, sorry, got my boy back in
NYC, my commission was fuckin' out of this world, and I don't
ever have to step foot in that frozen tundra you call home."

"Good to see you haven't lost your way with words."

"After that fuckin' show you put on with those dickbags,
you're gonna say something about my language?"

Curse you, big mouth! I just had to say something.

"Whatever. They were being jerks, and I didn't curse. There
are kids around. Going two hours without dropping an f-bomb
wouldn't kill you."

"It might and I don't want to fuckin' test it."

I have no response for him this time. Sometimes, it's better to
say nothing. An idea I've heard many times before . . . from my
mother . . . but don't use often.

"Gavin know you're here?" Donny says a few minutes later. I
think he's physically incapable of silence. He's just so loud and the
name Gavin draws the attention of the people sitting next to us,
including loudmouth number one.

"Nope," I hope Donny will catch the hint and drop it.

"Why not? You fly all the way out here to visit and don't tell
him? When are you going back?"

"None of your business, Donny." I know I should probably
correct him and tell him I moved here, but I'm not sure which
sounds more stalkerish, flying across the country to watch your
ex's football practice or moving across the country to the state
you broke up with him for when he suggested it.

"Stick with me after practice, he'll be thrilled to see you."

I came to this practice with the notion of seeing Gavin from
afar. I thought maybe being in the same vicinity as him would
give me the courage to call him. Under no circumstances whatso-

ever did I think I would talk to him today. And the thought of it happening causes my palms to sweat.

"Um. No. That's okay. I was actually getting ready to head out. Early morning tomorrow, you know how that goes."

"You're leaving tomorrow and you're not gonna say hi?" Donny sounds kind of appalled, and I wasn't sure anything appalled Donny. But it's not my fault he's jumping to conclusions, and it's also not my duty to correct him. "And you just got here. I was sitting two rows up, I watched you sit down."

"Stalker," I mutter under my breath, desperate for any kind of focus change.

"Cut the bullshit, Marlee. Man up and say hi. What's the worst that could happen?"

He could act like he doesn't know me. Worse than that, he could acknowledge that he knows me and not be happy to see me. He could have another girlfriend waiting for him. I mean, I've been thinking about this for the last three weeks. I have about ninety worst-case scenarios running through my head. Of course, I don't tell Donny any of them.

"Nothing. I have to get going. I wanted to swing by since I was in town. I did, he looks like he's doing great, I'm leaving."

I turn back around on the bleacher to grab my bag and when I do, loudmouth number one is staring at me with an expression I know well. You'd think the smug "gotcha" look would seem different on a three-hundred-pound man than it did on Courtney and Madison, but it really doesn't.

"So that's why your panties were in a twist, huh, babe?"

My lip curls in disgust at hearing him call me by the same name Gavin always did.

"You're just pissed because I was talking about your boyfriend down there."

"Let's get this straight, *babe*. I wasn't mad. I was annoyed because I came to watch football, not listen to a no-talent loud-mouth bash the players he's going to spend every Sunday watching for the next four months. You don't sound like a badass when you insult them. You sound like a douchebag, and you were making my head hurt." Not waiting to hear what else he has to say or the smart-ass comment that's inevitably coming from Donny's mouth, I toss my purse over my shoulder and make my way off the bleachers.

"Glad to see you haven't lost your spunk, Marlee!" Donny yells louder than I've ever heard him before, which is saying something because he is always loud. And because whoever is running the big show from above has an obvious bone to pick with me, he does so at the exact moment the crowd goes quiet because of an injury on the field. So everyone, fans and players alike, turn their attention to me.

Even the quarterback with the remarkable ass.

He's wearing a red jersey so the other players know not to touch him, but it's like I'm a bull and he's just pulling all of my attention. His mom must have broken him down because the hair that I loved so much is gone. He's staring at me, bronze skin glistening with sweat, mouth open. We stand frozen, looking at each other for I don't know, ten seconds . . . an hour . . . before my brain finally signals to my feet and I get the hell out of there.

Welp, I think to myself as I sit down on the train and text Naomi only minutes later, that most definitely did not go according to plan.

Forty-four

I GO STRAIGHT TO MY APARTMENT, FULLY INTENT ON GORGING FOR the rest of the night on wine, junk food, and reality TV.

Unfortunately for me, however, I still haven't gone grocery shopping, and I don't have cable.

Typical.

But I do have a cell phone to order out and internet to download movies. And while I might not have ventured to the grocery store to buy essentials like bread and milk, I most definitely hit the liquor store around the corner and stocked up on wine. It's called priorities, people, and I'm not questioning mine.

The sweet, newlywed couple next door told me about an awesome Chinese place that delivers, and today might be the fourth time I've ordered in the last five days. But they're fast, affordable, and after an afternoon like the one I just had, that's really all I could ask for.

Only thirty minutes after I order, I hear a knock on my door. They must have had my order waiting today because this is the fastest they've ever gotten here.

"Hold on!" I call from my favorite spot on the couch and grab the cash from my purse. "You were fast today."

"You really need to use your peephole," Gavin says when I swing the door open.

What.

The.

Fuck.

"Wh-what are you doing here?" I barely manage to ask the question over the lump in my throat threatening to choke me.

"I saw you at practice today. Did you really think I wasn't going to look for you after that? Are you going to let me in or are we going to do this in the hallway?"

I open the door wider, stepping out of the way, silently inviting Gavin in.

"Donny told me you're flying back to Colorado tomorrow, so imagine my shock when I call Dre to find out where you're staying and he tells me you're living here now."

I add Dre to #TeamTraitor and make a mental note to call Naomi later to bitch about her husband.

"Just to be clear, I never told Donny I was leaving tomorrow. You know how he is. He assumed and I didn't correct him."

"Why were you at practice today, Marlee?" There's my Gavin, straight to the point.

"I wanted to see you." I just didn't want him to see me. But Gavin is in front of me, his large body filling my small space and if this is the result of him seeing me, I can't pretend I'm mad he did. "I got a job in the city, and I've been thinking of you. Thinking about what you said when you left."

"I didn't leave, Marlee. You pushed me away."

"I know I did. I was a mess." I take a step back to prevent myself from doing something stupid, like jumping his bones. "I needed to finish what I started at HERS. I needed to know I could carry my own weight in a relationship."

"I told you to come and find me." He closes the space I created. "Is that what you were doing? Were you coming to find me or were you preparing to run again?"

"I . . . I . . ."

Gavin puts a finger in front of my lips.

"Take your time, Marlee. Because your answer matters." He sounds as cool and collected as ever while I'm sweating bullets and worried I'm going to vomit all over his white sneakers.

I gather all the wits I have left, which admittedly, aren't many, and take a deep breath before I answer.

"I was coming to find you." I clasp my hands together. Even though he came here, I'm terrified he's going to turn and walk away.

"Are you sure, Marlee? How do I know you're not going to run from me again?"

"Because." I look into his eyes. "I'm finally ready. I don't need you, but I want you. And I love you."

"Thank god." His hands come around my waist as he lets out a nervous laugh. "Because I'm not sure I was going to be able to let you go knowing you live one block over from me."

"Shut up. Again?"

"Yeah, again. It seems we can't stay apart from each other no matter where we go." He slowly drops his face down toward mine. "You're stuck with me."

"I can't think of anyplace else I'd rather be," I whisper just before his lips touch mine.

As soon as his lips are on mine, finally, after four long, lonely months, my body wakes up. He lights up a part of me that fades away without him. It's not that I'm not whole without him—I am. It's just that with him—next to him—everything shines brighter.

Gavin doesn't make my world, but I'll be damned if he doesn't enhance it.

His lips trail down my neck the way I've dreamt about for so long. "I missed you so fucking much."

"I missed you too." I pull his head in closer, my fingers on his freshly buzzed head. "I like your hair."

"Where's your bedroom?" is his marvelous response.

"The door that's not the one you came in through," is my very helpful answer.

When all is said and done, we are laying on hardwood floors, and calling to see if they can try to deliver again since we were too preoccupied to open the door when they came.

#SorryNotSorry

"SO . . . I WAS thinking . . ." In my head, this felt like a really good idea, but now, getting ready to say it out loud, I'm already questioning myself. "Never mind."

"Oh no you don't." Gavin pulls me on top of him, like the new angle will suddenly boost my courage. "What were you thinking?"

"Nothing. It's too soon." We've only been back together for a day, and I don't even know if we are together . . . just that we slept together. "Are we officially a couple again? Or am I jumping to conclusions?"

"Babe." He smiles with his eyes crinkling at the corners. I have no idea what the one word means, but I'm pretty sure he's laughing at me.

"Yup. Four months apart and I still don't know what 'babe' means."

"Marlee, you spent last night naked beneath me and on top of me before you fell asleep next to me. I went to practice because I had to, and then I came back and you were naked again. So yeah, babe, we are officially a couple. And as long as you don't plan on running from me, I don't plan on that ever changing."

"I already told you I'm not." I roll my eyes to try and distract him from the way my body melted on top of him hearing his bossy declaration. It fails, of course, and the grin on his face transforms into a full-blown smile that I feel straight to my core.

"So how long are you planning on sticking around then?" he asks.

I sober with the question. It wasn't one I was expecting, but one I've known the answer to since I decided to come find him.

I lace my fingers through his and look him straight in the eyes, hoping he can feel the sincerity of the words I am about to tell him.

"I was thinking forever . . . if that's okay with you."

The humor he had dancing in his eyes fades away and a look so fierce, it actually steals my breath, takes its place.

"Marlee," he whispers just before his lips touch mine. "Since the first time I saw you on that dance floor in Chicago, the only thing I've ever wanted was to hear those words fall out of the lips I am about kiss."

He doesn't even give me a chance to respond before he follows through and pulls my face to his, and his soft lips are on mine. We promise each other without words to never leave again and when he rolls us over so he's on top of me, he spends the rest of the night showing me how he will worship me.

The next day, Gavin gets his first ever fine for being late to practice.

But after the wake-up I gave him, he says it's well worth it. Which is good, because now that I have him, I plan on making him late a lot.

It might've taken us a long time to get here, but now that we've arrived? I'm taking my sweet time enjoying every single second of it. Who would've thought that the quarterback would be the one to catch my heart?

#Intercepted

Epilogue

"THROW THE FUCKIN' BALL, POPE!" YELLS THE LOUDMOUTH COV-
ered in what looks to be about two gallons of body paint. "I could
get rid of the ball faster than you!"

I seriously doubt that.

I start to turn around, but Naomi's hand on my massive belly
stops me.

"You're far too pregnant to start anything, and DJ is too little
to be a part of our tag team." She points to DJ bundled up in his
Giants jacket and hat, his little two-year-old legs dangling off of
his seat and watching a movie on the iPad, completely oblivious
to the game and my tendency to get a little nuts.

During Gavin's third season with the Giants, Dre was released
by the Mustangs and because my luck has drastically changed
over the past few years, he was picked up the next week by the
Giants. So now not only am I married to the man of my dreams
and expecting out first child, my best friend lives next door. #Jeal-
ousMuch? #YouShouldBe

"The excuse to eat extra tacos is wonderful, but this whole

biting-my-tongue-and-saying-no-to-beer thing is for the birds."
Not to mention the fact that my feet are so swollen, the only
things I can wear are flip-flops (not an option in January in Jersey)
or old lady orthopedic tennis shoes . . . with Velcro. Not hot.

Which, speaking of, I sit down and stretch my legs as much as
possible in the stadium seating. Gavin has been telling me to stay
home and watch the games on TV, but what do I look like? What
kind of football wife would I be if I didn't show up to cheer on my
man? Besides a warm, considerably less swollen and stressed one?

Gavin hands the ball off on the next play, but the running back
gets brought down well before the first down marker. I must have
missed the announcement, but Paint-man behind me takes this as
his cue to rip on Gavin again.

"Are you afraid now, Pope?" he yells like Gavin can hear him
on the field. "Do your fuckin' job!"

"Hey, fucker! How about you shut the hell up and sit the fuck
down?" Donny takes the words right out of my mouth. What?
There's a reason I force him to sit next to me every week.

"Who the hell are you?" Paint-man asks.

Donny glances over his shoulder. "The guy saving you from
the wrath of Pope's hormonal wife who's either about to rip you
a new one or get you kicked out of the game. All of the security
guards here love her and couldn't give a fuck at all about you.
Nobody would be sad to see you leave."

"Preach," Naomi and I say in unison with our hands in the air.

"I'll never understand why the fuck you two won't let your
husbands get a box—a temperature controlled, asshole-free box."
He shakes his bald, round head just as Gavin gets the ball back in
his hands.

"Between the three of you, I don't understand how I'm ever
supposed to enjoy another game," Emerson chimes in beside
Donny.

"You know you love us, Ems." I reach in front of Donny and grab her hand.

We might've had a rocky start, but Emerson's the sister I always wanted now.

"Yeah, yeah. I love you. Whatever. Can we watch the game?" Her attempt at serious fails mid-sentence as a smile takes over her face.

The game is tied fourteen to fourteen with the fourth quarter coming to an end. As much as I love watching the game, if I have to sit through another hour of overtime, I'm liable to kill someone.

Gavin must hear my silent pleas—or sense the impending murder charges—because as the humongous linebacker from the Cowboys is about to get the first sack of the night, Gavin spins out of the way. He crosses the field, running faster than I have ever seen him, and just as he's about to run out of bounds, he launches the football down the field to his receiver who shook his defender. It's a perfect throw and the catch in the end zone is effortless.

I jump up.

Wrong.

I stopped being able to jump at the beginning of the third trimester. I lumber up, screaming and punching the air on the way. As soon as I get on my feet, Naomi's arms wrap around my neck and we spin around in circles screaming like little girls at a pop concert.

When we let go of each other, I turn around, and my belly button that used to be an inny points at the man behind me. "What were you saying about Pope?" I don't drop eye contact for a second as he stutters and stumbles, trying, but failing, to come up with a response. So, like the exemplary football wife I happen to be, I do the reasonable thing—I scrunch my nose and stick my tongue out at him. Because while impending motherhood might've made my ass grow, it hasn't done much for my maturity levels. Some things never change.

DJ'S RUNNING AROUND with the other Giants offspring when Gavin and Dre make their way into the family room after the game.

"DJ, there's Daddy." Naomi points to Dre and DJ's friends are instantly forgotten. His little legs run across the room and he jumps into Dre's arms.

I have a similar reaction to Gavin.

"Hey, superstar." I roll onto my tip-toes and touch my mouth to his when we reach each other.

"Hey, gorgeous." He smiles down at me and rests his hand on my belly. "How are my girls doing?"

"We're good, happy you're still in the playoffs. Even though we wouldn't mind if you didn't wait until the last minute to win the game next time." I laugh as I say it, but I'm dead serious.

"I'll do my best." He drops his hand to mine and links our fingers together. "I don't want to be blamed for your water breaking all over the stadium seat."

"Gross. Could you imagine?" Just the thought causes me to shimmy-shake. "The headlines that could come from it?"

Gavin starts to laugh. I'm not sure if it's because of the way my lips are curled up in disgust, my serious fear of going into labor and having our daughter in the car or bathroom, or the hypothetical headlines, but I don't care.

It doesn't matter how often I see it. When Gavin laughs, the rest of the world disappears and mine lights up. The laugh lines around his eyes—a few more have popped up since we've been married—deepen, his single dimple makes an appearance, and his full lips part and frame his perfect smile. It's my favorite part of our life and lucky for me, we laugh a lot.

"You're crazy." He tightens his grip on mine as his laughter fades. "Ready to head home?"

"No place I'd rather be."

#HappyEndingsDoHappen

Alexa Martin is a writer and stay-at-home mom. She lives in Colorado with her husband—a former NFL player who now coaches at the high school where they met—four children, and German shepherd. When she's not telling her kids to put their shoes on . . . again, you can find her catching up with her latest book boyfriend or on Pinterest pinning meals she'll probably never make. Her first book, *Intercepted*, was inspired by the eight years she spent as an NFL wife.

You can find Alexa on Twitter and Instagram @alexambooks and at Alexa Martin Books on Pinterest.

Ready to find
your next great read?

Let us help.

Visit prh.com/nextread

Penguin
Random
House